COUNTING
BACKWARDS

Also by the author

Rabbits for Food

COUNTING BACKWARDS

Binnie Kirshenbaum

SOHO

Copyright © 2025 by Binnie Kirshenbaum

Published by
Soho Press, Inc.
227 W 17th Street
New York, NY 10011

Library of Congress Cataloging-in-Publication Data is available upon request.

ISBN 978-1-64129-468-3
eISBN 978-1-64129-469-0

Interior design by Janine Agro, Soho Press, Inc.

Printed in the United States of America

10 9 8 7 6 5 4 3 2 1

Carorum meus—Tony, Newton, Ferne, Isaac, Lucie, Susan, Babs, R.H., and Tony again and again—*ego te require magis ac magis inter transitum diem.*

PART ONE

7

PART ONE

Tonight or Tomorrow

You sit at the edge of the bed watching your husband who looks as if he were sleeping.

Hooked up to a high-flow oxygen tank, he might be sleeping, but mostly he is dying. A high-flow oxygen tank is not a ventilator. When the subject of things such as ventilators would come up, apropos of nothing other than stories on the news, stories of lawsuits and family battles, Leo invariably said, "No matter what. No artificial means of life support for me."

You have the document: *Do Not Resuscitate* and *No Artificial Means of Life Support*.

You, on the other hand, said, "I want to be freeze-dried. Or maybe one of those long-term induced comas."

The oxygen will not prolong his life, but it eases the pain of breathing.

The pain of breathing.

The oxygen eases the pain.

For him, the oxygen eases the pain.

But to ease the pain does not mean there is no pain.

For you, there is pain.

The hospice nurse says that if he shows indications of suffering, if he winces or groans or, because not all suffering is externalized, even if you just sense that he might be uncomfortable, you can give him morphine.

Not all suffering is externalized.

You eyeball the vial of morphine tablets.

The hospice nurse tells you that he will, most likely, die tonight. Tonight, or possibly tomorrow.

The hospice nurse leaves. She has other dying people to visit.

You take your husband's hand. You lean over, stroke his cheek, run your fingers through his hair. Such hair. Full. Thick. Boyish, the way it flops over his forehead, but not boyish because it's white. Eighteen years ago, soon after his fortieth birthday, his hair started going white. Within nine months, it was all white. Prematurely white. "It's you," he teased. "Living with you turned my hair white."

White hair, disease, death, all of it premature.

Now, you say, "I'm sorry that I wasn't always good to you. But more than anyone, anything, ever, I loved you. Do you know that I loved you?" *Loved.* Past tense. He's not yet dead, and already, you are in the in past tense.

Tonight, or possibly tomorrow.

Hurry up, *not all suffering is externalized*, please hurry up.

Because, for you, there is pain.

PART TWO

6

Do You See What I See?

Leo is at the living room window, the curtain pulled to one side, and he's peering out, like the nosy neighbor trolling for dogs peeing on flower beds or clandestine affairs, or—the snoop's jackpot—some perv peeking into a woman's bedroom. Except Leo is the opposite of a snoop. Insofar as the private lives of other people are concerned, he's pretty much a *So what?* kind of guy. But, as of late, every night he's posted himself there at the window. "Come here for second," he says.

Across the street, cars are parked bumper-to-bumper, and a sleek bicycle is chained to the streetlamp on the sidewalk in front of the red brick townhouse that's been there since 1902. Come late April or early May, tulips and daffodils will sprout and bloom from the patches of dirt that ring the trees, but it's neither late April nor early May. It's mid-February. When summer rolls around, the full view of the townhouse will be eclipsed by the foliage of the silver maples.

"What, who, is it now?" you ask.

"Under the light," Leo says. "You don't see Gandhi?"

"Gandhi?"

Leo sees Mahatma Gandhi stirring lentils in a pot. An iron pot that hangs from a tripod.

You don't see Gandhi. "Is he wearing anything more than a dhoti? If that's all he has on, he must be freezing. You might want to bring him a coat."

Because Leo realizes perfectly well that he is hallucinating, that Gandhi is not out there on the sidewalk stirring lentils in a pot, you feel free to add, "You might want to give him a pair of thick socks, too. I'm assuming he's barefoot."

Leo lets the curtain fall, and, not for the first time over the last couple of months, he says, "I should give Sam a call."

Sam is his ophthalmologist, and the way Thanksgiving happens not on a fixed date but firmly on the fourth Thursday in November, Leo's annual eye exam falls on the Tuesday after Labor Day. Sam examines Leo's eyes for glaucoma, cataracts, astigmatism, swollen corneas, misshapen corneas, torn or detached retinas, sun damage, any changes in his visual acuity, but, other than nearly imperceptible and inconsequential worsening of common myopia and presbyopia—near- and far-sightedness—the structural anatomy and physiology of Leo's eyes are healthy.

His eyes are healthy, although his vision stinks. His vision has always stunk. He got his first pair of eyeglasses when he was in kindergarten. Without them, Leo's world would be an impressionistic wash, and words on the page as easily read as streaks of smudged ink. Contact lenses are out of the question. As far as Leo is concerned, to go poking around your eyes is to court infection, which is fine with you. His glasses become him, in that bookish Clark Kent way.

Leo's previous appointment with Sam happened to coincide with the onset of his eyes playing tricks with the light at night. Shadows, pink-colored halos, stripes on the moon, and the incandescent glow of the streetlights turned skyward illuminating the row of rooftops populated with what looked like angels holding hands. *Angels* is your word. Leo is dead set against the likes of angels. He described the angels as something like a blurry string of cut-out paper dolls.

According to Sam, Leo's eyes were on the dry side. Nothing

serious. He recommended eye drops, Visine in the morning, and that *you* buy a humidifier. "And don't forget your sunglasses."

Sunglasses because blue eyes are more sensitive to the glare of the sun than dark eyes.

It's not only the ophthalmologist. Leo maintains annual appointments with a full compendium of physicians: a dermatologist, gastroenterologist, urologist, primary care physician, and although he's never had a cavity in his entire life nor any sign of gum disease, either—he brushes his teeth with a NASA-grade supersonic toothbrush, plus he flosses *and* uses a Waterpik—he wouldn't dream of blowing off the date with the dentist. Then there are the flu shots, and not just for himself. Come autumn, Leo starts in hounding you, "Addie, did you get your flu shot? Did you get your flu shot?" until you have no choice other than to lie to him. "I got it this morning. You can stop now."

On more than one occasion, you've asked him when he is going to make an appointment with a gynecologist. You've also suggested he see a psychiatrist. But Leo needs a psychiatrist no more than he needs a Pap smear. He's as sane as anyone who isn't mentally ill. This medical checkup religiosity of his has to do only with the dictum: *Early detection is the key difference between dying and living, and not merely living but living with all your vital organs intact, living free from pain.*

You bought a humidifier, and Leo incorporated Visine into his morning routine, but then one night, one of the angels took on the shape of a bald eagle, which flew from the roof and off into the unknown.

"It must have been the movement of the shadows," you said, and Leo agreed, but soon after the angel-turned-eagle, there came the man on stilts who walked the length of the block before turning the corner and out of view.

You wanted to know if the man on stilts was young or old. Did he have a beard, and what was he wearing? But Leo didn't catch the particulars. "He was moving at a brisk clip," Leo said. "On stilts."

The hallucinations occur only sporadically, one per week, two tops, but Leo has been keeping track of them, dates and times on a sheet of graph paper, and in a small spiral-bound notebook with a green cover, he writes the narrative descriptions in pencil. It's uncharacteristic of him not to document his notes on the computer, and his preference for using pencil and not a pen is equally baffling because of how, over time, pencil fades and how easily it is erased.

People who see ghosts tend to see the same ghost wafting down the same staircase, but none of the characters populating Leo's wacko hallucinations have returned for a repeat performance. However, a distinct pattern has emerged: these ornate, vividly articulated visions, like the earlier halos and angels, are seen exclusively from your living room window and they occur between nine and eleven at night, with two exceptions: the cauldron of bats emerged from a cave and flew en masse up to the moon at 8:32, and it was close to midnight when the troupe of actors arrived, smack in the middle of the street, illuminated by streetlamps like torches in an amphitheater, treating Leo to a snippet of *A Midsummer Night's Dream*, Act IV, scene i, Titania, Bottom, and the whole slew of fairies.

The following night, you called Leo to the window. "Look. It's Hitler and Leni Riefenstahl. They're making a movie."

"I'm not amused," he said, but he was amused, and you laughed as if these hallucinations were nothing but one more example of Leo's personality peculiarities, no different from the way he uses three towels, per shower, to dry off, or from that time he came home with eleven different kinds of salt: Himalayan pink, black lava, Alaskan flake, and who knows what else. They all tasted the same. They all tasted like salt.

The frequency of the hallucinations remains more or less constant, but your level of concern is rising to the point where it's become too tall to suppress, and now when, yet again, Leo mentions casually that he ought to check in with Sam, your response is not casual, as it was before. "Yes," you say. "You do. How about tomorrow, okay? First thing. Promise me?"

Promise. How many people keep, or even try to keep, every promise made? You know of no one, other than Leo. True to his word, first thing in the morning, he calls Sam's office, only to learn that Sam is on vacation, a month in Belize.

You suggest that, instead of waiting for Sam to return, maybe he should see someone else, but no. Leo is Boy Scout loyal to his physicians, all of whom have been carefully and critically vetted. *Physician* is Leo's word. Not *doctor*. *Physician*, which does not necessarily connote respect. The same way the FBI flags any applicant who's racked up frequent-flier miles with Aeroflot, Leo is highly suspicious of any physician who goes around blithely prescribing whatever newly approved FDA wonder drug that whichever pill-pusher from Pfizer happened to be selling that day. Leo's physicians investigate, for themselves, things like trial reliability, statistical efficacy, and potential side effects because, yes, this drug decidedly alleviates cluster headaches, but it's also possible that your liver will explode. Leo values their intellectual and professional curiosity, and he respects their expertise within their field, for the part of the body on which they've staked their claim, the same way he respects skilled electricians and the woman who cuts his hair.

Now, regardless of his high regard for Sam, a month is a long time, and you remind him, "What about early detection and all that?"

"He'll be back in three weeks," Leo says. "Whatever it is, it's not an emergency. There's no reason to worry. Trust me, okay?"

You do trust Leo. You trust him implicitly and always, but nonetheless you have to wonder how, from a sixth-floor window down to the street, he was able to see the lentils in Gandhi's pot.

The Sense of Smell

Leo doesn't play golf or build model boats in bottles, which isn't to say that he doesn't know how the little boat gets inside the bottle, or all about the physics behind a golf ball in flight. It's that, for the most part, he prefers knowledge over practice. His fleeting obsession with food—these obsessions, generally, are fleeting—had nothing to do with eating, but with reading. First he read *The Cuisine of the Roman Empire*, and from there he time traveled through the centuries and traversed the earth, both the flat and the round one, which is how you came to learn that, ounce for ounce, saffron might as well be gold. Despite knowing perfectly well that he'd never use it, this factoid led you to surprise him with the gift of a small, very small, packet of the royal spice, which, as you predicted, went directly into his drawer of treasures, a drawer like a safety-deposit box at the bank, except Leo's treasures are of no value to anyone other than Leo. A partial, very partial, list of things he's got squirreled away in there include: a bag of marbles, a slide ruler, a compass, a fossilized trilobite. Leo's treasures are another man's garbage, and that includes the saffron because by now, long past its expiration date, faded in color and scent, it would bring the same flavor to food as a light sprinkling of sawdust.

If you adhere strictly to the dictionary definition of the word, *to prepare food for eating by means of heat*, you can honestly claim that you cook. Once or twice a week, you broil packaged veggie burgers and steam broccoli. The one night you ventured beyond your culinary repertoire, whipping up scrambled eggs and melted cheese on an English muffin, Leo swooned. "You could sell these."

"Leo," you told him, "it's an Egg McMuffin."

You often have dinner out. Your social circle is wide: artists, academics, scientists, people who work in publishing or with not-for-profit organizations, and a handful of architects thrown into the mix. To define people by their professions is insultingly reductive, as if how they earn a living were their totality, which it's not, but you all do it anyway, like the way most people refer to those in their social circle as friends, but you don't consider those in your social circle to be friends. They are not, for the most part, people you would ask for favors or call in the middle of the night or put down as an emergency contact.

On the nights you don't dine out, you call in for delivery: Middle Eastern food, Chinese, Indian, Mexican, or brick-oven pizza.

Your cat, Roberta, is the only carnivore in the family.

Although the Gandhi sighting was devoid of any olfactory elements, it did conjure the memorable delights of cumin, turmeric, coriander, which is why tonight you order dinner from Tamarind Royale.

Not yet a year into your lives as a married couple, Leo asked you, "What do you think about moving to Long Island? Buy a house. Trees, grass, a yard, quiet."

Cambridge—where Leo was born, raised, and educated, a townie at Harvard—isn't Boston proper, but it's close enough. Then graduate school and a postdoc at a renowned medical research university where he made a significant discovery, one you've never been able to wrap your head around but you understood it was impressive enough for them to offer him a permanent position. Leo is, through and through, a city dweller.

Long Island?

Long Island was not where you grew up. You grew up in the suburbs of Connecticut. Six of one, half dozen of the other. "You do know," you said, "that in the suburbs there are no Indian restaurants that deliver. I'm not sure there *are* Indian restaurants in the suburbs." As Leo tried to absorb such deprivation, you added, "There *is* pizza delivery. From Domino's."

Your food arrives. Leo sets the table, and you spoon dal makhani over the mound of basmati rice on your plate. Leo got chana saag and mango chutney. Leo is mad for mango chutney, but it is too sweet for your taste. Nonetheless, as he unfailingly does when you get Indian food, he asks, "You're sure you don't want any?"

"I'm sure," you tell him.

It's not that he doesn't remember you consistently turn down his offer of mango chutney. It's that he finds your refusal incredulous.

He passes the container of chana saag your way, and you give him the remaining half of your dal makhani.

Except for the mango chutney, you and Leo always share.

Three, Only Three

The Virgin Mary nursing the baby Jesus on the hood of an illegally parked BMW was followed by a brief sighting of swans paddling placidly around in a small lake, but now, more than a week has come and gone, during which time Leo has yet to experience another hallucination.

It does happen. Inexplicable malfunctions will fix themselves without medical intervention or having to call customer service, like when your dishwasher quit but an hour later, when you tried it again, as if the dishwasher had only taken a bathroom break, it worked just fine.

You, on the other hand, are not working just fine.

You're an artist. *Artist.* It's a word that embarrasses you, as if there's something embarrassingly pretentious—*artiste*—about the whole enterprise, but that's what you are. An artist. Your medium is collage, and you're reasonably successful; reasonably successful insofar as you're represented by the Sandstone Gallery, which is a lesser known but reputable space, and a far cry from having your work on exhibit in a sandwich shop or in your mother's basement. Every now and again, another gallery will include your work in a group show, and from time to time you get a commission, which, aside from the one experience with the interior decorator, is flattering, and the money is nice. The interior decorator had requested a butterfly *in there, somewhere,* but when you delivered the piece, she was not happy. "A moth," she said, "is *not* a butterfly. I can't hang this in my client's foyer. Moths are depressing and icky," and you had to ask, "Have you ever seen my work? Or did you just pluck my name out of a bowl? Like a raffle ticket."

This is hardly your first dry spell, but with an upcoming show, a solo, it's particularly problematic. Sheila, the owner and curator of the Sandstone, wants eighteen collages. You've delivered fifteen of them already, five or six weeks ago, but in the timeline of the art world, never mind that an upcoming show could well be preceded by the upcoming resurrection of Christ, galleries insist they have the entirety of an exhibit two eons in advance of the opening. You swore to Sheila that you'd have the remaining three soon, but she is a Chihuahua in the shape of a person and has been calling every other day to ask how it's going, and because you don't want her to piddle on the floor, you tell her, "It's going great. I'm almost there." Almost there; that is if the distance between *there* and *almost there* were the same distance as nearing the finish line of a marathon before you've laced your running shoes.

In an earlier era, your studio, a small, windowless room in the back of your apartment, might've been a child's bedroom, a sad, wretched little child. The realtor had suggested you convert the Dickensian waif's room into a walk-in closet, but you didn't want a walk-in closet. You wanted a studio, at home, and because you've never been drawn to the large canvas nor to installation art, this room, although cramped and crammed with supplies in boxes, labeled and stacked, is ideal.

Now, the entirety of your worktable could be, except it's not, a collage unto itself: landscapes torn from *National Geographic*, a photograph of a teenage couple on prom night, a map of the South Pole, an obituary cut from the *Times*, a few deep-purple feathers, and scraps of black-on-black flocked wallpaper. It's like one of those 1000-piece jigsaw puzzles, a 1000-piece puzzle with 326 pieces missing, or maybe it's an additional 326 pieces from a different puzzle.

An old coffee can filled with paintbrushes, along with a glue pod, a tube of rubber adhesive, and two pairs of scissors, takes up the table's far-left corner, and dead center, propped up against the wall, is the same white canvas board that was there yesterday and the day before and before and before. You're not so much staring as you are squinting at it, wary, as if the canvas board were one of those plastic flowers that squirt water in your eye.

And then nothing.

You open your paint box.

More nothing.

Your phone rings. It's Sheila. You let it go to voicemail.

You call it quits for the day.

A Shared Vision

You could go for a walk or see if the cat wants to play, but it's about to rain, and Roberta is sleeping on top of Leo's desk. You contemplate waking her, but instead you open the middle drawer, the one where Leo keeps his hallucination notebook, the small spiral-bound notebook with a green cover. You open it to the first page, and after reading a few pages more, you put it back in the drawer and return to your studio.

Later, you hear Leo's key in the door. He doesn't call out for you, and you don't call out, "In here," nor do you look up from your table, but you sense his presence. He's leaning against the doorjamb, watching you. With the expectation that he'll occupy himself elsewhere, you say, "I'm kind of in the thick of it."

Not that you've ever made the trek up and across town to pester him when he's in his lab, but at home, when he's writing a paper or a grant proposal or is deep into reading, should you interrupt him, he snaps at you, "Can't you see I'm busy?"

You and Leo have different modes of expression. He snaps, whereas you grind your teeth and contemplate divorce. Now, your resentment at the intrusion dilates wide into resentment over the very fact that he exists.

But because he doesn't go away, something must be up, something that can't wait, and you have to ask, "Are you okay?"

"I'm fine," Leo says. "But do you have a minute?"

Because you'd rather Leo not see your work in progress, you suggest taking the conversation to the living room and having a glass of wine while you talk.

Leo goes to the kitchen to uncork a bottle of Malbec, and you cover what's on your table with the sheet of plexiglass to keep in place what could possibly blow away, then put a magazine on top of the plexiglass because plexiglass is transparent.

On the couch, you shift to face each other, and Leo tells you that, although Sam has returned from Belize, his first available appointment isn't until the twenty-third of April.

"He can't squeeze you in before then? You've been a steady customer since 1923, and how many times have we had dinner with him?" You like Sam's wife. She's a therapist but she never talks to you as if you might be a nutcase-in-training, and she has three pet rabbits.

"It's not urgent," Leo says. "I'm pretty sure I know what's wrong."

Leo's area of study is autoimmune disease, specifically lupus, and he works exclusively on a cellular level, and because hypotheses require a significant knowledge and a foundational basis of evidence, he categorically refuses to indulge in medical diagnostics. Try consulting him about stomach upsets, back pain, or the possibility of a concussion. Leo won't suggest so much as Rolaids, an ice pack, or acetaminophen. Instead, he'll say, "Call your physician."

Only once did Leo make an exception to this rule. You were out for a drink, standing at a crowded bar. A bald man had wedged himself in on Leo's other side. "Excuse me," Leo said to him, and then he tapped the same spot on his cheek where on the bald man's cheek was what looked like a splatted bug. "You should see a physician, a dermatologist. Soon. Like tomorrow."

Either gravely concerned or indignant at the audacity of some bozo in a bar pointing out his melanoma, the bald man put down his drink and walked off, and Leo said to you, "That guy is a couple of weeks away from dead."

Now, although stranger things have happened, especially as of late, you're incredulous that Leo went and diagnosed himself.

"No. I wouldn't diagnosis myself. Of course I'll consult with Sam, but I spent the day in the library. All the literature points to Charles Bonnet syndrome."

"And Charles Bonnet syndrome is what? In English," you remind him.

It's not arrogance; it's just that Leo tends to forget that the language of his profession is the same language as Martian to most people.

Charles Bonnet syndrome causes hallucinations and is primarily associated with glaucoma, but Leo's eyes don't hurt, they're neither swollen nor red, his vision isn't blurry, and the halos were not multicolored. Moreover, even in its nascent stage, Sam would've detected glaucoma. The secondary root cause for Charles Bonnet syndrome is macular degeneration. "When the eye is unable to accurately collect images, the brain responds with spontaneous nerve activity. It's like dreaming," Leo says. "The brain has to invent what is not visible."

The brain has to invent what is not visible.

You're mulling over those words when, as blasé as if he were letting you know that he feels a cold coming on, Leo tells you that, eventually, macular degeneration will result in a full loss of vision, all the way blind.

Flippancy is one way, your way of choice, to ward off fear, as if flippancy were like flipping a pancake, and it lands on the opposite side. "We can't have a Seeing Eye dog here," you say. "Not with Roberta."

"Relax, Addie. I'm not going to wake up blind tomorrow. The progression is slow. Twenty-years slow."

Twenty years is far enough into the future to believe it will never happen, but nonetheless, you suggest that he might want to start brushing up on braille. "You'll want to be fluent."

According to Leo's research, if it is macular degeneration, the hallucinations will diminish or even disappear entirely within six to nine months.

On your fingers, you count backwards. Five months if you include the angels.

"Who knows?" Leo says. "Maybe I'll get a glimpse of lions on the Serengeti before then."

To see a pride of lions on the Serengeti is something you and Leo have long intended to do. Not this year, but someday.

The brain has to invent what is not visible.

It's All in Your Head

The internal weather report for today: overcast with anxiety. What if Sheila gives you the thumbs down? What if Sam tells Leo, "Yep. You're going blind, all right," or worse, that he'll be blind not in twenty years but in two years, maybe three?

You should have popped another Xanax, but Leo's not wrong about your pharmaceutical intake, and it's too late now, regardless. Sheila's outside, on the sidewalk, looking left, right and left as if her head were an orange spiked on a metronome.

"You were supposed to be here at noon." She extends her arm and taps her watch. It could be she was exceedingly nervous that you might not show up at all, or else her irritation at your tardy arrival is bleeding into suppressed rage, but either way she's trembling like an aspen leaf in a crosswind. Her watch is a Movado, minimalist and black to match her black leggings and black-and-red poppy-print dress. You wear black, always, because in New York, you can't go wrong with black. You worry a lot about going wrong, which, inexplicably, you don't equate with being habitually late. You affect a get-over-it face and ask, "Since when have I been on time?"

The Sandstone Gallery occupies one of four spaces on the second floor of an old warehouse, since renovated and converted into art galleries, fashion showrooms, and offices for import-export businesses. The lobby is post-apocalyptic austere. Your high heels clickity-click on the gray tile floor. Sheila's ballet slippers are quiet shoes.

An intern, no doubt a student at Pratt or Cooper Union, is at the reception desk. Her hair is cut and dyed in homage to Andy Warhol. Her black turtleneck and blank expression complete the affectation. Her job is to ask visitors to sign in, to foist brochures on them, and answer questions like, "Where's the bathroom?" This current exhibit is titled *Women Run the Show: Contemporary Feminist Art.* Sheila must've blown herself away with that one. Track lighting with chrome fixtures runs the length of the high ceiling. A few tourists are milling about the room, barely glancing at the art on the walls. They are here for one reason only: to tell their friends back home that, while in New York, they went gallery hopping. The way you bypass a ladder to avoid bad luck, an older man sporting a spanking-new New York Yankees T-shirt, probably scouting for the bathroom, skirts around a red resin sculpture of a vagina displayed on an iron pedestal. You follow Sheila into her office, where you unzip your portfolio and arrange the three collages in a row on the table.

As if she were a homicide detective looking for a stray strand of hair, Sheila scrutinizes them, and then she points to the Virgin Mary perched on the wing of a plane nursing Baby Jesus. "Playful," she says, "yet it subverts the patriarchy with piercing wit." The theater troupe in the middle of the street is a satiric, yet sorrowful, rendering of American anti-intellectualism, and the trio of ostriches hiking to the summit of a snowcapped mountain is visually soft, deeply unsettling, *and* the articulation of the subconscious interrogating the irrationality of corporate greed.

Art-speak, as if it were a language created by a thesaurus without a dictionary, is a dialect that, even after all these years, you cannot fully comprehend. "So," you ask her, "do you like them?"

"Do I like them? Weren't you listening to me? Yes, I adore them."

She adores them, and now confident that your good news will beget more good news—your variation on the Matthew Effect—you float home to wait for Leo's call, for him to confirm that he's not going blind, that the problem was merely a speck of dust stuck in his eye.

Watching the clock does nothing to accelerate the movement of time, but the need to tell him how Sheila adores your deeply unsettling interrogation of articulation and to hear that whatever was in his eye has been removed are needs that compound like mounting pressure until you're on the verge of spontaneous combustion. You've got him on speed dial, and that fast, you hear his ringtone—Quantum Bell—emanating from the bedroom.

Whether it's his unconscious at play or one of those passive-aggressive things, to pay Leo's cell phone bill is to turn money into confetti. Eighteen hundred times, at a minimum, you've said to him, "What if there's an emergency? How will I reach you?" and invariably Leo gives you some kind of jackass response, such as, "There were emergencies before there were cell phones."

Of course he will call you the split-second he gets to his office. Nonetheless, despite the certainty that you'll be talking to his voicemail, you call him, which is why when Leo, the person, answers his phone, you're confused, and you ask, "Where are you?"

"I'm in my office," Leo says, as if the question were absurd because it is absurd. "I just got back."

To blurt out your good news before asking about his good news would be egregiously self-centered, even for you, a person who points in the direction of inward. "So, what's the verdict? What did Sam say?"

"Turns out I was wrong," Leo says. "There's no indication of macular degeneration."

A story, a true story, Leo often tells is that of a geneticist who claimed to have modified the DNA of white mice, to have produced white mice with black dots, mice with fur coats like the coat of a dalmatian dog. A groundbreaking discovery, except if you picked up a dalmatian-dog mouse, it would leave smudges of black ink on your fingers.

Never would Leo pull such a stunt. If it happens that his conclusion doesn't align with his hypothesis, when an experiment flops, when a theory proves incorrect, Leo is speed-of-light fast to admit he was wrong, except when it comes to you. When it comes to you, he is unable to locate those particular words.

The two of you rarely have a blow-up fight, but rarely is not never, and when it happens that Leo is the one at fault, he damn well knows he's the one at fault, but rather than own up to it, say he was wrong, say that he is sorry, he says, "I accept your apology," and when you point out that you most certainly did not apologize, he then says, "Yes you did." And that's how you get over it, because, however pathetic, he did apologize in his own special Leo way.

"So, no macular degeneration, that's fabulous." Now you can share your good news, except you can't, not when Leo says, "Sam thinks the disturbances could be originating in the occipital lobe. He wants me to see a neurologist."

A neurologist? Brain cancer, lesions, aneurysms, a hemorrhagic stroke?

There are two pathways to expedient medical care in this city. One is to go to the emergency room, but even then, unless you're riddled with bullet holes, they're not getting to you any too quick, either. The other, a perk of Leo's profession, is a kind of nepotism, colleagues who can pull the string that moves you to the front of the line, but now Leo says, "No. I don't want any of them knowing my personal business."

"Personal business? You're not asking about a sex therapist."

"I'll find my own neurologist, Addie," and again, the same way he sat twiddling his thumbs waiting to see Sam, his devout adherence to early detection is dismissed. "It won't take longer than a couple of weeks. I can wait."

"Wait for what? For your brain to melt or grow craters or whatever?"

"Craters don't grow," Leo says. "They flatten out."

"Yeah, fine. But you'll get right on it, yes?"

"Yes." Leo sounds as if you're pestering him about taking out the garbage, and he changes the subject. "How'd it go with Sheila?"

At this juncture, to go on about your stunning visual wit could be construed as an insensitive blunder, so you say only, "Good. Really good. I'll tell you more later. Don't forget you need to be home by six. We're meeting Jack and Alicia at seven."

"How could I possibly forget that?"

"I know. I know but buck up. We'll survive."

Silence Not Golden

When you lived uptown, Jack and Alicia were your next-door neighbors as well as the impetus behind your moving downtown. Somehow, they never learned the New York City Golden Rule: maintain a cordial relationship with your neighbors because things happen, like you lose your keys or need to borrow a plunger, but that's where the line is drawn. Anything more than that is an open invitation: feel free to drop by whenever it's convenient for them and most inopportune for you.

Your social circle runs the age gamut from late twenties to ninety-two, which renders the fact that Jack and Alicia are in their mid-seventies irrelevant to your dread at the prospect of dinner with them. Your dread is predicated on the colors that define them. Jack epitomizes khaki beige, and Alicia is the dull off-white of a button mushroom. But your bag of ready-made excuses provides cover for only so long before the excuses become a message, a hurtful message, which is why you're having dinner with them tonight.

When you get to the restaurant, Jack and Alicia, already seated, are waving at you with frantic enthusiasm, as if they've been sitting there for hours, half expecting that you might stand them up.

Alicia is a retired kindergarten teacher. All her blouses are patterned with tiny flowers, and she's wildly enthusiastic about tambourines. Jack taught history to sixth graders, which is all well and good, but you are already familiar with the Boston

Tea Party, which doesn't stop Jack from giving you a refresher course. "Of the three hundred and forty-two chests of tea that were destroyed," he says, "approximately seventy of them were hyson. A Chinese green tea that happened to be Washington's favorite. Jefferson's, too."

"Revolution requires sacrifice, doesn't it?" you say, nudging Leo with your foot, urging him to either say something less inane or, better yet, change the subject altogether, but tonight Leo is as chatty as a stick.

When the check arrives, Jack suggests moving this party to a café for coffee and dessert. You again turn to Leo, but his attention is fully focused on the folds of his crumpled napkin. You're flying solo here. "Oh, we'd love to," you say, "but we can't." You sneak a peek at your watch. "It's getting late." Like 8:27 is past your bedtime.

You promise them that you'll get together again soon, which you will do when you next run dry of excuses.

Jack and Alicia hail a cab, and now alone with Leo, you ask him, "Do you feel okay? You didn't say one word."

"I was bored," he says.

"Of course you were bored. They're boring, but, Leo, to say nothing at all was phenomenally rude."

"You wanted me to pretend?"

"Yes, I wanted you to pretend," and a silence comes between the two of you like a partition, until you ask, "Was it because you were thinking about your brain?"

"Not possible," Leo says. "My brain was comatose. But forget that. You still haven't told me how it went with Sheila."

"It was good. She's thrilled with my articulation of an interrogation. Or maybe it was the other way around."

Leo shakes his head at the Orwellian inanities. "If you'd

shown them to me first, I could've told you which it was. Now that I think of it, why *didn't* you show them to me?"

You slip your arm through his and say, "You'll see them at the opening. It'll be a surprise."

For the remainder of the walk home, you talk about what's playing at the Film Forum, about trying out that new Vietnamese restaurant and how you need to renew your driver's license. You talk of nothing that matters, and the conversation flows as seamlessly as a Möbius strip.

Something Is Broken

The money machines are broken. So says Leo. "I stopped at the bank to get cash," he tells you, "but the money machines were broken." To refer to the ATM as a money machine is a new one, but not without precedent. Leo has his own unique, albeit technically literal, linguistic spin for a handful of everyday objects, like how in summer he'll say, "It's hot in here. I'm going to turn on the cooling machine," to which you say, "On planet Earth, we call that an air conditioner."

"All of them were broken?" You're skeptical. "Was a notice posted? Maybe there's something wrong with your card."

"No." Leo is adamant. "The machines are broken. Come on, I'll show you."

You don't want to go out, but Leo insists he prove himself right, except when you get to the bank, after Leo inserts his card and enters his PIN, the "money machine" spits out the $200 requested. Sheepishly, Leo says, "They must've fixed them."

"Looks that way," you say.

It does happen. Inexplicable malfunctions will fix themselves.

But to have been fixed, they had to have been broken in the first place, and you tell him, "You should mention this to the neurologist."

"Why would the neurologist care that money machines were broken?"

"Because they weren't broken, Leo."

As if it's pointless to argue this with you, he lets it go, and you do the same.

Updates

If not once a week, then once every other week, you and Z meet up for a drink, but now it's been a month and a day since you last got together, a span of time that does not alter the inevitability: you are late and Z, Mr. Punctuality himself, is waiting for you at the bar. Your contention is that Z is anal-retentive, or else rigid punctuality is a requirement in German Studies departments worldwide. Z is of the opinion that your chronic tardiness is associated with ADHD creative daydreaming or that you're just inconsiderate, but the bottom line is that it's had no impact on your friendship and joking about it grew tired.

You order vodka on the rocks with a slice of lime. "To ward off scurvy," you say.

"The vodka? Or the lime?"

"Both." You raise your glass as if making a toast.

His name, of course, is not really Z. It's Zachary, but to you he is Z, a holdover from college when he went by Z for the duration of his freshman year, the same year he couldn't resist pontificating Wolfgang Iser *this* and Gerhard Lauer *that*, until you'd say, "Z, shut the fuck up. No one is interested," and he would shut the fuck up and take no offense either, because, as he put it, "Only your best friends will tell you that you've got bad breath. Everyone else, it's all about them avoiding the uncomfortable moment. Not you, Addison. You'd tell me."

So, you leaned in and whispered, "Z, your breath is bad.

Wicked bad." When his hand jumped to cover his mouth, you came clean. "I lied," you said. "Your breath is neutral."

Addison is your given name, but other than for professional and legal purposes, you're Addie. Only Z calls you Addison, just as to you he is forever Z. It's a best friend thing, and Z is your best friend. Not including Leo, that is. Leo is your *best* best friend. Leo is your *best* best everything.

Although you can't speak to Z's side of the equation, the lone exception to your mutual unvarnished honesty is your adherence to that commandment-type law: thou shalt not trash parents, partners, or children not your own. Z's wife, Katrine, runs a not-for-profit theater company where, over the years, you and Leo have endured the compost she force-feeds the audience, dramatic atrocities like that abridged version of *A Doll's House* starring Barbie, Ken, and Skipper dolls.

Leo is more tolerant, not of the insufferability of her dramatic "art" but of her insufferability as a person. "Think of her as a character in a play," he says. "A farcical comedy."

Leo has a point, but you can't make the leap.

Z watches you fish the lime from your drink and set it down on the cocktail napkin. "Why did you ask for that when you don't want it?"

"Because," you tell him, "only alcoholics order vodka straight." You take a sip, a very small and measured sip, and then turn your full attention to Z. "So, what's up with the gang at school?"

Another holdover from his goofy youth: Z never says *school*. Always *university*. For Z, *university* conveys intellectual rigor and European sophistication.

Rather than correcting you, he smirks because he knows you'll only say something jackassy like "Excuse-ay moi."

He never says *vacation*, either. It's *holiday*. He goes on *holiday*. Shaking his head, he tells you, "Machiavelli and the Borgias are back at it. Amusing, but really, who has time for their nonsense?" It's a rhetorical question. Writing a paper for the *New German Critique*, and with a speaking engagement at the German Linguistic Society Conference coming up in November, Z is the one who has no time for their nonsense. No time, but a modicum of interest. Of greater interest to him, although not necessarily to you, is that his son got accepted into one of those genius high schools, and his daughter got a prize for an essay she wrote, a spectacularly brilliant essay. His daughter is in the fourth grade. How brilliant could it be? Plus, you know the kid. There's nothing brilliant going on there. *Thou shalt not trash the kids.*

"What about you?" he asks.

"Sheila adored the new work. But I haven't done anything since. To tell you the truth, I'm a little worried about Leo. He's still hallucinating, nowhere near as often, and, not that this is a bad thing, but they're kind of mundane. A poodle. A bus. Although it was a double-decker bus. The ophthalmologist thinks it might be something with an occipital lobe."

"He'll probably have to do those eye exercises, right? To strengthen the muscles or whatever."

"No. He's going to go to a neurologist. The occipital lobe is a brain thing." You take a non-measured sip of your drink, more like a gulp, and all bitchy sounding, you add, "I'm shocked at your ignorance. I thought you knew everything." A swipe that, immediately, you regret. "I'm sorry. It's that there's more. Like last week, he came home with thirty-six rolls of paper towels."

"But that's Leo," Z says. "Remember the salt?"

"The salt was more like a wine tasting, but the paper towels were all Bounty. What's to compare? And then, a couple of days ago, he went to the bank and somehow screwed something up with the ATMs. He said they were broken. All of them broken."

"Maybe they were," Z says. "Don't make a big deal out of nothing, Addison. It was probably just a glitch in the system." To his credit, Z has a way, as does Leo, of putting things in perspective.

"A glitch in the system," you say. "That makes sense."

A glitch in the system.

False Positive

L eo flatly refuses your offer to go with him for the CAT scan. "It's not surgery, Addie. It's a scan. Twenty minutes start to finish."

"Okay," you say. "But if they have to give you an emergency lobotomy, I hope you'll be able to find your way home."

Because he is sympathetic to the rationale behind your idiot retorts, Leo takes no offense at them. Not even when his routine prostate screening came back with an elevated antigen level and you said, "Leo, if you wind up impotent, we'll work around that, but if you're peeing in the bed, I'm gone."

Leo laughed. "Thanks for the heads up. I'm seeing Kransky next Thursday."

Kransky. Dr. Kransky has a reputation. He's famous for a twenty-two-year run of prostate surgeries without a hitch and infamous for having run off with one of his patient's wives. But a shaky moral compass is irrelevant when stacked up against the ability to wield a scalpel with the precision of a mathematical equation. This is not to say that surgery, any and all surgery, regardless of the surgeon's reputation, is not without risk. Another fun fact of Leo's: one in ten thousand people dies on the operating table because the anesthesiologist goofed. One in ten thousand, although within the realm of possibility, is still highly improbable, unless you consider that the odds of winning the lottery are one in fourteen million, which brings one in ten thousand a lot closer to fifty-fifty. Not exactly the way you want to play Russian roulette.

Moreover, someday Kransky's unbroken record is bound to break. Nothing is perfect forever.

Leo put his arm around you and said, "Don't let your imagination run amok. False-positive PSA tests are as common as weeds."

Which is what it turned out to be, a false positive, common as a dandelion.

Now, you walk him to the door. "You promise you'll call me immediately after."

"I won't get results for a day or two. Addie, quit worrying."

"I can't help it."

One false positive is no indicator of future false positives, and perfect records are bound to break.

How can you not worry?

A String of Names

For two days you've been worrying yourself into knots, but now when he gets home, Leo tells you that the CAT scan detected nothing awry. No tumors, lesions, craters, or evidence of a stroke in the occipital lobe. "And I don't have spongiform encephalopathy, either." Without your having to ask, he translates for you. "Mad cow disease."

"I didn't know that mad cow disease was a thing in America. I thought only cows in England went mad. Maybe Wales, too."

"You should read more," Leo says, and you mutter, "Go fuck yourself."

The neurologist wants Leo to come back for an MRI, and you're back to worrying. "Why don't they call an MRI a DOG? Keep to the theme. CAT, PET, DOG."

"I'll bring it up with the neurologist." Leo is amused.

You sort of don't want to know, but nonetheless, you have to know what an MRI might detect that wouldn't have shown up in the CAT scan.

"Atrophy, fluid accumulation, things like amyloid plaques, neurofibrillary tangles," and as if it's no more deadly than a small cavity in a bicuspid tooth, Leo adds, "any indications of Alzheimer's."

Alzheimer's? No. Whatever this is, it's not Alzheimer's. Your grandmother had Alzheimer's. Her slow but steady swoop down the slope of cognitive decline started with where did she put her purse, her keys, her eyeglasses that were perched on the bridge of her nose. She lost sentences mid-stream, and words she wanted could not be found. She'd forget your name—"Tina, Lois, uh, Kate"—until you'd run out of patience. "Grandma, I'm Addie."

"Of course you're Addie. I know my own granddaughter."

She knew her own granddaughter, but her Social Security number and her phone number had evaporated from her memory bank.

Whatever it was with the ATM, Leo didn't hesitate when he keyed in his PIN, and if you ask him a question like when did Jonas Salk die? he'll reel off the year, month, day, and estimated time of death. Moreover, as far as forgetting where he put what, Leo's like a squirrel digging up the square-inch plot of earth with his little squirrel paws to retrieve a nut he buried eight months ago.

"You do *not* have Alzheimer's. For one thing, unless you've been lying to me about your age, you're way too young."

"It's not impossible, although statistically unlikely. Less than .16 percent, and I don't have the genetic marker, either. But, if it is Alzheimer's"—Leo gives you that wry smile of his, the one that gets you every time—"I want you to strip me of all identification, put me on the R train, and walk away."

"The R train? The R train goes to Queens. It would be better if you killed yourself."

"You're right," Leo says. "Good thinking."

Leo is sympathetic to suicide as a personal choice, believing that the decision to kill yourself can be, under certain circumstances, the sensible, wise, and compassionate thing to do for yourself and for your loved ones. Why prolong the agony when the agony is unbearable without respite or hope until you die an agonizing death?

Theoretically, you're on the same page, except when it comes to your cowardly self, although no matter what the circumstances, you never really know what you would do until you're there.

That's a Thought

To clear your mind of all thoughts is a relaxation technique, one you assume is easily accomplished if you're a corpse or an earthworm, but seeing as how you are neither, while you wait to hear from Leo, your thoughts accumulate and swirl like a sandstorm. You need a distraction.

Work is a distraction, and if nothing comes of it, failure is a distraction, too. Cobalt violet, crimson red, and Prussian blue create the desired deep burgundy. As you deliberate whether to paint the canvas with a palette knife or a thin size 2 brush, your phone rings. Leo! You don't bother looking at caller ID. It has to be Leo.

But it's not Leo. It's Judy, who, up until seven years ago, was a friend, a real friend, but that changed dramatically when she got pregnant. Not *because* she got pregnant but because when she got pregnant, she went all-out herbal-stupid: stinging nettles eradicate allergics, hibiscus lowers blood pressure, unprocessed cinnamon prevents measles, and women who don't have biological offspring don't have souls. It could be the remnants of fond memories, or something like a bad habit you should kick but haven't, holding together some semblance of a friendship.

She goes through the ritual blah-blah-blah. She's good. Robert, her husband, is good. Duncan is preter-human, like the Dalai Lama. That's the kid's name. Duncan.

"I'm good, too," you tell her. "Getting excited about my show. Invitations won't go out for a while yet, but, of course, you'll get one."

"I really do want to be there for you," she says, "but what

with the long drive into the city and Duncan gets his milk at bedtime, I don't know if it's possible."

Not that you give half a shit if she's at the opening or not, but nonetheless you ask why Robert can't give Duncan his milk before bedtime.

"Because Robert doesn't lactate. And I can't bring myself to use a pump. Feeding is about the bond between the *mother* and the baby."

Duncan is not a baby. He's in the first grade.

Judy couldn't care less about Roberta, but she does ask about Leo.

Because there couldn't be a worse time than now to listen to her proselytize about how brain scans cause epilepsy or arthritis, how his nose will fall off and drop to the floor, you say only, "He's much better. He's having far fewer hallucinations, almost none." And then, too late, you literally clamp your hand over your big mouth.

"Hallucinations? What hallucinations?"

"Oh. Nothing really. He was having trouble with his eyes. You know, blue eyes are more sensitive to light."

With the intractable force of ignorant certainty, Judy says, "It's not his eyes. It's his job. All these years of absorbing toxins."

Leaving off the apt adjectives, you say, "Well, that's a thought, isn't it?"

Before you hang up, Judy mentions that she doesn't know when exactly, but she will be coming into the city before too long. "I promised my sister we'd have lunch. I'd love to get together after. For tea." Then she adds, "I'm serious, Addie. He should sue that place for poisoning him."

Again, you say, "That's a thought."

The kind of thought you have if you're an earthworm.

Nothing to See

The MRI revealed what the CAT scan revealed. Not a damn thing, which was why the neurologist recommended that Leo consult with a neuropsychiatric physician. On a prescription pad, she wrote down the name and number for the one she said is tops in the field of oddball brain disorders.

"Oddball brain disorders?" you ask. "She actually said *oddball brain disorders?*"

"No, of course not."

"So, you'll make an appointment with this person?"

"Probably," Leo says. "I'll see."

"You'll see? You've been seeing plenty."

"Cute, Addie," Leo says. "Very cute," and he reminds you that it's been weeks since he last had a hallucination.

It has been a few weeks since he last called you to the window, to ask if you can see what is not there, and there have been no new additions to his notebook, either.

But still, something is out there.

On and Off

Two dinners in a row out with social circle friends, and then last night you went to a Greek restaurant in the Village with Miriam and Patrick, who are friends, in the genuine sense of the word. Miriam edits Young Adult books. Patrick is a sculptor who works with sheet metal. Tonight, you and Leo will be having dinner at home, alone, just the two of you, so nice, so right.

You make a bid for Mexican food. "How about Casa Rosa?"

"Sounds good," Leo says, "but can you wait? I want to look something up first."

"No problem. Will the television bother you?"

The television won't bother him. Leo's focus is that of a magnet on steel.

After hunting around for the remote control, which you finally find underneath the couch, but before you go channel surfing, you want to set yourself up with a glass of wine.

To get to the kitchen from the living room requires that you cut through the dining room, where Leo is at the table with his laptop open. Because you don't want to disturb him, you don't ask if he wants a glass of wine, too, but then he turns to you and asks, "Do you know how to turn this thing on?"

The screen is black, but the charger is connected and the green light is bright. You lean over his shoulder and press the power button. The computer boots up.

You don't tease him, but you don't walk away, either. You wait and watch as he dials up the library at the NIH, and, in less time than it took you to locate the remote control, he finds whatever it is he was looking for.

On the TV, two pundits are arguing about tax cuts. You're not paying attention. You're drinking your Chablis and mulling over the apocryphal story about Albert Einstein's inability to tie his own shoes.

You head back to the kitchen for a splash more wine.

Leo is intently reading the small print on the screen.

"Anything fascinating?" You're being facetious. Whenever Leo is reading something *fascinating*, his enthusiasm—an influx of energy that, unless shared, hazards an explosion like a bubble bomb—compels him to read whatever it is out loud to you until you say, "Leo, enough. The only words I've understood thus far are *the*, *is*, *molecule*, and *and*."

"No. Nothing fascinating." He logs off and shuts down the computer. The screen goes black, and when he gets up from the chair, you look down at his feet and ask, "Who tied your shoes for you?"

Beveled Edges

This notebook, like the one you've filled with charcoal depictions of Leo's hallucinations, is made of bevel-edged vellum paper. It's too small to use for a sketchpad and the paper is lined for writing. This one was a gift, a lovely gift, from Miriam, the sort of lovely gift you were sure would stay tucked away in the drawer, but no, and now on the first page, with a black Sakura Pigma pen, you write what comes to mind:

Mute at dinner with A&J
ATM broken
Paper towels
Put away dirty dishes
Wrote date on memo line on check
Couldn't turn computer on, but shoes were tied

Then you add:

Seems different, but not

Off the Tracks

No wonder you can't work. You haven't eaten a thing all day, but here's what's in your refrigerator: mustard, apricot preserves, orange juice, almond milk, wilted broccoli, and one egg. You get your bag and head out.

A sandwich board set up in front of a new bakery boasts in block letters: GLUTEN FREE. You don't have celiac disease, but your stomach is grumbling. A gluten-free blueberry muffin ought to be less expensive than a muffin not lacking an essential ingredient. But it's a wildly pricey muffin, which would be worth every penny had you been afflicted with pica, craving dirt for dinner or lead paint chips for a snack. You toss the gluten-free muffin—minus the two bites you took—into the trash.

Although you're shopping only to stock up on the necessities, you peruse the aisles as if you were in a market in another country, as if a jar of peanut butter, a bag of pretzels, and a bunch of bananas were exotic foods, worthy of examination. It's a way to kill time, to avoid your studio.

At home, you eat a spoonful of peanut butter straight from the jar, peanut butter that leaves a thick glaze in the back of your mouth, and then it hits you. You forgot club soda, but you should get to work. You *should* get to work.

Another way to kill time is to pick the lint out of the dryer, but you did that yesterday.

You look at the clock. It won't be long before Leo gets home. You get your computer and dial up Curiosity Stream, scrolling until you land on *Storm Chasing in Tornado Alley.*

Again, you take note of the time.

Periodically, you hit Pause to take pictures of the green-tinted sky, of a car flying over houses that have been reduced to rubble, of treetops, like brooms, sweeping the ground, until the last of the tornadoes funnels off to Oz. The closing credits are rolling. Leo is late.

Next up is *The Top Ten Most Devastating Tsunamis in History*. Leo will be here any minute now, but maybe you can catch one or two tsunamis before he's back.

Only two of the top ten most devastating tsunamis occurred after the moving image was invented. Without film footage, the screen's visuals are limited to still photographs in black and white, which makes no difference because, although you are listening, or half-listening, to the narrative, what you are watching is the clock.

Near to the conclusion of the eighth tsunami, the one that wiped out Nankaidō, you hear Leo's key in the door. With the boing of a manic jack-in-the-box puppet, you spring up from the couch.

"Where were you?" Your voice sounds more like you're squeaking as opposed to speaking. "I was worried."

"Sorry," he says. "The train derailed."

"The train *derailed*? Did anyone get hurt?"

"Hurt? No. No one got hurt. I didn't even know it happened until I saw we were at Chambers Street."

"So, the train didn't derail," you say. "You just missed your stop."

It wouldn't be the first time Leo missed his stop. Sometimes it was because he was overly absorbed in his reading and sometimes it was because the conductor's announcement that the local train is now running on the express track was incomprehensively garbled, but to reverse course never takes more than twenty minutes, thirty, tops.

"I didn't *miss* the stop," he says. "The train *derailed*. It went off the tracks. No big deal."

But it *is* a big deal, and you ask him for the umpteenth time when he's going to make an appointment with the neuropsychiatrist.

"I don't see the point," Leo says. "I feel fine."

"You're not fine."

"Do I look sick to you?"

"No. You don't *look* sick, but that doesn't mean you're fine."

"I'm fine," Leo repeats, as if stating an irrefutable fact.

"And what about me?" you ask. "I'm not feeling so fine."

"Well," he says, "in that case, you should see your physician."

"Not funny, Leo. Not funny."

What You Don't See

It was for twenty minutes, and without a scintilla of irony, that Leo stayed on the phone explaining to the slimeball selling vacation home time-shares how draining swampland does not decrease the mosquito population, that a degraded wetland can actually increase the mosquito population, and then he enumerated myriad viruses mosquitoes spread, including encephalitis.

You tell Z, "I mean, I get how it *could* be funny if he were simply amusing himself, but you know Leo doesn't amuse himself at the expense of others. Except me, but that's different. And for twenty minutes? No. He was not amusing himself."

"We all step out of character now and again," Z says. "Like when you're charming." You ignore the gibe, and Z scoots his barstool closer to yours. He puts his hand on your back and says, "Get a grip on yourself. The scans came up clean. Whatever it is, it can't be anything serious."

It was a different Curiosity Stream disaster documentary, not tornadoes and tsunamis, but one on hurricanes, flash flooding, and thunderstorms with bolts of lightning that must've inspired the myths of pissed-off gods, from which you learned what happens when lightning strikes a tree. Branches will break, the tree might split down the middle, or the bark might explode, rendering the trunk bare and vulnerable. Conversely, often the tree appears unscathed, with no indication of damage done, except there *is* damage done.

In the roots, or deep inside the tree trunk where the rings are distant from the bark, somewhere in there, the tree *is* damaged. Not apparent is the extent of the damage. How bad is it, and can the tree be saved?

If Not Him, Then You

Leo is snoring softly, and you get out of bed to snoop through his wallet, where, between three one-hundred-dollar bills and two restaurant receipts, you find the no longer crisp sheet of prescription-pad paper. You copy the neuropsychiatrist's name and number onto the back of an envelope, which you slip into your pocketbook.

It's like making an appointment with the President. Twice, the receptionist puts you on hold, and then she tells you that the first date available is December 7th at noon. After that, there's nothing until the 23rd of January.

"We'll take the seventh at noon," you say.

December 7th is six weeks from today. Six weeks to figure out how to tell Leo that he has an appointment with the neuropsychiatrist, an appointment that you made behind his back.

Turn the Page

The previous two lines on the first page of the beveled-paper notebook read:

Looked for carrots in silverware drawer
Poured full liter of club soda down kitchen sink

On the following line, you write:

Didn't realize sweater on backwards, V in the back

Over the River

To ask the same question again and again and expect a different answer is a definition of insanity, which is not terminology in any way applicable to Miriam and Patrick or Z and Katrine (discounting her theatrical productions). Yet, year after year after year, each of them invites you for Thanksgiving, to have dinner with them and their extended families, enough people to cast a Broadway musical. You assume these invitations are pro forma because your response is equally pro forma. "You're so sweet to ask, but you know, we always spend Thanksgiving with Leo's sister. She'd be crushed if we backed out."

Leo was seven and his sister was six when their mother died. Beyond their shared history and genetic material, Leo and Denise have a grand total of nothing in common except for deep and abiding devotion, which is enviable. You last heard from your brother a good seven or eight years ago when he sent an email. The subject line read *Dad died*, and you hit the little trash can icon. You were not quite yet teenagers when your brother first blamed your mother for the fact that your father was an alcoholic, but your mother would respond to his hateful remarks the same as she would to a waft of cigarette smoke, as if a wave of her hand were all it took clear the air. You can't attribute your brother's cruelty to youthful arrogant stupidity because even when your mother died, a decade before your father finally got around to dropping dead, while he did take the initiative to arrange her funeral, still your brother would express no regret for his vicious words. Your mother could forgive him, but you could not.

As fond as you are of Denise, and you are extremely fond of her, you'd walk barefoot on broken glass before you'd travel on Thanksgiving weekend. Also, there's this: you have limited patience for Denise's son.

You and Leo far prefer to spend Thanksgiving alone, to feast on your nod to the traditional dinner, a nod or a wink: Tofurky, Brussels sprouts, a couple of yams, and a Hubbard squash. Hubbard squash has no flavor, none, not even an aftertaste, but Leo insists that Thanksgiving is not Thanksgiving without a Hubbard squash. Every year, he goes to the Farmers' Market and comes home lugging a Hubbard squash of monstrous, prehistoric proportions. You once asked Denise if Hubbard squash had been the highlight of their family Thanksgiving dinners, to which Denise said, "A what?"

To slice a Hubbard squash is not unlike slicing a boulder, and it requires eleven years in the oven before it's soft enough to eat, had you had any desire to eat it, which you don't. Even Leo eats no more than a few forkfuls before he's had his fill of texture without flavor. And yet, year after year, he says, "Addie, Thanksgiving is not Thanksgiving without a Hubbard squash."

At Jeremy's Health Foods, where all the customers look sickly, you buy the Tofurky and a loaf of multigrain bread. Tofurky tastes like rubber, but between two slices of bread slathered with mayonnaise, it's edible.

You're half-hoping that this year Leo will experience a blip and buy a nice, small acorn squash, but no. Here he is, cradling a Hubbard squash the size of Moldavia.

Between November 18th and December 6th

Army of ants in bathtub
Put on two different shoes, insisted they were a pair
Ate entire Hubbard squash! All 112 lbs* in one sitting!
   (*hyperbole but, still, huge and flavorless)
Poured two full liters of club soda down bathroom sink

Apostate

More duplicitous, even, than making the appointment with the neuropsychiatrist without consulting Leo is that you don't tell him about it until tonight, after dinner, when you say, "We should probably leave around eleven fifteen."

Leo looks at his watch, and you say, "Tomorrow. The appointment is for noon."

"Appointment? Appointment for what?"

"The appointment with the brain specialist." Bad enough to be a sneak who committed deceit by omission, now you're a gaslighter, too. "Don't you remember?" you say. "You made an appointment weeks ago."

"I did?" he asks. "That's odd. I have no recollection of that. None."

"Well, that's why you're seeing him, isn't it? Because you're not cooking on all four burners, Leo."

He nods and looks down at the table, and you know that you did what had to be done, but it does not negate that it was a lousy thing to do. You push away from the table and go to the living room, where you look out the window. A few minutes later, Leo comes in and asks, "Anything interesting out there?"

"Not that I can see. Why don't you take a peek?"

Leo neither looks out the window nor does he respond to you. Instead, he picks a book up from the floor and goes to the bedroom. Roberta follows him. You stay where you are, looking for angels on rooftops.

Come Back Later

A power play, overbooking, or unexpected emergencies, whatever it is, physicians keep you waiting. They all do it, which doesn't make it any less of a piss-off, although Leo, engrossed in his reading, appears unperturbed, but you, as if you're the one with the brain problem, are coiling two-inch sections of your hair around your index finger. Coil, release, coil, release for thirty-two minutes until the receptionist calls Leo's name. Leo's name, but you go with him.

The neuropsychiatric physician gestures to the pair of chairs across from his desk and then juts his chin at the magazine, now rolled into a cylinder, that Leo holds in his left hand. "What are you reading?" he asks.

Unfurling *The Lancet*, Leo shows him the cover. *The Lancet* is perhaps the world's leading medical journal, and Leo says, "If you haven't seen this issue yet, there's a study on the chemical mapping of juvenile anxiety. It's fascinating."

The part about anxiety piques even your curiosity, but this neuropsychiatric physician's curiosity is not piqued. Instead, he asks, "What brings you here?"

Leo looks to you, as if you were the one having extravagant hallucinations, as if you were the one who couldn't figure out how to turn on the computer, or as if you are about to tell a story, one he's not heard before, Leo is on the edge of his seat, eager to hear what happens next. However, you're getting the distinct impression that the neuropsychiatric physician is bored to death by the story, although to be fair, maybe he has heard it countless times, and he shifts his attention to Leo. "Can you answer a few questions for me?"

"It depends on the questions," Leo says.

Ignoring the logic behind Leo's response, this neuropsychiatric physician says only, "Well, let's give it a try."

What is today's date? How many nickels are in eighty cents? Can you count backwards from twenty-five? Can you count backwards from one hundred by factors of seven?

Leo counts backwards, 93, 86, 79, 72, and you're counting along with him, but not out loud, which is fortuitous because in your head you go from 72 to 67. Unlike you, Leo runs the numbers the way water flows. Water does not stumble.

Now for the written part of the exam: Draw a Clock.

"A wall clock?" Leo asks.

"How about a cuckoo clock?" you say.

You're making every effort to cut this neuropsychiatrist some slack, but when he does not laugh as you and Leo do, your effort goes the same way it did after you went from 72 to 67. The hell with it.

The circle Leo draws is as perfect as if he had used a compass. "Roman numerals," he wants to know, "or Arabic? And set at what time?"

It doesn't matter. The decision is Leo's to make, and his Arabic numerals are evenly spaced, as are the strokes of the minutes. The clock is set at 12:34.

Next, Leo is instructed to write down a list of twelve animals and read the list out loud. "Cats, goats, dolphins, crows, peacocks, tortoises, trout, chameleons, earthworms, crocodiles, jellyfish, toads," and this neuropsychiatrist asks, "Are you sure you want to include worms and jellyfish?"

"Why would I not want to include them?" Leo says. "They *are* animals."

"He's right." Your voice is sour-cherry sweet. "If you don't believe us, you can look it up easily enough."

The same way a politician avoids a reporter's question, this physician of limited knowledge and lack of curiosity pivots seamlessly. "Have you been experiencing any trembling or twitching? In your hands."

In unison, you and Leo say no, but, as if you're not reliable on matters of such complexity, he tells Leo to extend his arms. Leo's hands are prostate-surgeon steady, but as if your having said as much were a fluke, a lucky guess, when he asks Leo if he shuffles when he walks, he doesn't take your word on that, either. "Let me see you walk across the room and back."

Leo does not shuffle, and Dr. Supposedly-Tops-in-the-Field makes a pronouncement. "I see no evidence of Parkinson's disease, and it's not Alzheimer's."

"Yes. I'm aware of that." Leo's smile is Mona Lisa ambiguous. "I assume you've looked over the scans and the neurologist's report."

"Of course I did."

"So, what is it?" you ask.

His best diagnosis: Come back in twelve weeks.

"That's it? Come back in twelve weeks?"

"Yes," he says. "And I'd like him to consult with a different ophthalmologist beforehand. Get a second opinion."

Leo walks out, but you lag behind. "I know he *seems* normal. He'll go days, weeks at a clip when nothing overtly weird happens, but I know something is off. He's not himself. He's not right."

"That's why I want to see him again in twelve weeks and why I suggested that he get his eyes reexamined. The hallucinations are indicative of an abnormality, but as of now, for me, no alarm bells are going off."

"Maybe no alarm bells are going off for you, but for me, they're ding-donging all over the place."

"Perhaps they are," he says, "but you should consider the possibility that you are overreacting. He might just be preoccupied or distracted by something else, and you're letting your imagination get the better of you."

"I don't have an imagination," you say, and Dr. Bozo tells you to make an appointment on your way out.

You do make an appointment for three months from today, which brings a modicum of satisfaction insofar as the odds that you will show up for this appointment are zero to none, and the odds that you will extend the courtesy of calling to cancel are negative four to zilch.

Leo is waiting for you outside on the sidewalk, and as if you don't trust him not to dash out into oncoming traffic or go picking through a trash can, you say, "Stay right here. Don't move. I'm going to hail a cab."

When a taxi pulls up, Leo rushes to open the door for you to get in first. He gives the driver your address, and it crosses your mind that maybe Dr. Neuropsychiatriquack wasn't entirely off the mark. Maybe you are overreacting, maybe the train *did* derail, maybe the ATMs *did* experience a technical glitch, and maybe Leo couldn't figure out how to turn on the computer because he was distracted by the television, and maybe he went to the silverware drawer to get a carrot simply because he was preoccupied with work. But no. When you told him to look in the refrigerator, he asked, "For carrots? Who would put carrots in the refrigerator?" What crossed your mind flies out the window, and you say to Leo, "We need to find someone else. Maybe a neuropsychiatric physician who actually reads *The Lancet.*"

He takes your hand in his and stares out the window.

Also Noted

Turning to the page where you last left off, you jot down the following:

Refused to go for dinner with Miriam and Patrick
Tore two pages from a book, threw them in garbage
*Bought dog biscuits for cat, then asked why I bought dog
    biscuits for cat*

Gift Wrapping

For you and Leo, Christmas, like Thanksgiving, is a private affair. What's different is when it comes to Christmas, you're a pair of sentimental goofballs, carrying on as if you were still children, except your Christmases bear no resemblance to those of your childhood nor to the majority of Leo's, either.

When he was five years old, having carefully considered the broad concepts pertaining to the laws of time and space, Leo came to a conclusion: Santa Claus is a hoax. But try as he did, there was no convincing Denise of the patent absurdity until two years later, when their mother died and took Denise's belief in Santa with her. Their father never failed to buy them gifts, but, while their mother wasn't exactly a ghost, she nonetheless hovered over the day as a haunting specter of loss.

Your mother did up Christmas as if Norman Rockwell were spending the holiday with your family. Gifts were wrapped with big red bows and arranged under a six-foot-tall tree decorated with candy canes, tinsel, and ornaments made of wood because ornaments made of wood aren't easily broken. Home-baked sugar cookies, red felt stockings, holiday cards displayed on shelves. But on Christmas Eve, your father would get drunk, kick the gifts as if they were soccer balls, smash the cookies to crumbs with his fist, and come Christmas Day, no one had an appetite for dinner. Year after year after year, and yet your mother never said fuck it, why bother?

Unlike Thanksgiving, Christmas is an unequivocally fixed date on the calendar, and equally unequivocal is that you and

Leo do the bulk of your Christmas shopping on December 20th. You want to avoid the mobs who push and shove their way through the stores, who step on your feet without apologizing, the elbow jabbers, all making a mockery of Peace on Earth and Goodwill Towards Men, but to wait any longer would leave you having to choose between a bobblehead elf for your special someone, or a fruitcake.

Leo is ready to go. You need a few minutes to put on your makeup, but by noon, you're out the door.

You take in the window displays and go into some of the shops to buy gifts for each other and something for Leo's sister and his nephew, which you'll send FedEx to be sure they arrive on time. Chestnuts from a street cart, another hour of shopping, and then you're ready to sit down for a meal.

There will be other gifts. In addition to two sweaters, a scarf, a pair of gloves, and the ultra-wifey, but always appreciated, six pairs of socks, you bought for him on eBay a rare book, in excellent condition, from 1921, on the physical and psychological effects of mustard gas. Tomorrow you'll go to the fancy-ass candy store, braving the long line for a box of hand-dipped chocolate-covered mints, and if he hasn't already, tomorrow Leo will go to your safe-bet jewelry store downtown to buy you a necklace or a pair of earrings. Leo has exquisite taste in jewelry.

It's on the early side for dinner, and you barely have time to set down your shopping bags and take off your coats before the waiter is there to take your drink order. You ask for a Merlot, and Leo says, "I'd like a carafe of lemonade."

You're in a French bistro. It's winter. They don't have lemonade.

Leo appears to be sulking. He does not open the menu.

The waiter returns with your wine and a glass of sparkling water with six lemon peels floating on top for Leo, which was kind of him. He asks if you're ready to order.

"I'll have the goat cheese salad," you say, and Leo says, "I'll have whatever she's having."

"Sounds good." The waiter heads to the kitchen, but when the food arrives, after one bite, Leo tells you that the goat cheese is rancid.

The goat cheese is not rancid.

"Eat around it," you say.

He picks at the greens.

You take a pass on dessert.

Traditionally, you buy your tree, always the smallest one, from the same vendor who drives in from Vermont and sets up shop on the avenue around the corner from your apartment. Rows of trees are propped up on both sides of a wooden A-frame. The scent of pine is strong in the air, but before you reach the stand, you say to Leo, "Let's skip the tree this year."

"Okay," Leo says.

He doesn't ask why.

Holiday Surprises

No jewelry for me
Calls sister to ask, Did you know Dad died? (Father died
*   12 yrs ago)*
Wants to rewrap gifts already opened
Asks if I want to go to Times Sq. to watch the ball drop*
*   *Stark raving mad question*

One Week and Six Days of Post-Holiday Surprises

No hallucinations, blips, glitches
Leo is perfectly Leo again

New Day, Old Subject, Next Line

Response to push to see different doctor: "I don't believe in going to physicians when I'm not sick" *
*Just hits me, he's been blowing off annual exams

Open and Shut

With the idea that frigid air will chill your anxiety, you and Leo walk to the Sandstone. It's not an unreasonable idea, except it has no more effect than the Xanax you popped, which is to say, none.

Sheila doesn't mention that you're late. Maybe because you're not *that* late, no more than twenty minutes, but more likely it's because, as she whispers in your ear, five of your eighteen collages have already sold. Five red-dot stickers giving you the red-dot sticker thumbs-up.

You turn to tell Leo that five, *five*, have sold, but he's already wandered off. However, an intern is there, balancing prosecco in plastic cups on a silver-plated tray. Maybe some other time you'll suggest to Sheila that she invest in wine glasses. Plastic, irrespective of the designated recycle bins, doesn't get recycled. Plus, plastic cups are chintzy, which doesn't stop you from taking one.

"Edwin Palace is here," Sheila says. "He wants to meet you."

Edwin Palace. The name rings a bell, but you can't put your finger on why, and you ask, "Who the fuck is Edwin Palace?"

"Edwin Palace. The *collector*. The *very* influential collector. He hasn't bought anything yet, but it would be a game-changer if he did. Come on. We don't want to keep him waiting."

You trail behind her, pausing only long enough to take a fresh cup of prosecco from the intern as she cuts through the crowd, and then again when you spy Leo, who does not see you because he's focused on the collage in front of him. You'd like to stop, ask what he thinks of it, but Sheila grabs your hand, the hand not holding the cup of prosecco, and, as if you were going to make a run for it, she pulls you over to Edwin Palace, or is it Castle? You're drawing a blank, and you're not really listening when Sheila introduces you, but you compliment him on his tie.

"It's hand-painted," he says. "I bought it in Venice. Last year. At the Biennale."

Whoop-de-doo, but you play your part, responding modestly to what you glean are words of praise, although he might as well be saying *wonk, wonk, wonk.*

When he reverts to speaking English, he asks you about the materials you use: Acrylic gel? Oil paint? Do you make your own paper?

"No. My paper is, almost exclusively, found paper. Old photographs, vintage postcards, magazines." And then you do that whip-your-hair thing, a clever move to look away on the chance that you'll catch sight of Leo. And you do.

As if he were a flagpole planted on a plot of a heretofore unknown planet, he has yet to budge from the spot where it seems he's staked his claim: dead center, fixated on your Virgin Mary nursing Baby Jesus on the wing of the plane.

Edwin Palace knows of a place where you can get top-grade washi paper, and you say, "I'll have to check that out. Thanks for the tip. It was a pleasure to meet you," and you beeline over to Leo. You slip your arm through his and say, "Looks familiar, does it? It should. It's yours."

"I know it's mine," he says. "What's it doing here?"

What's it doing here?

It's not his, not exactly his. The plane is yours, but there's no denying that conceptually it's his vision. It's a reflex, the way your chin tilts upward as the cup meets your mouth. You jiggle it, urging what remains of your prosecco to slide beyond the rim. The droplets evaporate on your tongue, and you give Leo's arm a tug. "I want to say hello to Z and Katrine. They'll want to see you, too."

To the left of the reception area, Z and Katrine are chatting away with Miriam and Patrick, which is its own curiosity. Z and Katrine's inability to stomach Patrick and Miriam is matched only by the degree of distaste returned in kind. Mutually exclusive of this symbiotic disdain is their friendship with you and Leo.

Miriam gives Leo a big hug. "Where have you been hiding?"

Z shakes his hand and claps him on the back. As if you'd all gotten together the week before, not all on the same night but in two foursomes, Leo is engaging in conversation the same as any normal person engages in conversation. You take advantage of the moment and say, "Sorry. I should circulate. You know, make nice. I'll find you later."

You *should* circulate, make nice, but you head straight for the bathroom, where you lock yourself in a stall, sit on the toilet, and shut your eyes, as if to see nothing is to think nothing, except *the brain invents what the eye cannot see*, and what your brain is inventing isn't doing you any good.

There's no need to flush the toilet, but you do because someone with a legitimate need for the bathroom might be lurking on the other side of the door, listening intently for the signal that relief is imminent. Ditto with running the faucet. You don't wash your hands, but you scrutinize your reflection in the mirror, searching for the reflection of an untroubled woman. But no, it's you. Worried and pale. You put on a fresh coat of lipstick.

Not *someone*. It's Leo lurking outside the bathroom, and you ask, "What are you doing here?"

"Good question," Leo says. "What *are* we doing here? Can we leave now?"

Oh, no. Please, Leo. Not tonight.

"I can't," you tell him. "You know I have to stay until the bitter end, but you seem tired. Why don't you go home?"

He's agreeable to your suggestion, and you experience a modicum of relief until he asks, "Do you want me to take our painting? Or will you bring it back?"

"Leo, that's not a painting. You know it's a collage. *My* collage."

"It's not really yours," he says. "It's mine."

Go home, Leo. Please go home. Please, Leo, just go away.

The Memory Palace

With his back resting against the arm of the couch, Leo is engrossed in whatever he's reading, or maybe he's just ignoring you again, but then he says, "Hey, how'd it go?"

"Great." You put your gloves in your coat pocket and drape the coat over the chair. "Really good. Seven pieces sold. Edwin Castle bought one."

"Edwin Castle? You mean Edwin Palace."

"You know who he is?"

"Of course I know who he is. He's a big collector." Leo reads you as well as he reads his book. "Addie," he says, "be happy."

"I am. Happy and exhausted. I'm going to go to sleep."

"I'll be in soon. I just want to finish this chapter."

One or two Ambien? Two.

You might've slept through the night, except at 3:08 in the morning, Leo is shaking your shoulder. "How can you sleep with this racket?"

"What racket?" You're groggy. "I don't hear anything."

"You don't hear the marching band in the hallway? Tuba, trombone, drum, cymbals. You need to see an otologist."

"I will when you do," you say.

"Me? What for?" Leo asks. "I'm not the one who is audio-impaired."

His hearing might be 20/20, but what's between his ears is a mess.

Hypocritic Oath

The worst thing about growing up with an alcoholic parent was not knowing who was coming through the door. Would it be the father who tousled your hair, asked what you learned at school today, and praised your drawings? Or would it be the father who threw a lamp at the wall, dumped dinner on the floor, and shoved your mother across the room?

What's happening with Leo is not at all the same, except it is the same insofar as you have no way to predict when Leo will not be Leo. His episodes of irregularities have increased exponentially. Increased, but they are still neither constant nor consistent, and it's getting to be like how you grew to wish that your father would come home drunk every night. Certainty prevents the shattering of hope.

When Leo leaves for work, you google: *Neuropsychiatric physicians NYC*. There aren't a whole hell of a lot, and two out of the five have no stars, although to cut them some slack, it could be because their patients, not right in the head, don't know that doctors, like restaurants, Uber drivers, and any damn purchase you make online, expect you to take the time to rate them. Of the remaining three, Dr. Head—Dr. Head, for real—has only two and a half stars, and Dr. Edrich has three. Dr. Tops-in-the-Field has four stars, which doesn't bode well for your confidence in the others. You call Dr. Edrich.

You explain to the receptionist that you want to make an appointment for a consultation, that you want to talk to the doctor, not about yourself but about your husband, that your husband won't be there, that what you want is a diagnosis and to know what can be done to fix it.

"I'm sorry," she says. "That's not possible. No reputable doctor would make a diagnosis without meeting the patient. It would be unethical."

Dr. No Stars might be more accommodating, hungry for business, less "ethical," but it turns out that he's not. Ditto with Dr. Head.

Ethical. Is *First Do No Harm* the equivalent of *Do Nothing*?

No Work, No Play

Drip, drip, drip, trickle, you're waiting for the coffee to brew, when Leo comes into the kitchen, and you ask if he wants some. "It'll be ready in a couple of years."

"No, thanks. I'm going to go for a walk. Do you need me to pick up anything on my way home?"

Leo is big on walking. His preferred walk is five blocks downtown and then across to the East Side, to the Strand Bookstore, where he roams the aisles, scans the tables, picks through bins, and, more often than not, buys two or three or fourteen books, books that he *had* to have.

"We're just about out of orange juice," you tell him, "and I think the bread has gone stale. So, juice and bread would be good. Should I write it down?"

"I think I can manage to remember orange juice and bread."

You pour yourself a mug of coffee, which you take to your studio.

A couple of hours pass before Leo returns, and because you weren't doing anything worth a shit anyway, you get up from your chair and find him in the kitchen. The bag of books from the Strand is on the counter, as is the grocery bag. Orange juice and two loaves of bread because he wasn't sure if you wanted multigrain or whole wheat. He puts the orange juice in the refrigerator and asks, "What have you been up to?"

"Nothing much," you tell him. "I've been trying to work, but it's been a bust."

"Don't give up," he says, and, with the bag of newly purchased books in hand, he goes off to read.

You return to your studio, where you stare at the wall as if waiting for it to crack, to reveal something hidden from somewhere you could not, heretofore, access, which does not happen, but Leo appears in the doorway. You assume he is going to ask about dinner, but instead he wants to know "Where's the little girl?"

"Little girl? What little girl?"

"The little girl with short brown hair. Yellow dress, pink sneakers. The one you've been playing with all day. *That* little girl."

"Leo, there's no little girl here."

And then, as if he's utterly exasperated with you, he says, "Great. You invited her over, and now you've lost her."

"Oh, *that* little girl," you say. "I sent her home."

"Why did you send her home?" Leo asks. "The two of you were having such a good time."

The man on stilts, the theater troupe, Mary and Baby Jesus, all the wacky visions he saw last year, Leo knew perfectly well that they were hallucinations. But this year, thus far, it's been different. This year, he's stubbornly refused to accept, for example, that your gloves were not in the freezer, that there was no marching band in the hallway, or that the handful of almonds he ate *were* almonds and not Roberta's Protein Puffs, and now this little girl? How do you challenge what you can't fathom? You don't. Instead you say, "Yeah, I know, but I really had to get back to work."

He nods his head. "Okay, then. I'll leave you to it."

From the box of Victorian cabinet cards, you select one. A child, a girl who looks to be five or six years old. Unless she's broken some kind of world record, she's long dead by now, so you have no qualms about decapitating her with an X-Acto knife. On a 9 × 11 inch sheet of heavy paper, you draw the outline of a headless body with disproportionately short legs and big feet, which you color up over the ankles with a pink oil-based pastel. On the top of the elongated neck, like that of a swan, you glue, slightly off-kilter, the girl's head. A few jagged lines of fine-liner pen on her face create the effect of a broken mirror. To craft a dress, you snip and fold a tattered swatch of yellow silk. You consider painting her eyes an icy blue. And her hair? Tree branches devoid of leaves? An upsweep of frogs? A bob of barbed wire? But first, you need to determine if this girl you are piecing together will be realized, or if you should send her home.

A Shot in the Dark

If the misconception that artists are most inspired when shrouded in gloom were accurate, you'd be churning out masterpieces on the assembly line of angst. But eleven days have come and gone since you put aside the girl with the yellow dress and you've done nothing except arrange your boxes along the walls, labels facing out, in alphabetical order: *Anatomy. Astronomy. Bugs. Buttons. Cars. Fabric. Fruit. Glass (broken). Landscapes.* But instead of stacking *Mail-Order Catalogs* on top of *Letters*, you sit on the floor and browse through catalogs from long-shuttered businesses that sold everything from toys to ladies' undergarments. Most of them have little stickers attached: $1 or 50 cents.

The flea market is where you buy the bulk of your material. Or, rather, where you *bought* the bulk of your material. Not that you're running low, but before all this, before Leo went haywire, every other Sunday the two of you would go to the flea market. While you scouted for myriad crap, of value to pretty much no one except collage artists and crackpots who stockpile defunct magazines or collect things like matchbooks and rubber bands, Leo sought out antique or vintage medical supplies: empty bottles once filled with snake oil that was probably castor oil, syringes that could baste a turkey, and pre–World War II medical textbooks, often illustrated. You, too, were attracted to the illustrations, particularly those that documented people afflicted with Boschian abnormalities: babies with a surfeit of limbs, faces without noses, eyeballs bleeding pus, a man with testicles like cantaloupes.

After the initial perusal, Leo wedged that decidedly not-for-children picture book under the bed with all the other books he'd never look at again, which doesn't mean he'd ever part with it. This hoarding is not confined to books alone. Magazines, journals, and tear-outs of academic papers and scholarly articles are jammed into his file cabinet to the point where drawers don't fully close. Whenever you'd accuse him of being a hoarder, he'd correct you. "Not a hoarder. I'm an *accumulator.*"

You gave up. People don't change. Leo is Leo, and you are you. You keep your trash confined to your studio, and you're a thief who has never confessed to taking for yourself a fair number of those horrific photographs or to tearing out pages of illustrations from anatomy books; acts of sabotage you justify with the maxim: *what you don't know can't hurt you*, a truism that has proven another maxim to be true: *there's an exception to every rule*, because now what you don't know hurts you the way surgery must've hurt before anesthesia.

The catalog of plumbing supplies, circa 1961, brings a revelation. There's a remarkable similarity between pipes and hoses fitted for sinks to the organs of the excretory system, but before you can get to your *Anatomy* box to fact-check your assertion, the phone rings. It's Sheila, and you ask her, "Did you know that a P trap is shaped exactly like a colon?"

Sheila expresses no interest in P traps or colons. She wants you to guess who called her. "You won't believe it," she says. "Go ahead. Guess."

So, you guess. "Mahatma Gandhi."

As if Gandhi calling were not outside the realm of possibility, she says, "Nope. Isabelle Weber. Calling about you."

Isabelle Weber, she of the Weber Gallery, wants to include your collages in a group exhibit of multi-textural work. "You have to call her today." Sheila is wetting her pants, and why shouldn't she be? There's a hefty commission in it for her, for doing nothing. "Between one forty-five and three. Today," she repeats.

"She's giving me an hour-and-fifteen-minute window? What if I can't call then? What if I'm at a doctor's appointment or something like that?"

"I know, I know," Sheila says. "She thinks that you'll be desperate enough to tell the doctor to wait."

"Thanks. That does wonders for my confidence."

To be overeager is not attractive. Play it cool, wait until 2:57 to call, but you chicken out of playing it cool because what if after an hour and twelve minutes she changes her mind?

The person who answers the phone asks if Ms. Weber is expecting your call, and then she puts you on hold. You get Rachmaninoff's Cello Sonata for your listening pleasure until it's interrupted by a cold, sharp "Yes." Not one to be bothered with the social graces, like a simple fucking hello, Isabelle Weber cuts to the chase. "I'll need to see twelve new pieces, no JPEGs. Bring the twelve to the gallery on June thirtieth between the hours of one and four."

"June of next year?" you ask. "Or the year after that?"

Isabelle Weber, so it seems, does not appreciate your wit. "This coming June," she says. "I'm aware it's short notice, but I've had a cancellation. Does this present a problem? Surely, you've been working."

As if you were the understudy for the lead in the play, the understudy who dozed off during rehearsals and never bothered to learn her lines, and now the star has come down with laryngitis, you affect a peppy can-do tone of voice. "No problem."

No problem.

Yes problem.

Your one shot to make it on the big stage, and you're going to blow it. In circumstances such as this, you rely on Leo to talk you down from the ledge. You could always rely on Leo. But not now. Now, Leo is not reliable.

You call his understudy.

Busy People

I t's disconcerting to find that Z is not here waiting for you. Did he get run over by a bus, or maybe a brick fell on his head? Ten minutes go by, and, perspective contingent, your glass is either half-full or half-empty when he blows through the door gushing apologies. "I'm really sorry. Really, really sorry. It's been insane. Scheduling meetings, itineraries, booking flights, hotels, I lost all track of time."

"Flights? Hotels? Where are you going?"

"I didn't tell you?" Whatever measure of no-big-whoop nonchalance he is hoping to achieve, it flops. "That lecture I gave, the one at the Waterloo Centre conference was, apparently, something of a resounding success. I've been invited to do a series of talks on the Continent."

Just for the fun of it, you ask, "Which continent?"

"Cute," Z says. "Very cute. The Goethe-Institut in Geneva at the end of September, Berlin in October, and Prague the following month. We'll fly over late June when the kids are done with school. Spend some time in Paris, and Katrine wants to go to Tuscany. They'll stay through August. I'll return the week before Christmas."

"This is really fantastic. I wish I could stow away in your suitcase," you say, "but I can't because, get this, I've been asked to be part of a group show. At the Weber."

"The Weber Gallery?"

"No. The Weber shoe store. Yes, the Weber Gallery."

"Addison, that is fabulous. More than fabulous. It's stupendous."

"Not everyone is of the same opinion." You recount the brief exchange you had yesterday. "I ran into Garth at Friedman's. He was agonizing over which brand of linseed oil to get. I don't know why, but I told him, and he let me know that the Weber Gallery *used* to be a really good space, but it's come down in the world."

"Garth is such a loser," Z says.

"No shit, but I'm worried. I haven't been working. I have one piece that's okay, but everything else, I've tossed it in the trash."

"You're too hard on yourself. What did Leo think?"

"He didn't see them." You shrug as if you have no explanation for this, but you do. "Yesterday morning, he poured orange juice on his Cheerios."

"So, he woke up groggy. I once brushed my teeth with Katrine's moisturizer. I didn't even notice the tube was pink."

"There's more," you say. "Last week he referred to Roberta as Concerta. Did I feed Concerta?"

"Concerta? That's pretty funny. I mean, it's not funny, but, you know, my son was on Concerta for a few years. For his ADHD."

"You're right. It's not funny, and he flatly refuses to consult with another doctor. He insists that there's nothing wrong, or else he says he's too busy with work. But when I ask about work, all he says is that the cafeteria ran out of rice pudding."

It was the way you said it, as if *the cafeteria ran out of rice pudding* were a betrayal. You need to take it back. "It's not as bad as I make it sound."

That's the truth. It's not as bad as you make it sound.

It's worse.

Three Days of Worse

8 A.M. calls sister, asks if he's interrupting her dinner
House keys don't work. Gets a new set made (from set
*   that "doesn't work")*
Offers cat a banana
Wakes at 3 A.M. Neighbor crying for help
Ignores me all night (again)

Tales In and Out of School

The train derailment is no longer an isolated incident. In the past two weeks, the downtown local train made a U-turn, making no stops, and went all the way to the Bronx. The week before, the train had to be evacuated because three people in one car had heart attacks, and yesterday the cab driver took him to Seventh Avenue in Brooklyn, not Seventh Avenue in Manhattan.

Nonetheless, the theory that impossibility and improbability, too, must be evidence based, coupled with the power of determined ignorance, allows you to cling to your hypothesis: Only you are aware of Leo's mishaps because you have no proof to the contrary. Yet analytic validity can just as easily be logical fallacy, and your validity disintegrates when Leo's secretary calls with the evidence required, required but not wanted.

"All morning," Thomas tells you, "Leo was in his office unfolding and refolding a tall stack of freshly laundered white lab coats."

Thomas is not Leo's personal secretary. He is the secretary for the department, all of whom want him muzzled, but preaching the Gospel falls under the protection of the First Amendment and isn't explicitly against any university policy. Also, he is very good at his job. Unlike his colleagues, Leo is neither rude nor cruel to Thomas. Rather, Leo responds to his proselytizing lightly, saying things like "Thomas, I got born once. That was enough."

Poor Thomas. A gay man deceived and manipulated by a pack of mentally twisted whack-jobs to undergo reverse-gay therapy and marry a reverse-lesbian from his church. His new life, he insists, is a gift from God. His reverse-lesbian wife tends a vegetable garden, and come late August or early September Thomas brings Leo a bag of fresh tomatoes. "Now these," Leo says, "*these* are a gift from God."

There's more than just the unfolding and refolding of the lab coats. Thomas runs down a few choice additional specifics: Sterilizing petri dishes containing carefully cultivated microbes; pestering his colleagues to turn on, then off, then on the sun button (a.k.a. the light switch); six ID cards lost, replaced, and spread across his desk as if he were playing a game of solitaire, and then there's the rice pudding. Every afternoon, Leo goes to the cafeteria and asks for rice pudding. "They don't serve rice pudding," Thomas says. "They've *never* served rice pudding. When Professor Schmidt tried to give him contact information for some specialist, Leo took the card, looked at it, and then gave it back. He said it was worth a fortune and advised Professor Schmidt to keep it in a safety-deposit box."

"Did anyone say what they think is causing this?" you ask. "Put a name to it?"

"I don't think they know, but even if they did, it would be highly unethical to tell me. All they say is that he's lost his mind, and he's driving them bananas."

"Explain this to me, Thomas. Why would it be unethical to tell you what is physically wrong with him, but it's not unethical to tell you that he's lost his mind and is driving them bananas?"

"I'm sorry," Thomas apologizes and clarifies that *bananas* is his word. "They wouldn't say bananas."

He's right. They wouldn't say bananas. Their words, surely,

would not be so soft. You picture them, Leo's colleagues, the students, and the cafeteria workers, trading stories, groaning over the inconveniences he's caused, and laughing. This is how it must feel to be the parent of a child who has no friends, a child who spends lunch hour trying to hide from the bullies who flick spitballs at his head. Is there solace to be had knowing that Leo is oblivious to the fact that he is the kid with cooties?

"I've prayed and prayed that this day would never come," Thomas says, "but the Lord has other plans. They can't have him here."

Barring crimes of moral turpitude, tenured faculty cannot be fired, not legally, and because in a court of law the Lord's plans aren't worth shit, the chair of the department, two representatives from Administration, two from Human Resources, and a quartet of attorneys convened around a conference table to cook up a temporal solution that would not result in litigation.

"They all want to do the best they can for him," Thomas says. "Everyone here likes him so much."

The best they can do amounts to this: a semester of medical leave bundled together with the sabbatical he's owed, his unused sick days, personal days, and vacation days, which will keep him on payroll, at his full salary, for one year and nine weeks. After that, he'll have to retire.

Retire? He's fifty-four years old. Even you, with your fiscal ineptitude, know that his Social Security won't kick in until he's sixty-two, and now his pension, which would've been substantial if he were to retire at retirement age, will amount to loose change. Leo's salary pays the bills and covers most everything else, too. The money you make is like money won in the lottery, and you blow through it like a gust of wind through an open door: swanky dinners, donations to PETA and the

Environmental Defense Fund, or indulging in some high-dollar item like the Persian carpet that Roberta uses as a scratching pad. With the idea that someday you would buy a cabin in the country, you've saved some money, but thus far, that money won't cover the down payment on an outhouse.

Thomas tells you that he's pretty sure that Leo will qualify for disability, that you should check with Social Security about that. "But there is one more thing," Thomas says. "They tried to explain everything to him, but nothing sunk in. You'll have to make him understand that he can't come back to work. The paperwork is all done. I'll send you the file now, but Leo has to sign the documents."

Leo's signature, his current signature, bears no resemblance to his former signature. As if his handwriting were a representation of the whole of him, it has diminished. You have to squint to read the now teeny-tiny and cramped lettering. The check he wrote to Con Edison looked like it had been written by a mouse, never mind that you had to remind him that you have auto-pay, that the bill was not a bill but a statement.

His signature isn't going to match his signature on any previous documents, but your hand-eye coordination, your ability to copy, is such that only a handwriting expert would be able to detect that it's a forgery.

Again, Thomas tells you how sorry he is. "I'll miss him. You know, he's the only one here who is kind to me."

You're on the verge of saying something nice, something about the tomatoes, but then the born-again reverse-gay man says, "Jesus loves you," and you're done.

To Tell the Truth

Only after the bartender sets down your drink, and you've taken a healthy gulp of vodka, can you turn your attention to Z, but with a deviation. Today, you go first. "Leo's on medical leave," you say.

"Oh, shit, Addison. They found out what's wrong? Is it something serious?"

"Haven't you been listening to me all this time? Yes, it's serious. We still don't know what's wrong, but whatever it is, work is too stressful." The words you choose, and those you leave out, are like veils. The general outline is clear, but the full picture is vague. "His colleagues agreed. He needs to take a break."

You can't bring yourself to tell Z the whole of it, not because you want to keep a secret from him but because if you say all the words, all of them, out loud, there'd be no way for you to escape the truth. The whole truth.

Sex and Death

L eo is wearing a suit and tie. His coat, knee-length, heavy black wool lined with thick silk, is slung over his arm. He doesn't want a cup of coffee. "I'm running late." He slips on his coat and says, "I'll be home by seven. If not before."

"Where are you going?"

"Where do you think I'm going? I'm going to work."

"Leo, you know that you don't work anymore. You quit."

His eyes narrow, befuddled or skeptical. "I did? When?"

"More than a month ago," you say.

"Why? Why would I have quit?"

You shrug, as if it didn't quite make sense to you, either. "You said you'd had enough, that you accomplished everything you set out to do there, and now you wanted to do other things."

"Okay. In that case, I'll go for a walk."

"Sounds good, but you don't need your heavy coat. A light jacket, at most. It's going up to seventy-six degrees today. Climate change."

"Maybe," he says, but he makes no move to take off his coat.

You walk him to the door and kiss him goodbye, the same chaste and sweet kiss you've come to exchange in the morning, and in bed before you go to sleep.

You kiss him as if you are apologizing for your thoughts.

You are apologizing for your thoughts.

It's a universal truth: over time, passion, the kind of passion where you can't keep your hands off each other, quiets down to sex a couple of times a week. By the time you hit the point of "more or less on a regular basis," foreplay has gone the way of daylight in winter, and for some couples, as if they've taken up residence in a polar circle, the sun never rises, and sex gets relegated to something like youthful indiscretion. Marriage becomes what marriage becomes. That's just how it goes.

As to be expected after twenty-four years together, your sex life had dwindled down. Twice a week, on average, unless you were traveling. As if hotel rooms were scented with Spanish fly, for the duration of your stay, the clock would roll back, not all the way back, but to the time of the twice-daily boink, at a minimum.

Granted, your glory days are behind you, but before, surely if a week had gone by with nothing, one of you, predicated on either the biological imperative or the need to be assured that you are loved and desired, would have asked, "Do you know how long it's been since we last had sex? Is something wrong?"

How long has it been since you last had sex?

The last time you had sex, which you didn't know then would be the *last* last time, was the night before your birthday, back when Leo was still more normal than not, normal enough so as not to be the stranger he's become. It wasn't exactly an out-of-body-experience kind of sex, but when you were done, you propped yourself up on your elbow and asked, "Was that my birthday eve present?"

There it was in his eyes and then spread across his face: *I forgot*. Not the *Oh shit, I forgot*, which accounts for the Hallmark line of *Belated Happy Birthday* cards—the abashed-faced cartoon character looking down at his feet. Leo's expression was one of fear. Leo had remembered that he never forgot your birthday. Until now.

But it was only a momentary memory lapse. The next day, he came home loosely swinging a Cerulean blue shopping bag by its gold-colored satin-braided handle. "Happy birthday," he said.

The size of the bag, made of high-end luxurious paper, hinted at a necklace, an expensive necklace.

Inside the Cerulean blue bag, something like nesting dolls, was a Cerulean blue box too big for a pendant but not for a statement necklace. The ribbon, tied with skill and flourish, was the same color gold as the bag's satin handles. Cerulean blue tissue paper fastened with a gold-colored sticker, textured to look like a wax seal, concealed what turned out not to be a necklace. It was an evening purse, an evening purse too small to hold more than a phone, a set of keys, and a tube of lipstick. An evening purse festooned with silver and red glass—no, not glass, plastic—cabochons glued to cheap filigreed brass. It was the kind of thing a little boy would pick out for his mother, and in that same way, if you were a little girl in your fairy princess stage of life, you would've swooned over it, but your fairy princess stage of life was long gone.

Even if he weren't standing there all puffed up with childlike pride, waiting, waiting expectantly for you to effuse over the utter gorgeousness of this *thing*, never would you have pointed out that one of the red plastic doodads was already coming unglued. Whatever your long list of faults, you are gracious. "It's so delicate," you said. "I'm almost afraid to use it. What do you think about keeping it on display? On a shelf. I mean, it's like a museum piece."

"That's a brilliant idea," he said, and so you put this grotesquerie on the top shelf of one of Leo's bookcases, where to look at it requires forethought and deliberate effort.

And that was the death of your desire for sex with your objectively handsome husband, just as it seems that he has lost all desire for sex with you, the difference being that with him you don't know why.

Do you know how long it's been?

Thirteen Days and Long Nights

Ten collages are ready to go. Ten, but Isabelle Weber is expecting twelve. Two more in eleven days explains why, at this late hour, you are in your studio, torturing yourself.

Against a backdrop of the solar system, you slide a two-inch plastic pink-and-green trout, up, down, left, right, off-center, herky-jerky, as if the pink-and-green trout were the planchette to a Ouija board. But the spirits are toying with you, refusing to give you a straight answer. You tell the spirits to go fuck themselves.

You pop an Ambien, which apparently you didn't need because as soon as your head meets the pillow, you fall from a troubled mind into the benevolence of oblivion.

But not for long.

It's nothing new, that your sleep is easily disrupted, disturbed by a shift of light, the call of a bird outside the window, the sound of rain, nightmares, ghosts, any thump in the dark, and now, as if you were in a trance and the hypnotist snapped his fingers, you're wide awake, as alert as a guard dog. No need to check the time. Give or take a few minutes in either direction, it's 3 A.M. The same way Leo's visual hallucinations occurred between nine and eleven at night, this is the hour when, once or twice a week, his brain invents an audial commotion. Now he's up and out of bed but standing as still as a brick.

"Leo," you ask, "what are you doing?"

"Shhh," he whispers. "That woman who lives next to us is in our bathroom."

"You were dreaming. Come back to bed. Go to sleep."

"I will," he says, but first he has to deal with our neighbor in the bathroom. Off he goes, and then, mission accomplished, he's back. "She's gone now," he tells you, "but get this. She washed her hands before she left. I put the towel in the washing machine."

You roll over and close your eyes, but you can forget about the oblivion of sleep.

One Big Mess

It looks as if a merry band of poltergeists had themselves one hell of a wild party in your studio. Images of vegetables, sea creatures, deserts, and dolls are strewn all over your table, and the floor is a crazy-quilt, littered with old postcards, sheet music, and illustrations of human anatomy.

If you can salvage the pink-and-green trout, that would leave you with just one more to do. One is only one. Two feels like two hundred. A trout on a cake plate? In a trash can? In a ski lift? No. No. No.

Roberta is sleeping on the couch. You sit beside her, stroking her, which is what you're doing when Leo returns from his daily all-day walk. He's wearing his coat. His scarf is wrapped around his neck. More disturbing than his dressing for midwinter in June is that he's as crisp as a cold apple. Perspiration should be dripping down his face, his hair should glisten as if slathered in Vaseline, but when he takes off his coat, his shirt looks as if it were freshly washed and ironed.

"I was just going to make a sandwich," you say. "Do you want one?"

"No, thanks. I'm going to take walk." He puts his coat back on, and the scarf, too. "I might stop at the store," he says. "Do you want anything?"

Do you want anything?

Yes. You want something.

You want Leo.

Your Leo.

Missing in Action

The day after tomorrow, Z is leaving for his six months on *the Continent*, and you are angry, furious, at him. You want to tell him that if he's going to leave now, *now*, then he should just stay on *the* fucking *Continent*, don't bother to come back. But you say no such thing because it's irrational. He's not leaving *you*. The timing, however, stinks. You're reduced to banalities. "So, you must be really excited. You're going to be the movie star of German Studies."

"Hardly," he says.

"Spare me the false modesty. You're going to blow them away."

He laughs. "You're right. I am. You, too. You have to email me the minute you hear from Isabelle Weber. I want to hear every word of the lavish praise."

"Lavish praise? From her? She's the original Ice Empress."

"Snow Queen," Z corrects you. "'Snedronningen.'"

"I thought I was going to miss you, but I'm not."

"Yes, you will. But you still have Leo."

"No. I don't still have Leo. He's been busy. Very busy."

"He's back at work? That's great."

"No. He's been busy walking. Every day, all day, he's out walking."

"Isn't that a good thing?" Z asks. "The exercise. Gets the blood flowing."

"Sure, it would be a good thing if he weren't wearing his winter coat. Eighty-something degrees out, and he's walking for hours on end with his coat on. And the weirdest part is that he doesn't sweat. Not a drop."

"I don't want to scare you," Z says, "but isn't that a symptom of schizophrenia?"

"I don't know. Except I'd think even Dr. Dum-Dum would've figured that one out. He's not talking to himself, and doesn't that start when you're young? I'd actually feel better if he were schizophrenic. At least then it would be *something*. A diagnosis. And I'm pretty sure that can be kept under control with medication."

"How about trying a regular psychiatrist instead of one of those specialists? Maybe he'd agree to that. It's not as daunting."

"The only way I could get Leo to a doctor now, any doctor, is if I stuffed him in a duffel bag and carried him over my shoulder."

"Addison, you've got to get him to a doctor. Maybe you could find one who makes house calls."

"We're not on the *Continent*, Z. Have you ever heard of an American doctor who makes house calls?" Your glass is empty. You ask Z if he wants another one.

"I can't," Z says. "I've got to get going. I still have a lot to do."

"I thought you were all packed, ready to board the plane."

"I am," Z says. "But the kids, they're kids. They haven't even started."

Z pays for your drinks. You're not ready to go, but you stand up when he does. You hug, and when you break apart, you say, "I'm happy for you, really I am, and you deserve all of it, but ..."

"But what?"

"Nothing. I'll miss you is all."

"I'll miss you, too. We'll keep in touch. Email me. Let me know what Isabelle Weber has to say," and with that, he, too, is gone.

A Day of Reckoning

You could tell Isabelle Weber that because her time constraint was unreasonable, you have only eleven collages to show her, not twelve, but you did say, "No problem." The only explanation is no explanation.

Plastic Bubble Wrap winds up in a landfill, or worse, the ocean, which is why you wrap the eleven collages in layers of newspaper and tie them into a bundle with brown twine. The Weber Gallery is well within walking distance, but it's brutally hot outside, and you'd be shocked if Isabelle Weber weren't repulsed by perspiration. You call an Uber.

As if art, like ice cream, melts if not frozen, the AC in the Weber Galley is on full blast and the white marble floors don't warm it up any. You should've worn a coat. Freezer-frigid and devoid of people. Maybe viewing is by appointment only. Also possible is that the tundra isn't a major New York tourist attraction. The paintings on exhibit are large-scale and brightly colored, like those of Gustavo Ramos Rivera, but you are afforded no more than a quick glance before the woman at the reception desk, who is not dressed in homage to Andy Warhol but rather like the assistant to a hedge fund manager, escorts you to Ms. Weber's office.

Isabelle Weber is as you'd imagined her: fashion-model tall, bone skinny, blond hair pulled back into a tight bun resting on the nape of her neck, someone for whom an arctic climate is room temperature. Fire-engine-red lipstick pops from her otherwise makeup-free face. You're not wearing lipstick, but your black eyeliner is winged into a perfect cat eye. The lone difference between your otherwise identical outfits, black T-shirts and black jeans, is that her T-shirt probably cost $699 at Bergdorf, whereas you got yours at Banana Republic.

By way of introduction, she says, "Isabelle Weber."

By way of welcome, she instructs, "You can put them over there, on the table behind you."

You tell her that you finished only eleven. "Not twelve. And one, I don't think, is up to snuff."

"Well, at least you're honest. I'll call you before the week is out."

And with that, you are dismissed.

Short Division

No more than eight, that's what Isabelle Weber said. No more than eight, but five? She wants only five. "I'm not at all keen on the others," she says. "I assume your reference to one as subpar was that thing with the fish."

That thing? True, it's not your best, or even the least bit good, but *that thing* stings.

Those that she is not keen on, you can retrieve at your own convenience. One of her assistants will bring them out to you.

It doesn't take Pythagoras to figure out that five out of eleven is less than half. Less than fifty percent is a solid F.

You could say that you have only yourself to blame.

But you don't blame yourself.

You blame Leo.

When he gets home, still wearing that damn coat, he finds you curled up in bed, and he asks, "Are you okay? What's wrong?"

You sit up, wipe your eyes, and leaving out the part about how it's all his fault and what's wrong is *him*, you say only, "Not okay. Isabelle Weber rejected six of my collages. Six out of eleven rejected."

"That's excellent," he says.

"Excellent? How is less than fifty percent excellent?"

"It's not less than fifty percent. She told you that she wasn't going to take more than eight. Five out of eight is 62.5 percent."

Your preoccupation with your dismal showing is interrupted by the fact that, in less time than it takes to sneeze, Leo did the math in his head. It's like when a film runs in reverse, as if a centripetal force gathers up the eggshells, which fly upward, the broken pieces snapping back into place, and there's Humpty-Dumpty, a whole egg with no visible scars, perched on the wall, spindly legs dangling over the edge.

"How is 62.5 percent any better?" you say. "It's a D. D-minus."

D-minus is the kind of grade that might get you into community college on probation, which would be okay had you not been counting on that letter of acceptance from Stanford.

"It's not a test, Addie. You didn't fail anything. Give yourself some credit. Five of your pieces are going to be in a show at the Weber Gallery. That's huge."

This is Leo. Your Leo, which is why when he tells you that he's going to take a walk, you want to beg him not to go, to please stay here, stay here like this, reasonable and wise, but you don't. Instead you say, "Would you please take off that damn coat?"

No, he won't take off the damn coat, and out he goes. He leaves you, and you are left hanging onto the precipice by your fingernails.

Hang on, Addie. Don't let go. Don't fall.

Ten Days in July

*Overdue homeowner's insurance bill and three subsequent
warning notices hidden under stack of books
Watches 5–10 minutes of movie and walks away (Bored?
    Unable to concentrate?)
Bookmarks (minimum dozen) 3–11 pages in (Attention
    span?)
Ignores me all night
Ditto
Pouring rain, refuses to take umbrella
Mumbles (garbles) some words
Walk, walk, walk (coat)
Otherwise fine, whatever that means*

The Ephemera of Dreams

This morning, after eating a bowl of Cheerios with *milk*, Leo leaves (*no coat!*) to buy the newspaper, and in no time at all, he's back with the *Times* and the weather report.

"It's not exactly balmy," he says, "but it's not humid. We should do something. Go somewhere. You've been cooped up for weeks. How about the flea market?"

"Yes. Absolutely." You grab your bag, and, despite the fact that he's not wearing it now, you tell him, "You don't need your coat."

"Thanks for the tip." Leo is laughing at you. "I said it wasn't humid. I didn't say it was snowing."

How can it be that in ninety-degree weather, when the city is an expansive sauna, Leo can walk for hours wearing that heavy wool coat of his and sweat not so much as a teardrop, yet after a fifteen-minute leisurely mosey to the flea market, his forehead is slick with perspiration? You can't make sense of it because there is no sense to be made of it.

You don't bother with the table that's all about lamps, and you can skip the one with the Hummel figurines on display, but you stop at the next table, where three large cartons take up half the surface. Three large cartons filled with authentic junk: a chipped bud vase, spools of thread, rhinestone brooches with all but one or two rhinestones missing, a plate with a fault line, one knitting needle. You turn over a card of four intricately carved jet buttons to look at the price: $10.

The dealer says, "I'll take eight."

She's none too quick counting out the two dollars, in coins, and you crane your neck looking for Leo. When you spy him across the aisle examining an antique microscope, you say to the vendor, "Forget it. Keep the change."

Not to be as mindful of money as would be prudent is one thing, but those microscopes don't come cheap, and Leo already has two of them. You put your hand on his forearm to stop him from pulling out his wallet. "Leo, you've got this exact same one at home."

"It's not *exactly* the same," he says, "but you're right. It's similar. I don't need it."

Of course he doesn't *need* it, nor is there a place in your apartment for another antique microscope, not to mention the extravagance, yet now you want him to buy it. You want him to be happy. But then he lights up when he discovers a dented aluminum tin of Dr. Dodd's Sunlight Pills. He wonders if Sunlight Pills were a cocaine compound or flour bonded with corn syrup. You ease the tin from his hands, and, as if your money weren't his money, you say, "My treat."

The tin of Sunlight Pills is somewhat larger than a tin of Altoids, and Leo asks if you'd put it in your bag. "It won't fit in my pocket."

You're about to quip, "You should've worn your coat," and then you think, *What am I? Stupid?*

Neither of you comes across anything else that you can't live without until, at the second-to-last table before you exit, you happen on a row of cartons filled with books. You and Leo browse through the boxes. None of the books pique Leo's interest, but you score a prize, a 1950s Dick and Jane primer.

Leo suggests you have brunch before going home.

After the waiter takes your order—two spinach omelets,

coffee for Leo, and a Bloody Mary for you—you open the primer and, toying with the words on the page, you say, "Look, Jane. Look. See Dick."

It's a sweet smirk that Leo gives you, and he says, "You're such a child. It's Spot. 'Look, Jane. See Spot.'"

"You memorized *Fun with Dick and Jane*?"

"It was a memorable book," he says. "Moronic, but memorable," and he adds, "We should go to the flea market more often. Today was nice, don't you think?"

"Better than nice. It was perfect."

Every now and again, when you are in a deep-down sleep, you dream about your grandfather, that he is with you, teaching you how to paint, how to mix colors on the palette board with a palette knife, how to create shadow, how light isn't yellow, it's white, and you are awash with awe and love, but then it happens, as it has to happen, in that flash between dreaming and the state of being fully conscious, you get consumed with the dread of waking, of knowing that when you wake, you will not be sitting with your grandfather cleaning your brushes in a can of turpentine, and you will have to relive that loss of awe and love all over again. Your grandfather died when you were eleven.

If only you didn't have to wake up.

Post-Perfect

Light bulbs in sock drawer
Calls sister, talks 20 minutes, hangs up, no goodbye
Calls sister, 7 minutes, says goodbye, doesn't hang up
Mumbles, sentences trail off into garble, babble
Heat wave, wears sweater under coat
5 days in a row, wearing same shirt. Refuses to change.
Told him it smells. Told me I smell
Watching TV. Asks me to quit talking. Not talking

The Doleful Sound of Howling

It's 3 A.M., and according to Leo, a pack of Siberian huskies is in your living room, howling. "They're fine," he assures you. "It's primal. Their ancestry. The wolf genes." Leo explains that they howl when they want to go out, but sometimes they howl because they get lonely without their human companion. "If that's the case," he says, "I'll stay with them. Otherwise, they could go on like this all night."

Leo goes off to comfort the Siberian huskies, who, needless to say, are *not* in your living room howling.

Except now you hear it, too, the howling, the doleful howling, but this is howling only you can hear, and it goes on like this for the remainder of the night.

Radioactive

Across the board, it's been a long summer devoid of human connection. After all, you can refuse only X number of dinner invitations before they quit coming. Even Jack and Alicia have stopped asking.

It has not escaped your attention that not so much as one of Leo's former colleagues has called to say hello or ask how he is doing, and unless Leo's made new friends you don't know about, he talks with no one other than his sister and you. The full extent of your communication with anyone other than Leo consists of the twice-weekly phone calls with Miriam and your email exchanges with Z, but Miriam, who avoids the subject of Leo entirely, monopolizes the conversations by recapping the plots of the YA vampire series she's editing, and with Z, emails are like postcards: *The weather is here. Wish you were beautiful.*

Face it. You are lonely, and worst of all is when Leo is with you. He's there but not there, not Leo, like how no matter how hard you press a conch shell to your ear, you're no nearer to the Jersey Shore. The only possible explanation for your enthusiastic yes to Judy's invitation to meet for tea is that you're craving human interaction. You don't even drink tea.

The saving grace is that you're not making a day of it, because Judy is squeezing you in between lunch with her sister and the drive back to Garrison.

Only now when any chance of punctuality has come and gone does it dawn on you that you don't have a gift for Duncan. Bringing gifts for the children is something you do. A new toy tends to keep the whining to a minimum. It's too late to stop at the store, but ever resourceful, you pick through Roberta's toy basket. You don't have to have children to know that no kid will be enthralled with a catnip mouse or a chewed-up crinkle ball, but surely a laser pointer is a toy that transcends species.

Judy is mildly peeved that you are late, but when she sees the gift you've given to her son, mildly peeved is instantly subsumed by wildly pissed off.

"What is wrong with you?" Her voice comes from a dark place, guttural, demonic. "That is an outrageously inappropriate gift for a child. For anyone." But when she turns her attention to her son, her tone shifts, all sweetie pie. "Duncan, honey, that's not a toy. Give it to Mommy."

But Duncan is aiming the pointer at some college girl, who, texting away, is oblivious to the red dot flitting from the wall to her forehead, and his mouth falls open, wide enough for you to step inside.

The way an alligator clamps a small mammal in its jaws, Judy clamps her hand around Duncan's wrist and her voice drops an octave, less sweetie pie. "Duncan, please give it to me. Now. It's radioactive. Do you know what *radioactive* means?"

You tell her that it's not radioactive. "It's one milliwatt. One milliwatt is not radioactive. Do you really think Leo would give Roberta something dangerous? It's a toy. A cat's toy."

Judy is attempting to pry open Duncan's fingers. Good luck with that. Duncan's fist is tight, as if he were gearing up to punch her. Because no mother wants her kid making a scene in public, Judy compromises. "Keep it aimed at the floor. If the red gets anywhere near a person's eyes, they'll go blind. Do you understand?"

"What about at my feet?" Duncan asks.

"No. Absolutely not. The floor. Radiation is poison."

"It's one milliwatt."

Judy glares at you. Her silence is aggressive, and you don't bother to explain that playing with a one-milliwatt laser pointer is not the same as playing in puddles in Chernobyl.

As if this café offers complimentary coordinated metaphors, your coffee tastes like the burnt dregs of the pot and the croissant is stale. Judy squeezes extra lemon into her caffeine-free ginger tea. Duncan couldn't give a flying fuck about his carrot juice.

Judy's physiognomy has not changed. She looks like the same Judy, the one who smoked baggies of weed and laughed over everything and nothing. If you could get Judy to laugh now, maybe then you could laugh, too, and this little get-together might transport you back to how things used to be. But laugh about what? There must be something to make her laugh.

Something.

Something, but what?

And then, something comes to you, and you perk up. "I have the most hilarious story to tell you. Remember when Leo was having those insane hallucinations?"

"He's not still hallucinating, is he? Really, he should sue that place."

"No, no. Nothing like that. Nothing like it was before." Omission is not prevarication. It *is* nothing like it was before. "But there was this one he had, I don't even remember when it was, but it was a doozy."

Judy sneaks a quick peek under the table, and once she's satisfied that Duncan isn't going all-out Marie Curie on himself, you then tell her about the little girl, how Leo accused you of losing her, but Judy's not laughing. She's misty-eyed, oozing concern, treacly concern, and creepy, too.

"I have to ask," she says. "Did you ever have an abortion?"

You clutch the handle of your coffee mug, not to take a sip but as if to get a tight grip on the coffee cup handle were the same as to get a grip on yourself. "What's that got to do with Leo's hallucination?"

"Isn't it obvious?" Judy says. "He was envisioning the child you denied him. You denied him a child, and now it's too late."

The words you want are stuck in your throat, stuck as if stuck in a muck of bile, black bile that you'd like to spit in her face. But your mouth is dry. Although nowhere near as satisfying as a gob of spit would be, you take a ten-dollar bill from your wallet and fling it at her. Paper money, lacking sufficient mass to travel the distance, flutters like a dying moth and lands on the table, and you are out the door.

It's all noise in your head, noise like a souped-up car without a muffler, but when you get to the corner, while waiting for the light to change, the noise gives way to a coherent thought: *I should go back there. I should go back and snatch the laser pointer away from her kid*, but then you think, *No, no, don't do that.* You want Judy to be the one to take it away from him, which you know she will do. You want Judy to be the one to make her child cry.

One Pea in a Pod

L eo takes off his coat and asks you, "Where's my wife?"
You glance over your shoulder as if someone might really be there, standing behind you.

But looking you square in the face, Leo repeats his question. "Where is my wife?"

"Where's your wife? Leo, I'm your wife."

"No," Leo says. "You're not my wife. Where is my wife?" And then as if you were not his wife, as if you were someone else's wife, Lot's wife, you freeze, go mute, go blank, until Leo, in a way that is unmistakably accusatory, as if demanding you answer the question, asks again, "Where is my wife?"

"Leo, *I'm* your wife."

"No. You are *not* my wife. You look like my wife, but you are *not* my wife," and as if to confirm this for a fact, he says, "My wife is prettier than you are."

In the abstract, out of context, you would have deliberated if you should be insulted that he considers you, because *you* are you, to be less attractive, or if you should be flattered that he believes you are prettier than this woman, this impostor of his wife.

But this is not in the abstract, this is *in* context, and you're too rattled to care which of you is the fairest in the land.

You tell him that his wife is sleeping. "Leave her be," you say. "She needs to rest," and you go to the bedroom, where you get into bed and pull the top sheet, pale blue, up and over your head.

From Bad to Worse and Repeat*

Books in bathtub
3 A.M. Siberian huskies howling in living room
Six $100 bills in the freezer; five $100 bills between towels
  in linen closet (no problem with "money machine")
Thought I was impostor (Capgras syndrome?)
3 A.M. (3 A.M. witching hour?) someone on 7th floor needs
  help. Couldn't say help with what
3 A.M. wakes me holding thermometer to check if my fever
  came down (not sick)
Bit into pear "laced with cyanide," dropped poison pear in
  toilet (didn't flush)
3 A.M. got dressed to go to bookstore
Bought dog biscuits for cat, asked if I wanted one
Accused me of having affair
3 A.M. gets dressed to go to work
3 A.M. gets dressed to go for haircut
Accused me of stealing "his things" (wouldn't /couldn't say
  which things)

*Calls sister incessantly
*Mumbles, garbles, sentences trail off
*3 A.M. outings
*Mixes up words, uses wrong words (aphasia?)

*Ignores me (even when I ask questions)
*Reads 3–5 pages, then opens a different book
*Won't watch more than 10 minutes of movies
* Some days seems okay, but still won't acknowledge problems
*Rarely laughs

This Night Is Different

On those nights when Leo gets up for a 3 A.M. foray to the hardware store, or to join the search party looking for a lost poodle, you try to reason with him, cajole him, plead with him to get back into bed. Some nights you succeed, but when he refuses to believe that the post office is closed, or that he isn't going to miss his flight, or that *everyone* isn't waiting for him and out he goes, your imagination pulls out all the stops: a crazed meth head with a gun shoots him in the stomach, and he's left there to die, alone on the street in a pool of his own blood; he gets run over by a drunk driver who doesn't bother to stop, and he dies, alone, on the street, a string of blood coming from his mouth; he falls off the pier into the Hudson River and drowns, his body found the next day floating and bloated.

Tonight is different. Tonight, you don't sit up and say, "Leo, it's three in the morning. Where are you going?" Instead, you pretend to be asleep, but when you hear the door close behind him, those same scenarios, that same film noir footage, loops through your head. What's different about the torment tonight is now you *want* the crazed meth head to shoot him; you *want* him to be the victim, DOA, of a hit-and-run; you *want* him to drown, an accidental death, in the Hudson River.

Maybe he was prescient when he said you *look like my wife, but you're not my wife*, because you don't recognize yourself as yourself, either. How, when, did you get this cold? So cold, so cold that on a hot summer day, you could park yourself on a bench under the mid-afternoon sun wearing your winter coat, and still you'd be too cold to break a sweat.

The Report

With a good deal more oomph than necessary, you're yanking his shirts and jackets from their hangers, all the while shrieking the shriek of a madwoman, "Get out! Get the fuck out," but Leo responds as if you were doing something like loading the washing machine or clearing the table, and not flinging his pants, shirts, sweaters, socks, and underwear out the door, where a few feet into the hallway they've accumulated like a mound of dried leaves raked in autumn.

It is autumn, but the leaves didn't change colors with the season. Nothing is as it should be.

Only when you toss out a few books for good measure does he get the fuck out, but unlike the way you might walk through a mound of dried leaves crunching underfoot, he sticks to the perimeter as if circumventing a puddle.

He's not wearing a coat. When he gets in the elevator, you go to the bathroom. The Xanax is in the medicine cabinet. The vial is the kind with a childproof cap, but because you're shaking enough to make your bones bleed, you have to open it with your teeth. The two tablets dissolve under your tongue, which speeds up the rate of absorption. In a matter of minutes, you are not serene, but you are reasonably calm. Calm enough to embark on the task of returning his things, neatly, to their respective closets and drawers. You've put the books back on the shelf, and while you're collecting his socks and underwear, the elevator stops and the doors open. Leo emerges, but he is not alone. Trailing close behind him, like a pair of pull toys, are two policewomen.

Police*women*, police*men*, police*people*, no difference. Their faces are set in that same look, the look that might as well be part of the uniform. The cap, badge, baton, gun, and the look that says: You're guilty of . . . I don't know what, but you are guilty of something, or you're right there, right on the verge of committing a criminal act, as if by virtue of simply entering the subway station means you're about to jump the turnstile.

The gum-chewing policewoman with a bovine jawline asks, "You want to tell us what happened here?"

As if what's going on out here were no business of his, Leo goes inside, and you explain, "There's something wrong with him. With his brain." You're not crying in what would have been a vain attempt to soften them up. You're crying because you are crying. "I just lost it."

"Yeah, well. But you can't do this. We'll have to write up a report."

"A report?"

Her partner, clearly a rookie trying to act like a full-blown cop, says, "We're talking about domestic violence here."

"Domestic violence? There was no violence."

"It's in the category," she says, and you ask, "Do I need a lawyer?"

"No. But we have to write it up. It'll get filed somewhere. Just don't do anything like this again."

If you ever wondered how it happens that women who previously reported real incidents of domestic violence wind up getting murdered, now you know: the reports get filed "somewhere," and the husband or boyfriend need not bother calling a lawyer.

When again the elevator stops at your floor, one of your

neighbors, the banker who lives at the other end of the hall, steps out. He should turn left, but when he sees the two policewomen, and you holding an armful of Leo's socks and underwear, some of it still on the floor, he asks, "Everything okay?"

You wouldn't mind if one of the policewomen were to tell him that there's nothing to see here, that he should move along, mind his own business, but they act like they didn't hear him, so you say, "Everything's fine."

As if he's not sure whether or not to believe you, he hesitates, until you repeat, "Everything is fine. Really."

Fine? Everything is not fine. Nothing is fine.

Help

You call the NYC Suicide Hotline because there's no such thing as a Homicide Hotline, and you are desperate.

PART THREE

5

Someone Is Listening

The Suicide Hotline volunteer picks up on the first ring, which makes sense. Think about it: a suicidal person is about to jump but holds off to make that last-ditch cry for help, only to listen to the phone ring once, twice, five times, as if all representatives were busy assisting other customers. How many times does the phone have to ring before a suicidal person takes a flier off a tall building?

You probably shouldn't tie up the line. You probably should say, "Sorry, wrong number," but what if she doesn't believe you? Suppose she thinks that before she's had the chance to talk you down, you decided not to postpone the inevitable? That could devastate a Good Samaritan or, at the very least, ruin her day. But you do tell her, "I'm not going to kill myself."

"So, why are you calling?" she asks.

Good question. Why *are* you calling when this woman has lives to save, *really* save? But doesn't your life needs saving, too? "Because," you say, "because I don't know what to do."

"Do about what?" she asks.

"My husband. There's something wrong. Very wrong. For nearly two years now, he's been seeing things, and hearing things, and his words are all mixed up, and he can't work, and he thought I was an impostor of myself, and ..." You're spilling your guts in the way food poisoning happens, relentless spasms, until every crumb, every word, is purged. To release the words is what you needed most of all, to say the words out loud, out loud to someone, even if that someone might be doodling the whole time, or texting, or clipping her toenails, there is respite to be had. Temporary respite. The dry heaves will come soon enough, but for now, you can rest your head on the cool tile of the bathroom floor.

You express sincere appreciation for her listening to you, but you want to hang up before she can wish you luck or tell you to take it one day at a time, which isn't all that different from what she does say. "I know a therapist who might be able to help you. Can you get to Brooklyn?"

"That's thoughtful of you, but I don't need therapy." You probably *do* need therapy, but who doesn't?

"She's not that kind of a therapist. She's a consultant. A facilitator." The Suicide Hotline volunteer tells you her mother had Alzheimer's. "I was at my wit's end," she says. "Marcy helped me with everything. What to expect, how to prepare, who to call, experimental treatments, where I could find the best care. Everything."

"But he doesn't have Alzheimer's."

"She deals with all kinds of mental health issues. Really, she can help you."

As if this woman on the phone were actually standing there alongside you, looking over your shoulder, you write down Marcy's name and number and then crumple up the piece of paper and drop it in your trash can.

Now what are you going to do?

You retrieve the ball of paper and smooth out the creases.

It's Warm in Here

Tall, big-boned, long brown hair worn in a single braid, Marcy is the sort of woman you'd describe as "earthy," as if she might smell like an Idaho potato dug fresh from the dirt. The path to her office is through the kitchen, a country-quaint, gingham, calico, cringe-worthy kitchen. Perched on the windowsill, a white porcelain duck sporting a glazed blue-and-white checkered bandanna around its neck speaks to you: *This is a colossal waste of time and three hundred bucks down the toilet.*

"Would you like a cup of tea?" Marcy asks.

A cup of vodka you wouldn't turn down, but tea? "No, thank you."

You are not enchanted by the decor of Marcy's office, either, not the needlepoint sampler nor the quilted wreaths hanging on the walls, and the two chairs, the way they are arranged side by side behind her desk is alarming. Marcy sits in the one closest to the wall, directly facing her computer, and she pats the seat of the chair where you decidedly would prefer not to sit.

"I know it seems awkward, at first," Marcy says. "But the desk creates a barrier. That's not helpful."

It's a comfortable chair, but you can't escape the icky sensation that the seat is damp, moist from the milk of human kindness.

Marcy opens a new file. "Let's start with a general overview, the first indications that something was amiss, the progression of symptoms, changes in abilities, shifts in behavior. Did you write any of it down?"

You fish around in your bag for your notebook, the pages and pages of lists that could just as well be tracking the progression of kudzu: a plant soon to grow out of control, block the sunlight, smother all forms of life in its ever-widening path, until there's nothing but devastation and destruction left in its wake. "I don't know that I wrote down everything," you tell her, "but I've got a whole lot of it."

"Good." It's almost curt, the way Marcy says, "Good, very good," as if you work for her and did a reasonably decent job at an assigned task.

You start at the beginning, almost two years ago now. "But back then, he knew he was hallucinating. Not like now."

Without looking up from her keyboard, Marcy asks, "He *knew* or he *suspected*? I mean, did he actually say that he was hallucinating, or did he ask if you were seeing what he was seeing?"

This distinction had not occurred to you. "It seemed like he knew. He certainly didn't argue with me, and we laughed about them. At first, he thought it was an eye problem. Macular degeneration, but it wasn't. Then he went for all the brain scans, but they showed nothing out of order." Because you're not about to read the entirety of your notebook, you pick and choose, making selections that, pieced together, create a picture. "But there are still days, or good chunks of days, when it seems like nothing is wrong. Except he's not himself. He's different."

Although there's no absolution to be had, you confess how you threw his clothes out into the hall, how all too often you can't even look at him, how you no longer try to stop him when he goes out in the middle of the night because you want something terrible to happen to him.

Marcy seems to be possessed with the binocular vision of an owl, the way she's bent over the keyboard but sees that you're biting down hard on your lower lip. She slides the box of tissues over to you.

You blow your nose into what is already a wet tissue. A big glob of snot breaks through and sticks to your hand. Now, you're a disgusting person inside and out.

Typing away, Marcy still doesn't look at you, not even when she stops to ask questions about things you wrote down but didn't include in your rundown: Difficulty with numbers? Does he have disturbed heat regulation? Is he sleeping during the day? Do his hands shake? Or twitch? Do his feet shuffle when he walks?

"No. Leo walks the way a fish swims, except that he stops to eat and sleep." Then you say, "I might be wrong about that. Do fish stop to sleep?"

Marcy lets go with one of those self-deprecating laughs that are half-laugh and half-snort and says, "I haven't got a clue."

"That neuropsychiatrist we went to, he asked the same questions about the walking and his hands."

"You saw a neuropsychiatrist? When was that?"

"After the scans came up clean, but it was a waste of time. He had Leo draw a clock. I tried to get him to see someone else, but he refused."

Marcy quits typing, and she swivels her chair in your direction, to look at you face-to-face. You take another tissue from the box, and then two more.

"The problem with a lot of these doctors," she says, "is that their diagnostic scope is limited to the norm. They don't consider the exceptions beyond the ninety-eighth percentile. They forget that two percent is not the same as zero."

Maybe because that's what Leo would've said, or maybe because she knew that you needed a tissue without your having to ask, but whatever the reason, you find that you're flooded with warmth for Marcy. You trust her. You respect her. You forgive her the needlepoint sampler, the gingham and calico, the porcelain duck in her kitchen.

"Your husband is far younger than the statistical age range, and the tremors and shuffling generally develop prior to, or concurrent with, the onset of the hallucinations." She stops there, but only to retrieve a white wicker trash basket from under her desk, which she holds out for you to deposit the used tissues. Then she picks up where she left off. "But, with the erratic behavior, symptoms that mimic multiple brain disorders, symptoms that *do* vary from person to person, the ups and downs and stretches of plateau, the neuropsychiatrist should have known."

"Known what?" you ask, and Marcy tells you, "Your husband has Lewy body disease."

Lewy body disease. It's a thing! With a name, corralled and definitive. Lewy body disease. It's a disease, and there are all kinds of cures and treatments for diseases. Expecting an answer along the lines of amoxicillin or naproxen or vitamin B injections, you ask Marcy, "So, what's next?"

"It's hard to predict," she says, "but now that the bad days far outweigh the good ones, I'd say he's coming to a steep drop. You need to make plans."

"Steep drop? Plans? What kind of plans?"

"Dementia patients require special care," she says.

"Dementia? You said *disease*. Lewy body *disease*."

"Sometimes it's referred to as a disease. Other times dementia. It's a matter of semantics," she says.

A matter of semantics is defined as either a trivial distinction of word choice or an essential distinction, like how *submerge* and *drown* share a definition, but the distinction is decidedly essential: what is submerged will reemerge, but to drown is to stay down, down in the depths of Lake Tanganyika, a vantage point from where, despite the geographical proximity, you'll never see a pride of lions sunning themselves on the Serengeti plain.

Marcy waits until you no longer need another tissue, at least for the moment, before asking if your papers are in order. "A will, power of attorney, health care proxy. I can recommend a lawyer who will prepare everything in advance, and on one of the days when your husband is lucid, you can scoot over to the lawyer's office for him to sign the documents."

No thanks to you, your documents *are* in order. It was one of the ways in which Leo was like a Boy Scout: *Be Prepared.*

How could you possibly have been prepared for this?

"You never know," Leo said. "I could get hit by a car tomorrow."

Hit by a car, a drunk driver, and left there to die alone on the street.

Marcy outlines how consecutive hours of lucidity will continue, at least for a while, but there will be days when lucid hours are reduced to minutes, which could then be followed by uninterrupted days of full cognition. "There really is no way to predict what will happen when. The decline is erratic," she says.

If you were a child, you'd have clamped your hands over your ears, refused to listen, but you're not a child. Instead, you pick apart a tissue, rolling the torn pieces between your fingers into little cylinders that fall on your lap, as Marcy tells you, "Ups, downs, plateaus, but eventually, there are radical and steep drops, and the ups are not up much. Later, when his mind is completely gone, it can happen that there's a sudden flash, like a spasm, of full cognition. It doesn't necessarily happen," she says, "but if it does, it can be alarming."

For now, for today, these are your preliminary instructions: First, order an identification bracelet for Leo, something like one of those medical alert bracelets. Next on the list, you have to find a way to give yourself a break, time away from Leo. Marcy asks if you have family or friends who can stay with him.

"He has a sister," you say. "My closest friend is out of the country. I haven't been talking much with anyone else."

"People tend to isolate themselves when things like this happen. It's a mistake. You need your friends, but for now, ask his sister if she can stay with him for a few days. And you should consider joining a support group. Even if only an online forum to engage with people who are going through the same thing."

A support group? Online, offline, end of the line, no way, never, but you keep that to yourself, and you thank her for the clarity, for telling it to you straight, and for her no-nonsense brand of kindness. You write out the check for $300, and while buttoning your coat, you thank her again, profusely, as if she has given you a gift, something you've always wanted, as opposed to what she has given you; a gift in a plastic bag heavy with human waste.

Blessed Are the Good

The price of an identification bracelet includes three lines of free engraving and free advice: *Avoid last names, addresses, and Social Security numbers. We suggest first names and phone numbers only.*

On the first line: *Leo.* No additional information. Just *Leo.* Next, *Addie* along with your phone number, and then, on the third line, *Denise* and her phone number. You pay extra for express delivery.

Between the successive phone calls from Leo and the conversations you and she have had in private, it's not as if Denise doesn't know that something is wrong, very wrong, with Leo. But this? If there were any way to put a good spin on it, you would. But there isn't, so you can't.

"No, I can't believe this," Denise says. "Not him. He's so smart."

Leo was the only person in his family who finished high school, and later when he went to graduate school, they were confused. Hadn't he already finished college?

Denise was not yet Sweet Sixteen when she got knocked up and married her loser boyfriend. They moved into one half of a two-family house that was only a few blocks away from the house where she and Leo grew up, and where their father lived until he died. On top of being a loser, Denise's adolescent husband was also a drunk. A year later, Denise got pregnant again. Two babies before she was old enough to vote, but unlike your mother, Denise is no fool. In short order, her drunk of a husband got the boot.

Now, again she says, "But he's so smart. How can this be true?"

"I don't know. Never in my wildest dreams . . ." You correct yourself: ". . . worst nightmares. But listen, I have a favor to ask. A big favor. I'll understand if you say no, but Marcy told me that I've got to find some time for myself. Alone. Is there any chance that Leo could spend Thanksgiving weekend with you?"

"That's not a favor," she says. "Of course he can stay here. He's my brother, and it's not like I don't have the room."

Flying in the face of the conventional ideology about high school dropouts, Denise has done very well for herself. Working two jobs, leaving a cousin to babysit the kids, Denise was able to buy her half of the two-family house. Three years later, she bought the other half, which she rented out. Still working two jobs, combined with the rent she collected, she invested in a second two-family house. With three rental properties, and the Cambridge of Harvard rapidly subsuming the Cambridge of the working class, Denise retired. Unlike Leo, the decision was hers to make. Now, instead of bagging groceries and slinging hamburgers, she spends her days doing what she likes best: dusting, scrubbing, sweeping, polishing, and cooking for Joey, her son. Denise can't abide a house that doesn't sparkle, and Joey can't abide the idea of employment.

Joey is her son, *her* son, but he takes after his father, except never, ever, would Denise give Joey the boot. Her daughter left home on her own accord, but when she's in desperate need of a fix, she shows up at Denise's door for a handout. In contemporary parlance, Denise is the classic enabler, but what Denise says is "He's my son. She's my daughter."

He's my brother.

You're quick to offer to accompany Leo there and back, by

train, because you're confident that Denise will say what she does say. "Don't be ridiculous. Joey will come to you, and after, he'll drive him home. It's not like he's busy."

Because truth and manipulation need not be mutually exclusive, as if it were an afterthought, you say, "I'm wondering if Joey might prefer to drive down on Tuesday. Or Monday, even. You know there are more car accidents on Thanksgiving weekend than any other time of the year."

"I'm glad one of us is thinking," Denise says. "He can pick him up on Monday and bring him back the following Monday or Tuesday. Avoid the traffic, and I'll get to have Leo here longer. We'll have a ball."

"Denise, I can't tell you how much . . ." but before you can finish the thought, she cuts you off. "He's my brother," she says.

He's my son.

She's my daughter.

He's my brother.

Denise is a good person, but she hasn't had much good luck with the people she loves.

Skip to the End

While Leo sleeps, you google: *Lewy body disease.*

The first website you open is associated with a highly prestigious medical institution, but right off the bat, you're confronted with that word: *dementia.* You click on different site, one also connected to a hot-shot place, and then you try another one and another, all of them semantically wedded to *dementia.* Not you. In your head, as you read, you doggedly substitute their word for your word.

Lewy body *disease* is tracked in Seven Stages like the way Hell is delineated in Nine Circles.

Stage 1: devoid of symptoms.

Devoid of symptoms?

It's a terrifying syllogism: if diagnosis is predicated on the symptoms alone, and Stage 1 is devoid of symptoms, is it not logical to conclude that anyone and everyone who is devoid of symptoms has, in fact, entered Stage 1 of Lewy body disease, and therefore Stage 2 is waiting in the wings for us all?

That can't be right. You go back to those other *d*-word sites, but it's unanimous. Stage 1 is asymptomatic, and they are also of one mind when it comes to the onset of Stage 2.

Stage 2: symptoms that mimic those of Parkinson's disease occurring prior to, or concurrent with, vivid hallucinations.

Of one mind, and more points for Marcy, as it's a closed mind, a collectively closed mind.

After that, it's like you've been suckered into a game of three-card monte. Behavioral changes are not fixed. Depending on which expert is running the deck, some sites list things like difficulty operating simple machinery (ATM, computer), aphasia, antisocial behavior, and loss of libido can be found in the column under Stage 2, whereas other sites have aphasia and loss of libido in Stage 3. Auditory hallucinations, Capgras syndrome, paranoia—pick a card, any card—are listed in Stage 2, Stage 3, and some you find early into Stage 4. You do discover a bit of additional consensus, such as how they've all got garbled speech slotted midway down into Stage 2. Okay, that fits except their garbled speech commences right around the same time as chronic and significant nasal discharge, an assertion that does not comport with your experience. You've never seen nasal discharge sliming out like a raw egg from Leo's nose, and that is the sort of thing you'd have noticed, for sure. Equally baffling is that, although some sites put diminished attention span in Stage 2 and others have it in Stage 3, they all claim a diminished attention span is preceded by excessive sleeping. Leo's attention span might be diminished to that of a fruit fly, but excessive sleeping? You wish. None of these sites make mention of excessive walking nor of wearing a winter coat in summer, and there is nothing about trying to feed a banana to a cat.

You go to a different site altogether, one less impressively credentialed, but not crackpot, either. In the same way that Marcy with her Master's degree in social work made mincemeat of that neuropsychiatric nincompoop, sure enough, this site, like Marcy, concludes that the only site worth consulting is the one that, like Marcy, acknowledges the exceptions, the two percent whose hands don't tremble, who don't shuffle when they walk. Moreover, this site assures you, such as any of this is assuring, that not everyone with Lewy body disease experiences every associated symptom nor do their symptoms necessarily appear in the designated Stages, which is to say that stashing cash in the freezer might well show up on the list of symptoms associated with Stage 5, and that the Stages as this site lists them are general guideposts only. This website, you conclude, is the lone honest one. You keep scrolling, reading until, as if it were written in bold, there it is: Frequent Episodes of Incontinence—*Leo, if you start peeing in the bed, I'm out of here*—and you *are* out of here, and fast. You jump to the end.

Stage 7: Life Expectancy.

Life Expectancy is calculated After Diagnosis, but how do you calculate After Diagnosis? If Stage 1 is No Symptoms, do the hallucinations qualify as After Diagnosis? Are you two years A.D.? Or did the clock start today, with Marcy's diagnosis? But even with a definitive date of A.D., Life Expectancy is wishy-washy: Some sites say 3 to 8 years, others say 5 to 8 years, and one of them puts it at 8 to 12 years. That one, as if 8 to 12 years weren't sufficiently tortuous, follows with *although cases of up to 20 years have been reported.* Something in the tone of that, of *up to 20 years* implies an exclamation point at the end of the sentence: *up to 20 years!*

Up to 20 years!

Twice the Price

On the not-so-off chance that Leo will pack spoons instead of socks, you're packing his suitcase for him. "Are you going away?" he asks.

"No, you are. Remember, you're going to Denise's for Thanksgiving."

"It's only Saturday. Thanksgiving isn't until Thursday."

"Yeah, but Joey's picking you up on Monday. To avoid the traffic."

"Right. Good idea." He goes to the closet and takes out a jacket. "Thank you for packing for me. I'm going to go for a walk."

"Leo," you say, "you'll need something warmer than that jacket. It's cold out," to which he says, "Be sure to leave room for books. I'll decide which to take later."

Shirts, jeans, underwear, socks, three sweaters, an extra pair of gloves, toothbrush, hairbrush, and you're done. You stretch out on the couch to relax, to relish the prospect of the coming days when Leo will be Denise's problem, not yours. You fall, not asleep but into a fugue state, like you're floating on a lake, and you stay there, floating, until Leo gets home carrying two Cerulean blue bags.

"I got you something," he says. "Two things."

"Why?" You swing your legs around to sit upright. "Leo, you're so sweet, but there's no reason to buy me anything."

"Since when does there have to be a reason?" He puts the bags on the coffee table and sits down next to you. "Open them," he says.

As if these boxes were like Pandora's box, you know that to open them will release misery. If you don't open them, whatever hope is in there will remain inside.

You tell him that you have an idea. "Put one away, save it for Christmas, and the other one, why not give it to Denise? A special gift like that, from you, would make her so happy."

"You're right," Leo says. "I should've thought of that before."

You ask Leo which of them he'd prefer to give to Denise. "Or," you suggest, "you could give her both of them. Make her twice as happy."

"No. I want you to have one." As if he were able to see what's inside the boxes, he takes a peek into both bags and decides that the smaller one is for you. "Do me a favor," he says. "Hide it somewhere, okay? Just in case I forget where I put it."

"Since when do you forget where you put something?"

"Never." Leo gives you a big smile, which ought to, but doesn't, fade away when he adds, "But stranger things have happened."

To respond requires you to open your mouth, but who knows what misery would come flying out? You put the larger of the two bags in Leo's suitcase and look around for a good place to hide the smaller one, somewhere where it can't be found.

I'll Miss You When You're Gone

It's a four-hour drive from Cambridge to New York, yet no sooner does Joey walk in the door, than right off the bat he says, "We should hit the road before rush hour," and although you are equally eager for them to hit the road, you offer to make him a sandwich before they head out.

"No, thanks," Joey says, but he sits down and asks if you happen to have a cold beer handy.

"I might. Let me check."

You don't need to check. Neither you nor Leo drinks beer, but on the top shelf of the refrigerator, behind the milk, there's a six-pack of Brooklyn Lager. It's been there since August, when Leo brought it home. "A cold beer might be nice in this hot weather," he said, to which you said, "Maybe taking off your coat would help." Now, you set one bottle on the counter, put one back on the shelf, and stash the remaining four in the vegetable bin.

Joey eyeballs the bottle as if it were something along the lines of celery soda or beet juice. "You New Yorkers," he chides, "with your designer beer. This shit's expensive."

"Don't blame me," you say. "Leo bought it."

"Well, I got to admit, it's good."

Joey is drinking his beer, Leo goes to the bathroom, and you open his suitcase to double-check that he didn't pack anything like batteries or a can opener. Leo emerges from the bathroom, and Joey sets the empty bottle on the coffee table. Easing himself up from the chair, he arches his back and twists his torso clockwise and counterclockwise and then picks up the beer bottle as if he were about to ask where he can find the trash can, but instead he says, "You got another one of these? It's a long trip."

"I think there's one left," you tell him. "Top shelf in the fridge."

Joey light-foots it to the kitchen, returns with the bottle of beer snug in the pocket of his coat, and then picks up Leo's suitcase. "Jesus, Uncle Leo," he says. "Whadda you got in here? Books?"

Four books, and he's got three pens in his shirt pocket. You once gave him one of those plastic pocket protectors, and, for real, you had to explain to him that it was a goof gift. "Leo," you said, "if it weren't for me, you'd be a full-fledged geek."

If the Seven Stages of Lewy body disease were at all consistent or accurate, Leo would've forgotten how to read just before or soon after he began going out at three in the morning, which was when he was supposed to lose his sense of smell. Leo's sense of smell remains that of a bloodhound. And lose his ability to read? That will never happen, or at least not until he reaches the end of Life Expectancy.

Joey is already out the door when you take Leo's hand and tug on his identification bracelet. Satisfied that the strap is securely fastened, you stand on the tips of your toes and give him a quick kiss. "I'll call you later. Tonight."

"I'll miss you," he says. "I miss you already."

You look at him, puppy-eyed, at this man who looks like Leo but isn't Leo, and you want to say, "My husband always kept pens in his pocket, too."

I miss you already.

Martyrs in Cyberland

When you were in college, some twit in your dorm asked if you wanted to come along to a meeting for children of alcoholics, to which you said, "Maybe in my next life." But here you are, sitting at your computer, searching for a Lewy body support group. Not to join, definitely not to join, but to read about what other people do, other people whose lives, like yours, have been upended and shattered.

> I am 78 years old. My husband is 80 and was diagnosed with Lewy body 5 years ago. I have to dress him, feed him, bathe him. My hope is that I will be able to continue to care for him. We've been married for almost 60 years.

> God bless you.

> Yes, but you should consider getting an aide to come in for one or two afternoons a week. You need to be careful that you don't overdo it.

> I could never put my husband in one of those assisted living places. Our children come to visit him and help me out some. They have children of their own so they can't come more than once or twice a week. But they show him a lot of love, but it's sad that our grandchildren are afraid of him.

Has anyone tried acupuncture?

Little children are often afraid of dementia patients. They don't understand.

We didn't know what was wrong with my mother for such a long time. Years. One week she'd be her old self. Then the next day, she'd put her socks on over her shoes. But when I discovered she had no food in her house except bags and bags of corn chips, I had to accept that she could not live alone.

Even the worst aide is better than the best of those places.

I wouldn't trust a stranger with my husband.

One of the doctors said my wife was a paranoid schizophrenic because she was talking to herself and accusing me of sleeping with all the women at our church.

The doctors are useless.

At first, I thought my father was going insane.

We go to a geriatric psychiatrist. She can't help my mother, but she helps me.

Does your mother live with you now?

My husband and I decided that we would move into her house. It's better that she stay in her own home.

That's true. It distresses them something awful to be in unfamiliar surroundings.

Does Medicare pay for that psychiatrist?

You can't do this alone. There's no shame in having an aide come a couple of times a week.

Does anyone know of a daycare kind of place?

I thought I was going to go insane.

Lol

I AM going insane. But what can I do?

I am my wife's 24/7 caregiver. It's frustrating and there are times when I feel unappreciated, but this is God's will.

My mother's hallucinations went away years ago, but just recently she started talking to pictures on the wall like she's at a party. Is that normal?

Normal? None of this is normal.

Dream On

You've fed the cat. Tuna Medley. You've fed yourself. Gouda cheese and crackers. Now you call Leo and listen to the ringtone coming from the hall closet. You neglected to pack his phone. The only reason to hesitate calling Denise's number is the time. It's 9:08, not late by most people's standards, except Denise is one of those early-to-bed, early-to-rise types, but you told Leo you'd call. You promised.

Denise picks up with a buoyant hello, almost as if she were singing the word. No, you didn't wake her. Yes, everything is fine. "We're having a ball," she says. "You know, with our stories, we're laughing like a pack of hyenas."

You know their stories. When they're together, they go on for hours, recounting side-splitting scenes from childhood: deranged Aunt Marie handcuffing them to a banister, Leo setting off stink bombs in church, the time Denise opened a "beauty parlor" and cut Leo's hair into the style of a dog with mange, all of it a laugh-riot in that you-really-had-to-be-there sort of way.

That they are having a ball sparks a thought, and you indulge the fantasy: two or three days from now, Denise will call, and she'll say, "Listen, don't take this the wrong way, but I'm thinking. I've got plenty of room here. I'm home all day. Joey's home all day doing nothing, and you're busy. The streets are safe here. Maybe he'd be better off staying with me."

You'd do your best not to leap in the air the way a dog jumps high off the ground to catch a Frisbee. You'd pretend to mull it over, or maybe the way you feared that Isabelle Weber would change her mind had you delayed, you'd leap to catch the Frisbee before it lands. "You know," you'd say, "you might be right."

It's a fantasy, which doesn't mean it can't happen, but it's not happening tonight. "Hold on," Denise says, and Leo gets on the phone. He tells you he's having an excellent time, Denise made a fantastic dinner, but he's getting tired and will go to bed soon. He says, "I love you," and that's it. He hangs up.

Homecoming

Thanksgiving Day, just before noon, you call Denise. "How's it going?"

"Great," Denise says. "The turkey still needs a few more hours in the oven. I've got so much food here, a feast. We'll be eating the leftovers for a week."

It's a feast, all right: a turkey the size of a Volvo, the cavity filled with Stouffer's breadcrumb stuffing gussied up with chestnuts, the ample overflow of stuffing baked in a casserole dish; Heinz HomeStyle Roasted Turkey Gravy; Ocean Spray canned cranberry sauce; candied yams with marshmallows; mashed potatoes; and an apple pie from Stop & Shop because who can be bothered to bake a pie?

"Wow," you say because what else can you say, and then you ask her to put Leo on the phone. "I just want to say hello, tell him I love him, you know."

"He's out. Taking a walk. Again. Four times yesterday, in the pouring rain, he walked all the way to the Harvard Coop, and four times he was back with a bag of books." The Harvard Coop is relatively near to Denise's house, but she doesn't walk the way Leo does. "Him with the books." She laughs and you laugh because it's a bonding thing with you and Denise, the way you joke about Leo. "Honest to God," she says, "I don't know how you put up with him."

Although you know perfectly well that she's referring to the Leo from before, and not the Leo as he is now, nonetheless in one fell swoop, the way a head on a chopping block drops into the basket, your laughter cuts off and lands with a thud, and you say, "I know you're busy with the cooking. I'll let you go. Have him give me a call. Later. After you've had your dinner."

Having wasted a few hours cutting pictures from magazines—dark clouds, mouths, a fire hydrant, and horses because you couldn't find any ponies—either you're exhausted or else you've worked yourself into a stupor of boredom. Whichever, you get into bed to take a nap, which turns out not to be a nap but something more like the recommended eight hours of sleep. Except when you wake up, it's not morning. It's ten at night, too late to call without disturbing Denise.

You open a can of food for Roberta, then open a bottle of wine for yourself, and while you're scrutinizing what's in the refrigerator, your phone rings.

"Everything's fine," Denise assures you. "But we had a little adventure here. I thought you should know. It's quite a story."

And here it begins: After dinner, Joey and Leo went to watch the football game, and Denise got to work cleaning up.

Leo was never much of a football fan, and now with a significantly diminished attention span, it took all of five minutes after kickoff before he got antsy and went out for a walk, which was when Joey went to get a six-pack from the refrigerator.

Denise was scouring the pots and pans, by hand with Brillo pads, because the dishwasher doesn't clean them well enough to suit her. Next, she set about sweeping, then mopping the kitchen floor before going at the grout with a toothbrush. With her kitchen twinkling like Tinker Bell in flight, Denise then tackled the dining room, vacuuming the carpet and polishing the table to a high gloss. Now, although dog-tired, before going to bed she thought to ask Joey if he wanted a turkey sandwich and if Leo would like another slice of pie or maybe a plate of candied yams.

Finding Joey alone in the living room, stretched out on the couch, no doubt sufficiently tanked to the point where he couldn't tell you who won the game, Denise asked, "Where's your uncle?"

"He went for a walk."

Leo's coat was hanging on the rack by the door. "He went out without his coat? When did he leave? How could you be so stupid?"

Never mind that he was looped, Denise sent Joey off to drive through the streets of Cambridge to find Leo.

But Joey returned home alone and said to his mother, "Maybe we should call the cops?"

If Denise deliberated it was only because she is even less fond of law enforcement than you are, but she was spared from having to make a decision because suddenly that was when a squad car pulled up in front of her house. A squad car with Leo in the back seat. The two cops escorted him to the door, where Denise was waiting, shivering against the cold air. Without a word of explanation, Leo waltzed into the house and sat down on the couch. Before Denise could shut the door, the cops asked if they could come in, to discuss the situation with her.

Denise digresses from the story to tell you, "It was good that you bought him that bracelet. They saw my phone number was local and got my address from a reverse directory. It wasn't major case detective work."

According to the cops, Leo walked from Denise's house over to Sargent Street, landing like a homing pigeon at the very same house on Sargent Street where they grew up. Leo turned the doorknob, but it was locked, so he knocked.

Again, Denise digresses. "I told those bastards that when we lived there, the door was never locked. It was a safe neighborhood then. You know, making it sound like it's not a safe neighborhood now because they're slacking off on the job."

You can picture it, Denise giving them something like the evil eye.

When the owner of the house opened the door, Leo said to him, "You're not my father." The man told Leo that he must have the wrong address. He wasn't rude about it, but the cold air was blowing inside his warm house, and he closed the door. Not until a half hour or so later, when Leo returned, did it register with the man that Leo wasn't wearing a coat, and the man was less than pleasant. "Your father doesn't live here," he said, and he shut the door in Leo's face.

When Leo showed up for the third time, the man ignored his knocking, until Leo was kicking at it, yelling, "Aunt Marie, let me in." Then the man called the police.

It was obvious to the cops that Leo was not a homicidal maniac, he didn't stink from booze, and he was too young to have Alzheimer's, but something was wrong with him. It was freezing cold, and he wasn't wearing a coat. One of them said to Denise, "We thought maybe he's mentally retarded."

His partner stepped in to remind him that they can't say *mentally retarded* anymore. "You got to say *challenged*. Or *special* or something like that."

"Okay, so we thought he was mentally special."

The cops gave Denise and Joey a bit of shit for letting Leo go out alone. "You got to watch him because he's what, like, special, right?"

"Yeah, he's special," Denise said. "He's my brother."

"Not that kind of special. I mean, retarded special?"

"Thank you for bringing him home." Denise wanted these cops gone, and they were just about to leave when Leo got up from the couch and took a pair of twenty-dollar bills from his wallet. As if a ride in a squad car were the same as a ride in a taxicab, Leo thought to give them a tip, a generous tip.

Another bonding moment between you and Denise. "You know how he is with tipping. I thought for sure the old one was going take it, but his partner jumped in about how they're just doing their job, blah, blah, blah. I guess not all of them are crooked. But really, he's fine now. He's with Joey. They're watching TV. Hang on, I'll get him."

You ask Leo how he's doing, and he says, "Great. I'm going to have another piece of pie. Denise made a huge dinner. I didn't have any turkey, but I was stuffed to the gills. What about you? What did you have?"

"Hubbard squash," you say. "Thanksgiving isn't Thanksgiving without a Hubbard squash, right?"

Leo laughs and you laugh, but he laughs more than you do.

Black Friday

As if the night before never happened, Denise says, "I made him waffles for breakfast. Now he's reading. Joey's still sleeping it off. I was thinking about going shopping, to Target, near here. For the sales. But I don't know. The people out there are nuts."

Your hunch is that Denise has opted to forgo the Black Friday bargains to stay home to watch over Leo, but you say, "I hear you. I'm going to do my shopping online."

"Maybe I'll do that, too." Then she says, "Hold on. Let me get him for you."

Leo takes the phone and asks, "Where are you? Why aren't you here?"

"I'm home. Working."

"Oh, okay, I don't want to keep you, then. Goodbye." He hangs up.

Your work amounts to staring at the 12 × 16 inch piece of particle board papered over with stunted pine trees and a red-breasted eastern bluebird, cut from *The Sibley Guide*. You glue the bird belly-up on forest floor. One of its eyes is staring up at you as if it were asking, "Now what?"

Now what? Good question.

In the box labeled *Words & Numbers* is a ream of correspondence written on elegant linen stationary, and some on the lightweight blue paper folded into lightweight blue envelopes designated for Airmail, one of which you open. Not to use it. You'll never use it. Intact, it is its own kind of art form: blue ink, cursive handwriting, dated July 7, 1943, to a soldier from his fiancée. *Dear Elias, I can't marry you. I've fallen in love with someone else. Sorry. Good luck in the war. Sincerely yours, Charlotte.*

Victorian cabinet cards are a different medium, but you do have one that, like the kiss-off letter, you would never desecrate. The photograph is blurry, and there's nothing alluring about the man or woman, both middle-aged, standing side by side, their faces unremarkable. What makes it important is what's written on the flip side, *Joseph and Margaret Hemon*, and below their names reads: *No decedents.*

No decedents.

Someone needs to remember them.

Who will remember you and Leo?

You put the letter back in its box and take out a calendar. 1974, which you bought because of the font. American Type-writer Semibold. From the days of the week, you cut out Friday, and then the B and the A from FEBRUARY, the L from APRIL, and then you flip back to MARCH for the C. Neither the days of the week nor months of the year contains the letter K. You take a pair of scissors to a square of black paper.

BLACK　　Friday

Black Sunday

Denise is not about to let Leo go out unchaperoned. Joey is with him. "They went over to the pool hall," she tells you. "I'll have him call you when they're back. Or when we finish dinner. We'll be eating early."

"Whenever is fine. I'm not going anywhere."

You're not going anywhere and you're not doing much of anything worthwhile, which you justify with the idea that this is your restorative time to yourself. You're expected to fritter away the day when you're on vacation, and so late in the afternoon, when it's nearing dusk, you get into bed with your laptop and a fresh bag of kettle corn. The movie you dial up is based on a Stephen King novel about a demonic washing machine. You don't watch it all the way to the end. Not because it's a spectacularly crappy movie, which it is, but because your eyes flutter and close, and you drift into a bottomless sleep.

You slept as if you were practicing to be dead, and you wake up groggy and fuzzy-headed, hugging a now half-empty bag of kettle corn. It's dark out and eerie-quiet. 10:47. Roberta must be famished, and you must not have heard the phone ring when Leo called.

But now, just as you set down the bowl of cat food, your phone rings, and it's as jarring as an alarm clock set for too early in the morning.

Denise has got to be the only person in the world and throughout history who would ask how you are before saying,

"It's not as bad as it sounds, but we just got back from the hospital. Leo stabbed Joey. With a knife."

"What?" Roberta is rubbing up against your legs, wanting to be fed. "What did you say?"

"Leo stabbed Joey with a knife."

"No. No, he didn't." Not *No, he didn't* as if you don't believe her, but *No, he didn't* because you refuse to believe her. "No," you repeat. "No, no, no."

"It was just a flesh wound," Denise says, almost dismissively. "On his arm, above the elbow. A couple of stitches and a gauze pad. He barely felt it."

What pops into your head is a hateful thought: *Joey barely felt it because he probably was too drunk to feel it.* Decidedly not a thought to share with a mother when your husband has stabbed her son with a knife, even if it was only a flesh wound.

"I don't understand," you say, as if pleading for an explanation. "I don't understand any of it. Leo doesn't hurt people or animals. He's never even punched a wall or kicked the couch. And he loves Joey."

"You don't have to tell me. I know. But listen," she says. "There's something else. God forgive me, but I had to call the cops. On my own brother, I had to call the cops. It all happened so fast. I didn't know what to do."

Joey was taking a nap. Leo was in the kitchen with Denise, who was preparing dinner. "Nothing fancy. Just spaghetti and meatballs, and I was going to fry up some eggplant for him. Because of the vegetarian thing."

Leo was standing next to Denise but facing the other way, his back to the counter, which, although it might seem otherwise, makes for easier conversation. "And he was yakking up a storm, but to be honest, he wasn't making a whole lot of sense."

Leo's talk ricocheted from the optimum cholesterol levels to the probability of life on other planets to the amount of lead in drinking water, and if it weren't already problematic to follow the conversation, a lot of his sentences trailed off into garble. "Gobbledygook," Denise says. "And a couple of the stories he told, as best as I could make them out, were batshit crazy, like how the FBI raided all the apartments on Seventeenth Street, and wolves were in your living room, and that his secretary got trained out of being gay."

"That one's real. His secretary is gay but got brainwashed to pretend he's not."

"Are you kidding? That's insane." Denise then picks up where she left off.

While she was mixing the egg into the chopped meat, Joey came in to get a beer from the refrigerator. The next thing she knew, Leo was yelling at her to get down, shouting, "The guy's armed, he's got a gun."

But before Denise could tell him there's no guy with a gun, that it's Joey with a can of beer, he pushed her away like she was in the line of fire, and grabbing a knife from the butcher block on the counter, he stabbed Joey in the arm. Then he dropped the knife and walked out of the kitchen like nothing happened. "He thought he was protecting me," she says. "But I didn't know what to do. I wasn't thinking. The cops. I can't begin to tell you how bad I feel."

"What choice did you have? What matters most is that Joey's okay." But you can dance around it for only so long. "Leo," you ask, "is he in jail?"

"No. Thank God for that, too. You wouldn't believe it, but the cops who came were the same two from before. They weren't total assholes, and it's not like Joey is going to press charges. They took him to Mass General, to the psych ward."

"I'll catch the first train out in the morning," you say, although you know you won't catch the first train out because that leaves before the sun rises. "I should get there by early or midafternoon."

Because things do happen, like your sink clogs and you need to borrow a plunger, or your husband stabs his nephew with a kitchen knife and you've got to catch the first train out to Boston, how wise you were to adhere to the golden rule: *maintain a cordial relationship with your neighbors.* You grab an extra set of keys from Leo's desk drawer. Only when you knock on Caroline's door does it occur to you that she might be sleeping. But, no. She's up and dressed as if she's just come home from a party.

"I'm sorry to bother you, but I have a big favor to ask. Would you be able to take care of my cat for a few days? I have a family emergency."

"Definitely. Absolutely. I love cats. Honest, I wish I could have one, but my boyfriend is allergic."

You tell her that you don't yet know for sure exactly when you'll be back, but that you'll call her tomorrow night or the day after. "I should have a better idea by then. Is that okay?"

You don't know for sure when you'll be coming home, but what you do know for sure is that Leo won't be coming home with you, or ever again, and isn't that what you were hoping would happen?

There's Nothing Wrong with His Heart

Joey picks you up at the train station. Denise isn't with him because the hospital is in Boston proper, and Denise can't tolerate city traffic because of her panic attacks. "She breaks into a cold sweat," Joey explains. "She can't breathe. She's nuts."

After driving around and around the parking lot, looking for an empty spot, Joey states the obvious. "This could take a while. Let me drop you off. I'll meet you up there."

"You're sure you want to come up? You don't have to."

"I know I don't *have* to," he says. "I love my uncle. I want him to know there's no hard feelings."

The man at the reception desk, wearing a blue uniform like the uniform of a security guard, checks his computer and tells you that Leo is in room 702. "Take the elevator to the seventh floor and turn left for the cardiac unit."

"The cardiac unit? That can't be right. There's nothing wrong with his heart."

"That's what it says here." He points at the computer screen as if you were standing next to him and could read it yourself. "Room 702. The cardiac unit."

Maybe Leo did have a heart attack. It was a heart attack that killed his mother. You recall Leo once telling you that heart attacks are often one of those genetic things, handed down from generation to generation, like a set of china and no one wants that, either. Now that you think of it, it's miraculous that Denise didn't wind up in the cardiac unit along with him.

You recall having heard that one heart attack is often

followed, in rapid sequence, like a roll of somersaults, by another and another until you're dead. Leo would know, but it's not a question you can ask when he's in the cardiac unit.

How clever of this hospital to sandwich the gift shop between the reception desk and the elevator banks. Glide right in to buy a gift or feel guilty if you don't. As is, you're choking on guilt.

The pickings are slim. A teddy bear? A coffee mug? Flowers already wilting? There's a Mylar balloon with a unicorn on one side and a rainbow on the back. The other balloons all sport those yellow emoji smiley faces grinning *Get Well Soon*. Mylar balloons are not biodegradable, but you rationalize the purchase: regardless of whether you buy it, it's going to wind up in a landfill or else in the ocean where it will clog a whale's intestines. A candy rack is set up between the two cash registers. You swipe your credit card and then exit the gift shop with the Mylar balloon, three Peppermint Patties, and no less guilt.

On the seventh floor, before turning left, you stop at the nurses' station to ask if the dufus downstairs got it wrong, but the nurse on desk duty confirms it: 702. She strikes you as too young to be a real nurse. If not for the badge pinned to her scrubs—*Maureen Dugan, LPN*—you'd have pegged her as one of those kids who wheel the cart of magazines from room to room, as if dying people were desperate to read *Golf Digest* or *Family Circle*, but fuck it. Volunteer work looks good on college applications.

"Did he have a heart attack?" you ask.

Information on a patient's condition can be shared only with family. "Are you his daughter?"

"No, I'm his wife. He's my husband."

"Oh, I'm so sorry. I just thought he was older because of his hair."

"Premature," you tell her. "It turned white years ago."

"Oh, that explains it. I was trying to figure out why his skin is so smooth. And he sure isn't frail."

Leo did not have a heart attack. He's in the cardiac unit because the psych ward is full. "You know, what with the holidays. But," Maureen says, "before you go in, I should explain the situation." Her expression conveys a curious blend of fear and optimism, as if she'd broken something valuable, but don't worry, she's pretty sure she can glue it back together. "He's okay, but he's still in restraints. You know, strapped to the bed. Last night he punched a nurse. In the face."

You react as if she'd just punched you; not in the face, the blow lands closer to your spleen. Stabbing Joey? Punching a nurse? As if he were a condemned man and you were pleading for his life, you say, "He has a disease. It's affected his mind. Before this, he was like Gandhi."

"I understand," she says. "My grandfather has Alzheimer's. He sometimes gets violent." Maureen's intention, clearly, is to be sympathetic, but her grandfather is not her husband, and even if she does look as if she hit puberty last week, her grandfather has got to be old.

"He doesn't have Alzheimer's. He has Lewy body disease."

"Oh, I've heard of that. It's some other kind of dementia, right?"

You ask if you can speak to a doctor.

"I'm sorry. They're all in surgery or else making rounds. With the cardiac patients," she adds.

Leo is not a cardiac patient. His heart is healthy, which serves only to make everything worse.

A Smiley Face

Room 702, like a table in the back of a restaurant, the one closest to the bathroom, is the last room on the left at the end of a long corridor. You take a moment to pull yourself together, the kind of moment you'd take to smooth out the wrinkles on your dress or tuck strands of flyaway hair behind your ears.

The curtain that separates Leo's bed from the other bed in the room is drawn closed for privacy, but there's no indication of a roommate, which is all for the best, given that this is the cardiac unit.

If it were you strapped to a bed, you'd be twisting every which way, trying to break free of the restraints, all the while yowling and hurling expletives like that girl in *The Exorcist* until your eyes rolled back into their sockets. But Leo, strapped in flat on his back, his arms pinned to his sides, his ankles shackled, unable to sit up to watch the idiot show on the television, is listening to celebrity gossip with the same serenity as if he were at home listening to chamber music.

Because his head and neck are not pinned to the bed, when you say hello, he can turn to look at you, and he grins as if he were the yellow smiley face on the Mylar balloons you rejected. "You're here," he says.

"Of course I'm here. I'm here to visit you." You lean over and kiss him somewhere between his cheek and his ear, and then jiggle the string attached to the unicorn and rainbow balloon. "The gift shop didn't have much to offer."

"It's beautiful," he says, as if the balloon were a Botticelli bobbing and weaving in the air, instead of something more like an evening bag decorated with plastic jewels. You tie the balloon to the foot of the bed.

To eat when fully supine is to risk choking, and how do you perform the Heimlich maneuver on someone who can neither sit nor stand? You should hold off giving him the candy and banish that thought of yours, the thought of him choking on a Peppermint Pattie.

One of the three chairs for visitors has armrests and a padded seat covered with tweed, the upholstery equivalent of industrial carpet. You sit in one of the plastic chairs, as if you don't deserve even that one small vestige of comfort.

You don't recognize any of these celebrities on this TV show, but you get caught up in the story that one of them who could be Paris Hilton, except she's not Paris Hilton, is relating about her time as a Scientologist. But just as you're about to find out how she managed to make her escape from the cuckoo cult, Joey shows up. Now you'll never know. Not that you care. Not really. Joey, too, got a Mylar balloon for Leo, one of the yellow smiley face balloons and its impossible request on the flip side.

Whatever else you think of him, Joey has qualities that you both admire and envy. He's not faking it when he tells Leo that it's great to see him, and they're shooting the shit the same as if Leo had not, the night before, stabbed him in the arm with a knife meant for slicing steak.

It had not occurred to you, as it does to Joey, to reach for the remote that controls the position of the bed to raise Leo into a sitting position. Sitting up, he won't choke, and you get the Peppermint Patties from your bag. Leo reacts to the Peppermint Patties as if they were hand-dipped chocolate-covered mints, and you ask Joey, "Do you mind feeding one to him? I want to see if there's a doctor around." Not that you're expecting a doctor to have wrapped up heart surgery in the past thirty-two minutes, but it's a good excuse for you to make *your* escape, even if not for long. Joey peels away the silver foil, and just to be on the safe side, you say, "Be sure to break it into small pieces. So he doesn't choke or anything."

"Hey, Addie," Joey says, "what do you think? That I'm a moron?"

"No. I think you are good. You're a good person, Joey. Like your mother."

Maureen is no longer at the nurses' station. Another one, an RN, is there. Probably not the one Leo punched, because when you ask her if she can remove the restraints, her apology comes off as sincere. "I'm really sorry. We can't. Not yet."

"I understand, but I would like to speak with a doctor. Do you have any idea when one will be available?"

"No. I'm sorry. I don't, but our administrator is here, and he asked to have a word with you before you leave."

"Is now okay?"

She points to an open door diagonally across the hall. "That's his office. You can go right in."

The administrator has the eyes of a basset hound and a sweet smile, neither of which prepares you for the blow he delivers. Leo will be discharged tomorrow, in the morning, because there's nothing wrong with him, or, rather, nothing wrong with his heart, and the psych ward still has no beds available. "But even if one did open up, he doesn't meet our standards for admission. We can't do anything for him here."

"Please, you have to keep him at least for another day or two. I need more time. I live in New York. He can't come home. I have to find a place for him to stay."

"I'm sorry," he says. "I really am. But you understand. Hospital rules, Insurance regulations. There's nothing I can do."

You resist falling to your knees, but the blubbering, the pleading, *that* you can't control. "Please, who can do something? Who can help me? Please. Who can help me?"

Where to Go

The very decent hospital administrator managed to wangle one day extra in the hospital, which you have to appreciate, despite the fact that it's like a one-day stay of execution, and the clock is ticking.

Denise puts up a fresh pot of coffee. You're at the kitchen table with your laptop, googling to find a place in Cambridge or Boston, an assisted living facility or a home, for Leo, a home like a storage unit for the contents of your apartment while it's undergoing a renovation.

"How about this one?" You read out loud, "Private rooms, home-cooked meals, round-the-clock nursing staff, garden, therapy dog. He loves dogs."

You call the number on the website, but they are full. "If you'd like," the woman says, "we can put you on the wait list."

No. You can't wait.

Denise sets down a mug coffee for you and one for herself.

You call another place, and another, and as if you're calling on a Thursday to book a room at a quaint bed-and-breakfast for the upcoming holiday weekend, they're all fully booked, and the words, *I'm sorry, but* . . . come to take on the shape of a faulty neon sign: *No Vacanc es.*

But then there's hope. No garden, no dog, but they do have a room, which they will hold if you can FedEx a check for the deposit.

"Sure, I can do that now, no problem," you tell the man, "but maybe it would be better if I brought it to you in person. Now, or in the morning. He's being discharged from the hospital the day after tomorrow."

"What's he in the hospital for?" the man asks.

It doesn't occur to you to lie, to say he got food poisoning or you thought he might've had a heart attack but it was a false alarm. No, you tell the truth, which does not set you free. No garden, no dog, and no room for people who have a history of violence.

"It's not a history. It was just this one time. Really. He's the most nonviolent person ever."

"Please understand," the man says. "We have to protect the safety of our residents."

Hope goes like a plate thrown against a brick wall.

You move on to the next one, which gets you a recorded message: "The office is closed. We are open Mondays through Fridays from eight A.M. to six P.M. Please call back then."

The day is over.

"It'll be okay," Denise says. "We've got all of tomorrow. We'll find a place. How about for now, we call in for a pizza? I'll get half sausage for Joey and, what? Green peppers for you?"

You say yes to pizza with green peppers, and then you go to the window, where beyond your reflection the neon sign, further forlorn, blinks: *S ve Me.*

The Circular Driveway

In the morning, before you start making calls again, Denise has a suggestion: maybe you'd shouldn't bother with Boston and Cambridge; New York, a bigger city, probably has more facilities, homes, dumping grounds, whatever you want to call them. "Chances might be better of finding one with a room available there," she says. "If you do, Joey can drive you back tomorrow."

"I don't know," you say. "I think I should keep trying here first. Without the time constraint, I can look around for a place, a really nice place in New York. Even put him on a wait list."

What you don't say is that if you can find a room for him in the Boston area, you can opt not to look for a place in New York. If you were to leave Leo here, maybe it would be as if geographical distance were a measure of all distance.

Your first call in the morning is to Dickerson House, the place whose recorded message yesterday signaled that the day was done, but that was yesterday.

Today is a new day, and Dickerson House has a room! They have a room, and they will hold it for you if you can get there by noon.

Denise can't go with you because of the Boston address. While Joey drives, you look out the window, noting nothing remotely urban about this outlying part of the city. It's all trees, and a quarter mile back, you passed by a bucolic, albeit slightly disconcerting, cemetery. Denise might be willing to brave this drive, which you hope she can. You need someone to visit Leo when you can't visit him. Can't? Or won't?

You arrive at your destination. So far, so good. Dickerson House is the very picture of one of those sanatoriums where rich people go to take the cure, where, when the weather is warm, they can sit outside under a tree with a sketchbook or wander the grounds with their psychiatrist. The driveway is circular. The parking lot is in the back.

No doubt there was once a time when Persian carpets were arranged over what are sure to be oak floors, but now royal blue carpeting goes wall to wall. Joey sits himself down in one of four armchairs arranged around a Bombay Company replica of an antique coffee table. On the opposite wall hangs a Christmas wreath, unadorned except for a red plaid bow. Posh WASP.

The woman behind the desk greets you with a groundswell of good cheer, when exactly zero amount of good cheer is appropriate. "Are you here to visit a resident?" she asks.

"No," you say. "I have an appointment with Joan."

"Great. You have to sign in, and then I'll let her know you're here."

The sign-in book is not a clipboard but one of those flower-print cloth-covered *Guest Books*. On the far end of the desk, in a red foil-covered pot, is a miniature Christmas tree festooned with gold balls smaller than marbles. "It's real," the woman says. "You can smell the balsam. Go ahead."

You choose not to smell the balsam, but you do ask what she plans to do with the bonsai-size fir tree after Christmas. "You're not going to just toss it in the trash, are you?"

Goodbye and good riddance to her good cheer. "Have a seat. Joan will be with you shortly."

Joey is reading one of the pamphlets taken from the array carefully fanned around a vase filled with fake flowers; fake, but decent-quality fake.

A middle-aged man and woman who match the wreath on the door, insofar as they, too, exude understated wealth, are on their way out, but then, as if they were the welcome wagon and you were someone newly admitted to their club, they stop. The woman asks if you have a family member moving in. "Your mother? Or your father?"

"My husband," you tell her.

"But you're so . . ." She was going to say, "Young. You are so young," but she makes a save. "You're very lucky that they have a room available. This is one of the finest assisted living facilities in all of New England. You're doing the right thing."

The Message Board gang would beg to differ.

Even the worst aide is better than the best of those places.

Most definitely that little fir tree is going to wind up in the trash.

The Cost of Living

She of the mauve suit, white silk blouse, and square scarf patterned with mauve, navy blue, and yellow swirls draped around her neck, Joan is the sort of woman who inexplicably intimidates you in that way where you think that she thinks you might have head lice. Her soliloquy of sympathetic words is delivered with the warmth of an automaton, but when she moves on to the sales pitch, although equally well-rehearsed, she speaks with the enthusiasm of a goofy docent giving a guided tour around the former dwelling of some person of little historical importance. You could give a flying fuck that the mansion was built in 1896 or that four generations of Dickersons lived here, but your curiosity is piqued when you learn that in 1972, Albert and Helen Dickerson died in a plane crash. They had no descendants. *No descendants.*

"The Dickerson Foundation sold the house, and subsequently it was revamped into an assisted living home, *home,*" Joan emphasizes, "not facility. We have a perfect rating from the government's Department of Health and Human Services *and* nothing but five-star ratings on Yelp!"

The contract is, literally, eleven pages long, but Joan asks that you first turn to page four, to *Rules and Regulations,* which she reads out loud as if you were illiterate. You try to pay attention, but her voice goes in and out, like when you're on the phone and the reception is poor, as if she might at any moment stop and ask, "Are you there? Can you hear me?" But when she gets to Rule 7, *Aggressive behavior will not be accommodated,* that one comes through like a fire bell: exceedingly loud and shrill. The only difference is when a fire alarm goes off, you can stick your fingers in your ears to muffle the sound.

"Has he had any history of aggression?" Joan asks.

"No," you say. "Never."

Rule 10: *No pictures, photographs, calendars, etc. fixed to the walls.*

Rule 11: *Name tags must be sewn into all articles of clothing and securely taped to all other property (books, magazines, puzzles, radios, etc.).*

Now, Joan gets down to business. A double room is $12,875 per month. A single room is $14,995. An additional $600 gets you a Presidential Suite, a private room overlooking the garden, but the garden is off-limits to residents, unless supervised.

Thirteen, fifteen, sixteen thousand dollars a month is Monopoly money, the kind of money that can buy you three hotels on Park Place. In terms of real money, you can afford a room in a Super 8 motel. Maybe.

If the situation were reversed, for you, whatever the cost, Leo would've sprung for the Presidential Suite, which is why it comes as a relief to learn that none of the deluxe rooms are available just now. No single rooms, either, but despite the savings, the idea of Leo having to share a room does not sit well with you.

"I'll put him down for the first single that opens up," Joan says. "Now, let's go over what the fee covers."

For umpteen million dollars a month, Leo gets a room he has to share, three meals a day, plus snacks, and a wide range of activities led by professionals (art teachers, music teachers, yoga instructors). A nurse is on call around the clock. At night, after lights out, three aides are on duty, and during the day, six aides are on the floor at all times to assist with feeding, toileting, showering, dressing, and walking.

Toileting? "He's not . . . He's fully self-sufficient. He even remembers to flush the toilet. A lot of men, normal men of sound mind, forget to flush the toilet. He doesn't need help with any of that." It strikes you as unfair that you'll be subsidizing the cost of other people's dressing, showering, *toileting.* It's not like paying taxes that go toward funding schools and food stamps, things for a greater good. This is a private enterprise. There should be a sliding scale.

Sheets, towels, and weekly laundry service are included.

Umpteen million dollars, and yet they do *not* provide toothpaste, a toothbrush, shampoo, or soap. Even a Super 8 motel gives you a free bar of soap. Doctor and dental visits and medications, those are on you, too.

After you sign both copies of the contract, here, here, and here, Joan tells you that you can pay monthly by check, but today you're required to fork over, up front, payment for the first two months and a $3,000 security payment, *plus,* she's going to gouge you for the few days left until the end of November. Then, as if she were feeling for raindrops, Joan extends her hand, palm up, and says. "I'll need your credit card."

You should know, except you don't, the maximum you can put on any one card, but this sort of extra-large hunk of money could well trigger an alarm like those anti-theft tags used to nab shoplifters or like when you try to sneak a nail clipper though airport security. You give her two Visa cards and one Mastercard and ask her to put a third on each.

One by one, the cards go through, and then Joan asks if you have any questions.

You do have questions. Two questions: 1) How the hell are you going afford this? and 2) Where do you get name tags?

How the Hell *Are* You Going to Afford This?

Summer camp–style name tags need to be pre-ordered with an estimated wait time of seven to ten days for delivery, but Denise, ever resourceful, has devised a temporary solution. With a permanent gel ink pen, she's written Leo's name on white fabric bias tape, which she is sewing onto the cuffs of Leo's socks.

Sitting across the table, you've got the computer open to the calculator app. The sum total of your now exponentially increased monthly expenses subtracted from Leo's paycheck, will cover the cost of Dickerson House with enough left over to buy Roberta's food, litter, and the occasional cat toy.

A less expensive place might not have a five-star Yelp review or a circular driveway, but how bad could it be?

How bad could it be? Even without the Message Board's two cents, you know damn well how bad it could be. You saw that episode on *60 Minutes*, the one where an undercover reporter with a hidden camera infiltrated assisted living facilities or "homes," where dilapidated people, half-awake or half-dead, are clothed in crusty hospital gowns, their beds covered with disheveled sheets that might've been white decades ago but now are the same color as the rats scurrying across the floors, and even those rats have maggots breeding in their bedsores.

You'll have to start cutting coupons. You'll have to cut your own hair or let it grow to your knees. You'll have to eat Kraft American cheese, cancel Netflix, HBO, Curiosity Stream, and your subscriptions to *Artforum*, *ArtNexus*, and *Juxtapoz*. You'll have to tell the homeless man who camps out on your block that you no longer have any dollars to spare. You'll have to get a job, but who would hire you, and to do what? Your gainful past employment experience is limited to babysitting when you were in high school, a stint at Banana Republic where you were fired for not having a good personality, and waiting tables.

Travel expenses. You forgot to factor in transportation. Round trip, New York to Boston, $250 off-peak. If you were to come every other week, you would save $500, as if that rationalization justifies a greater motivation. You don't want to come every week. You don't want to come every other week. You don't want to come once a month or even once a year, or ever.

What you're trying not to think about is that Leo's paycheck has a definitive expiration date, whereas Leo... *3 to 8 years, 5 to 8, 8 to 12, and cases of...*

Sa e Me

Proof Positive

You google: *Lewy body life expectancy.*

Google tells you that you have visited this site nine times.

Yes, but it's not impossible that a new study has been released, an update.

Neither possible nor impossible without the evidence, but the evidence is what it was each of the eight times before. Nothing has changed, and nothing, absolutely nothing, will ever be even remotely the same.

Now What?

Under the fluorescent lights at a table in the dining room, you're surrounded by old, frail, and demented people who shout into space and pee on themselves. Leo might not be Leo, but he's nothing like these people, either.

"Let's go somewhere quiet," you suggest.

With two books cradled against his chest, Leo follows you to the small room set aside for private visits. The chairs are identical to those in the lobby, but these are hand-me-down chairs, a bit worn and shabby. The carpet is stained, and the coffee table is scratched. The lamps, too, are lobby castoffs, but you appreciate that they are lamps with shades instead of those overhead tracks of fluorescent light. You scoot your chair closer to Leo's. Your knees touch, and you take his hands, hold them, softly.

Now what?

You ask how he is feeling and if he likes it here, and Leo says, "It's okay."

"And the food? How's the food?"

"Excellent."

Excellent? You've seen the food. It's steam table glop.

"So, what did you have for lunch?"

"Chicken and rice. Last night, for dinner we had beef stew."

To give them the benefit of the doubt, it could be they simply forgot that Leo doesn't eat meat, as opposed to the more likely explanation, which is that they don't give a fuck and figure what does he know anyway? One week ago, he knew that he didn't eat meat. One week ago, he didn't eat Denise's Thanksgiving turkey.

From desperation springs banality, and you are reduced to talking about the weather. "It's nice and warm in here, but it's freezing cold outside. Not technically freezing. More like thirty-eight or thirty-nine degrees."

"If it goes below thirty-six," Leo says, "plant life can die from the frost."

You take out your phone to check the weather report and take note of the time. "It's warmed up a bit. Forty degrees. The plants are safe."

Forty degrees, and you've been here for one hour, sixteen minutes, and eleven years. "I have to get going," you say. "I can't miss my train. But I'll be back soon."

His words are unintelligible until he gets to the tail end, ". . . not ready to go," and you have to explain to him that you are going home alone, that he'll be staying here. "But I'll be back soon. Is there anything special I can bring for you next time?"

"No," Leo says. "Nothing comes to mind."

Nothing comes to mind.

You squeeze his hands, three squeezes in a row, as if a squeeze of the hand were one word in Morse code. Three words.

"You're going home?" Leo asks.

"I have to. Caroline, our neighbor next door, has been watching Roberta all week."

"She's nice," Leo says.

"Yes, she is. I don't want to take further advantage of her. Denise and Joey will be here tomorrow." You press your palms flat against the armrests, about to ease up from the chair, when, the way a magician will make a quarter disappear right before your eyes but too fast for you to catch how he did it, that's how fast the whites of Leo's eyes go pink. Pink, like the eyes of the white rabbit pulled from the very same magician's hat, and tears collect at the brim of Leo's eyes, like floodwater ready to breach the seawall, and he asks you a question he's never asked before: "Why did this happen to me?"

"I don't know, Leo. I don't know." You have no words of comfort to give because there is no comfort to give, no comfort to be had, and you must not cry.

And then, in defiance of the laws of physics, biology, gravity, and human nature, Leo's tears, like a film running in reverse, go backwards into the sanctuary of his tear ducts. The whites of his eyes are white again.

"Now that I think of it," he says, "you could bring me a box of those oatmeal raisin cookies from Chelsea Market, and *The Life and Legacy of Marie Curie*. It's in the living room, in the far-left bookcase, the third shelf from the top."

This disease that is destroying Leo's brain makes you question your own sanity.

Cancellations

Five days, five days of suffocating under a blanket of guilt conjoined with a love that, despite everything, is like the indestructible constant of energy. You shelved the twice-monthly visitation plan in favor of one day once a week. At least for now, at least until you're confident that Leo has settled in at Dickerson House, that he is as happy there as such a thing is possible. You can't stay overnight because of Roberta. Your cat is your excuse.

The train headed to Boston arrived at Penn Station on time, but you did not. The next train departs in two hours. All around you people are bustling, rushing, wheeling their suitcases, heading out of town for the holidays. College kids with backpacks slung over their shoulders, parents with children keeping a keen eye on the rambunctious ones running in circles, all off for a cozy Christmas with family. A group of five young-professional types are carrying their skis.

At Dunkin' Donuts, you are among your own kind: alone, joyless, going nowhere for Christmas. Many of them homeless. You order coffee and a cruller and look around for somewhere to sit. The tables are a painful shade of orange. Only one of them is vacant, and with the napkin from the waxy Dunkin' Donuts bag, you brush away the previous slob's crumbs. The cruller is stale. The coffee is too hot to drink. You blow on it until it's cool enough to sip without burning the outer layers of your tongue to raw pulp. Nursing your coffee in a paper cup as if it were a fine after-dinner cognac in a snifter until it's empty, you drop the cup in the trash bin along with the cruller. You go back to the counter to buy a dozen jelly-filled Munchkins for Leo, which you put in your tote bag on top of a jar of macadamia nuts, the box of oatmeal raisin cookies from Chelsea Market, and *The Life and Legacy of Marie Curie*.

The train rocks like a cradle, rocking you to sleep, and you sleep all way the from New York to Boston, where you're jolted awake by the conductor's booming announcement: *Next stop, South Station. South Station, next stop.*

The deep blue hour of dusk, and it's snowing! Snowflakes the size of dimes. Snow! Snow blankets the branches of trees. Snow freezes time, and the world goes silent. Snow! It rarely snows in New York anymore. It *used* to snow. Not like in Anchorage, Alaska, or Billings, Montana, but still you could rely on some snow in winter. Now, even when it does snow, the flakes are no bigger than crystals of salt and the accumulation amounts to a layer of dust.

But in Boston, it's snowing, really snowing, and you picture yourself twirling like a ballerina in *The Snow Maiden*, but you trudge to the taxi stand, where the line is long and growing longer. Directly behind you, a woman is gabbing on her phone. You want to tell her to take her noise elsewhere, but you don't because of the child with her. The little girl has tilted her head all the way back, eyes closed, mouth open, catching snowflakes on her tongue. You could let the kid know that she ought to think twice about eating snow, that, sure, it looks clean, but as it falls from the clouds, all kinds of crap gets netted in the latticework, the kind of crap that can give you cancer. But no. What's a little cancer down the road compared with the magic of catching snowflakes on your tongue?

The taxi line moves in increments of inches.

If it continues to snow like this, this little girl could well wake up tomorrow to the best news: *School is canceled.* Her mother will swaddle her into a snowsuit, the kind of snowsuit that allows for all the mobility of a penguin, and send her outside, where she'll make snow angels while simultaneously courting frostbite. She might even build a snowman or, rather, *try* to build a snowman. It's no simple thing to build a snowman, and the requisite materials—two lumps of coal, a carrot, two bare branches cut to size, and a top hat—are not always readily available. When you were the same age as this girl, you had to make do with a pair of bottle caps for eyes, a pencil for a nose, and your snowman did not have arms. A knitted beanie didn't quite fit its lopsided head, which was set precariously on its lopsided body. Your snowman was the Quasimodo of snowmen, but still, he was *your* snowman. The next morning, the sky was a clear, sharp blue. The sun was bright, and your snowman's head had melted away. The knitted beanie lay on the ground, and you wept. A snowman is the winter equivalent of a sandcastle, except a snowman is like a person, sort of.

By the time you reach Dickerson House, the snow is a good three inches deep, and shows no sign of letting up, and you can't yet bring yourself to go inside. Your shoes will get ruined, but you watch the snow fall, until, as hard and unexpected as a snowball lobbed at your head by some dick kid, the memory thwacks you: You never built a snowman. You had *tried* to build a snowman, but the snow you rolled failed to get any bigger than an orange and was shaped more like a banana. Your snowman was a memory that didn't happen. There must be other memories like that one, memories that never happened, and what of those that did? Will they, too, melt away under the next day's sharp, bright winter sun?

The Gift of the Magi

The recreation room is not actually a discrete room, a room unto itself. Rather, it's the far side of the dining room cleared of tables, and it's now done up with the trappings of Christmas. Taped to the walls are dismal cardboard snowmen, Santa and Mrs. Claus, and elves, their glitter balding. The three plastic trees decorated with faded plastic ornaments are without tinsel or candy canes. Unlike the wreath in the lobby, the ribbons on these wreaths are bedraggled, as if it's not worth investing in new decorations when half the people here don't even know what an elf is, never mind that one of the elves is missing a foot.

Four rows of folding chairs are arranged in a semicircle around a piano, where a woman wearing a red sweater is pounding out "Jingle Bells." Some of the residents are singing along, or somewhat singing, "*Oh what fun, duh, duh, la, la, duh, snow.*" The others, heads lolled, have nodded out. Because surely Leo is hiding out in his room, it comes as a bit of a shock, or more like a blow, to spy him in the second row, center seat, between two women whose combined age has got to be in the low four figures. Neither woman is singing, although one of them is either swaying to the music or maybe she's just trying to stay awake, but Leo is bopping his head as if "Jingle Bells" had a syncopated rhythm, and he's singing along as if he were Frank Sinatra. He needs a haircut.

Had you happened upon this scenario under different circumstances, say at an office Christmas party, a party where, uncharacteristically, Leo went way too heavy on the hooch, you'd be counting the minutes until he sobered up, until you could tell him how you found him among a crowd of dementia patients sitting around a piano belting out "Jingle Bells," to which he would say, "You're making that up," and then, by way of illustration, you'd sing "Jingle Bells" as if you were Ella Fitzgerald, scatting the first two lines before going all in. It would have been one of those private jokes between the two of you, yours alone.

"Jingle Bells" concludes with some intermittent clapping. You set the tote bag down on one of the tables and drape your coat over the back of a chair. Leo, staring straight ahead, doesn't see you. The way you do in a movie theater when the only available seats are in the middle of the row, you take care to avoid knee contact with the other people. To get Leo's attention, you tap him on the shoulder, and he asks, "What are you doing here?"

"What am I doing here? I'm here to visit you. Come. Come be with me." You tug at his hand until he stands up, and you lead him away from the recreation area to the table where you left your things. You pat the seat of the chair next to yours. "Sit with me. I've got all kinds of goodies for you." Like a bowerbird trying to attract a mate, you arrange the Munchkins, the jar of macadamia nuts, the box of oatmeal raisin cookies from Chelsea Market, and *The Life and Legacy of Marie Curie* in an aesthetically pleasing row. "Sit with me," you repeat, but Leo won't sit with you, and when the woman at the piano hits the first notes of "Deck the Halls," he glances over his shoulder. "I'm sorry," he says, "but I'm busy now. Can you come back later?"

Later?

But before you can say no, no you can't come back later, Leo is already walking away, to return to the group, his gang. You put the jar of nuts back into your tote bag. You'll eat them on the train. The Munchkins, the cookies, and the book you'll leave with the aides, for them to give to Leo later. *Later*. While you're fumbling to button your coat, Leo comes hurrying back to you. A Christmas ornament, a hollow plastic reindeer, Rudolph, time-worn, the red nose faded closer to pink, dangles from the string gripped between his fingers. As if it were a fresh plum, he says, "This is for you," and off he goes. Again.

As a precautionary measure, as if they'll bust you for stealing a crappy plastic ornament, you scope out the room before you slip Rudolph the Pink-Nosed Reindeer into your tote bag. After you drop off the Munchkins, the cookies, and the book at the aides' station, you ask about getting Leo a haircut. They can make the arrangements, but you have to pay for it. Maybe Denise knows how to give a decent haircut, although, really, how good does it have to be?

You call for a car to take you to the train station, away from here.

The snow on the ground sparkles under the moonlight, but no longer is it falling from the sky.

The First Noel

A Christmas gift from Denise arrived earlier in the week, which was the same day you opened it. The card was less flashy than her cards of Christmases past. No crystal stickers, no ornate embossed gold lettering, but you know that this card, a cat wearing a red Santa-style suit *Wishing You a Meowy Christmas*, was chosen with care. The gift, a pair of multicolored striped mittens with a matching scarf. You know that Denise put thought into what she chose for you, but you'd wear socks on your hands and a towel around your neck before you'd wear multicolored mittens with a matching scarf. Caroline, who generously cat-sat for you, wears things like mitten-and-scarf sets. You, less generously but money is tight, tied a ribbon around the box, and you left it outside her door. Then you went online and ordered a basket of holiday-inspired junk food to be delivered to Denise and Joey, which should have arrived on the twenty-third. Denise will open it after she and Joey have finished their Christmas breakfast.

Excluding what's in the Cerulean blue bag, there are no gifts for you to open today, but no. You can't. You'll save it for next year or some other year.

You would get out of bed to feed Roberta, but she is sleeping on the pillow that was Leo's. It's not as if with Leo gone she's called dibs on his pillow, his side of the bed. Roberta and Leo shared a pillow from the get-go. She was the itty-bittiest little kitten living in a cage at the Humane Society, which is a wretched place but preferable to living where she was found, huddled in a corner of an abandoned shop near Times Square that once sold New York City souvenirs made in China. You were giving her a real home, which did not fully assuage the guilt over choosing an adorable kitten instead of one of the other cats, older cats, cats that were blind in one eye or missing part of an ear, the cats that no one wanted. It wasn't as if you didn't know that kittens aren't kittens forever, that in four or five months, her time as a kitten would end, but you wanted those four or five months enough to leave behind those old, gnarly cats, to walk away and try to forget them.

You wanted those months.

For six years now, she's been a cat. You roll onto your side to stroke her back. "Do you know how much I love you?" Animals do communicate. They'll let you know when they are hungry or want to play. They'll convey affection, what can be construed as love, but unless Roberta is eating her dinner with a knife and fork, she's not engaging in conversation with you. Nonetheless you say, "I miss him, too."

Your bed is too big for one person and one cat, and despite her inability to fathom so much as one word, you nonetheless ask, "How would you feel about a sibling? A big scruffy brother? Or maybe a sister, one who is missing an ear?"

Roberta yawns. Pink tongue, small teeth, sweet fangs. She gets up, stretches, and hops off the bed. It's time for her breakfast.

Instead of popping open a can, you fill her bowl with cat treats, which are the cat equivalent of sugar cookies, a Christmas breakfast.

Two Turtle Doves

This cat sitting on your lap is ugly, spectacularly ugly, and in the fourteen months he's been warehoused at the Humane Society, according to Ellen, who is in charge of adoptions, no one, not one person, has expressed any interest in him. You sort of get it. His fur is dirty white with splotches of orange. He's huge, but his ears are far too small for his size.

"He's a big boy," Ellen says. "Just shy of twenty-two pounds. A big bag of candy. He loves everyone. Dogs, cats, people, rabbits. Doesn't matter. He loves them all."

"He is sweet, but I'm worried about my cat. She might be afraid of him. She's on the small side."

"This guy is one hundred percent beta," Ellen says. "Your girl is going to rule the roost. It might take her a few days to adjust. But after that, they'll be best buddies."

Just shy of twenty-two pounds crushing your lap, purring like a well-oiled purr machine, he rubs his nose hard against your nose, a cat kiss.

His name is Peaches. You change his name to Howard.

Roberta hates his guts. She hisses and spits and swats at him, but he just sits there, as if he were the Buddha. When she is done letting him know that he disgusts her, she goes to your studio and sulks between a stack of boxes. You try to coax her out with treats. She doesn't want treats, and she wants no part of that fat ugly thing you brought home, either.

Two days running, and nothing has changed.

You call Denise to let her know that you can't come up on

Friday, as planned. "I got another cat, and Roberta isn't exactly happy about it. She'll adjust, but I can't leave them alone just yet. She might kill him."

"Don't worry about it." Denise laughs. "Like when I was born, my father said they had to watch Leo like a hawk. Joey and I will be there."

Denise and Joey visit Leo almost every day. And you? You'd rather stay home and break up catfights.

You check to see if Roberta ate the treats you left for her this morning, but she hasn't touched them. She'd rather starve than forgive you.

What have you done?

You sit on the couch, and immediately Howard jumps into your lap. "You're such a sweet boy." You stroke his head. "What am I going to do? Tell me, Howie." *Howie.* Already he's Howie. "I can't bring you back to that place."

That place.

Hugging him tight, maybe too tight, because you want to keep him, you want to take care of him, you want him to be loved. But Roberta wants him gone. "Oh, Wee-Wee," you say, "what are we going to do?"

Wee-Wee, an even greater, or lower, diminutive.

Returning to your studio, you get down on the floor and reach between the boxes to pet Roberta. "You're going to like this," you say. "I'm calling him Wee-Wee. Like pee. Like you do in your box. If you want, we can even call him Poop."

Roberta licks her left paw, licks it excessively as if it were filthy, as if there were a spot that will never come out.

Show-and-Tell

You're showing Leo the pictures on your phone. "Roberta has a brother now. At first, she wanted nothing to do with him, but look. She's cleaning his ears."

"He's beautiful," Leo says. "What's his name?"

"Howard. I named him Howard."

"Howard?" Leo repeats, as if Howard is someone he *knows* that he knows, but from where? A friend of yours, maybe? Or perhaps Leo is just mulling over the name, trying to determine if it's a good fit for this cat in the picture.

You show Leo more pictures: Roberta and Wee-Wee curled up in bed, Roberta and Wee-Wee eating dinner side by side, the two of them sharing a spot of sunlight on the floor. Then, as if you owe Leo an explanation, you say, "I didn't want Roberta to be lonely when I'm away. When I'm here. When I come to visit you."

"Oh, that reminds me," Leo says. "Don't come tomorrow. My wife will be here, and she doesn't like you. I have no idea why, but don't take it personally." Then Leo gets up from the table. "You'll have to excuse me, but there's some reading I really need to get done. Kiss Roberta for me and give Howard my regards."

And here you are, sitting at a table, alone, alone with that woman you don't like.

The Truth Hurts

S ummer, autumn, the holiday season, and now two weeks into his spring semester do not literally add up to a decade, but it feels as if at least nine years have passed since you last saw Z. That is, until after you hug and he says, "You look dreadful. Are you okay?" Then nine years melts into two weeks.

"Thanks," you say. "Nothing like a little flattery." You ignore the second half of his greeting. You're in no hurry to talk, and why deny him the delight he derives from sharing the minute-by-minute recount of his presentations, the praise he garnered, the parties, the sightseeing, and the menu for four out of every five meals he ate? Now that he's done dribbling the ball, he tosses it to you, and you tell him, "The show at the Weber is opening in three weeks."

"Three weeks? You didn't send me an invitation?"

Invitations. You forgot about them. No one needs an invitation to the opening, but the reception is a private party. "Shit," you say. "I forgot. I'll send you one tonight."

"You forgot? Thanks a heap."

"Don't take it personally. No one got one."

"What is it, really? Something's off with you. Is it Leo? Did you find out what's wrong?"

Z has barely touched his drink, but you order another round. "It's not good," you say. "It's bad. Really bad. Horrible." Unlike Z's pointillistic recap of his glorious excursion, you go with broken brushstrokes: the escalation of Leo's weirdness in frequency and subject matter, and then how he'd be back to his old self for days, or most of the day, and then how the weird-ness would come back with a vengeance, your inability to cope, Marcy's diagnosis of Lewy body disease, Thanksgiving weekend, Dickerson House. "I've been going there once a week, bringing him cookies, candy, and books. One week I didn't go because I got another cat. Howard. Roberta wasn't at all pleased. In fact, she was furious. I—"

Z cuts you off. "Enough with the cats," which is kind of rude. You don't interrupt him when he drones on about his kids and his wife. "What is Lewy body disease?" he asks.

With Z, you don't have to sugar-coat the truth, and you tell him, "It's a kind of dementia."

"Dementia? Leo? Jesus, Addison. This is a nightmare."

"It was for a few days, the hissing and spitting, but they're getting along great now."

"Would you please stop with the cats," he says. "Why didn't you tell me?"

"In email? It's not exactly email subject matter."

"You could've called. I assumed no news was good news, that you found a doctor, a medication that worked. Really, why didn't you call me?"

"Because I knew you were having a great time. You were happy. Besides, there wasn't anything you could do."

"Oh, damn, I am so sorry. I'm so very sorry. I don't know what else to say I mean, I get how you must be feeling. Of course, not from experience"—he raps his knuckles on the bar, knock wood—"but I can't begin to tell you how sorry I am. For you."

Something about the way he says that, that he is sorry for *you*, doesn't sit well with you. "I'm not the one with Lewy body disease. Why are you sorry for *me*?"

"Well, because of how humiliating this is, how humiliated you must feel."

Humiliated?

"Humiliated?" You can feel it on your face, as surely as if you were sculpting it from clay, the mix of fury, fear, heartbreak, and despair. "He's sick, Z. He has a disease."

"Yeah, yes, but it's not like heart disease or something. It's like the difference between getting arrested for civil disobedience and getting arrested for exposing yourself in public. You know how it is with dementia. People with dementia are ridiculed, the butt of jokes. You can't respect someone with dementia. They have no dignity. Everyone will be talking about how pathetic he is, and they will pity you and avoid you. No one wants to be around that."

"It's not a virus. I'm not contagious."

"No, but you've seen this happen. I can't even imagine what it's like to be pitied. It's so humiliating." He closes his eyes and shakes his head hard, as if to dislodge the very idea that he would ever be pitied. "I hurt for you, Addie. I really do."

"Addie? Since when am I Addie? Is that your pity name for me?"

He doesn't answer your question in a direct way. Instead he says, "I don't want you to feel humiliated around me. I'm your best friend."

"I have to go." You signal the bartender for the check. Z reaches into his jacket for his wallet, but never mind that you can't afford it, you say, "No. My treat," as if to pick up the tab might mitigate the humiliation Z has bestowed upon you and restore some of the dignity that his pity has stripped away.

Z notes that you've left a hefty tip. "Generous," he says.

"Yes," you say. "I am generous." You put on your coat, and Z says, "Don't forget the invitation."

"Don't worry. I won't forget. You can count on it."

But generosity does not restore dignity or diminish pity. Humiliation cannot be erased with a big tip, or with anything, and then there's the burning shame of it, that, as he does with you, Z spoke the truth.

PART FOUR

4

It's All Over

The opening is tonight, and this afternoon, yet again, there's another email from Z. Three weeks, 802 emails, plus the voice messages asking about his invitation. You delete it, as you deleted all of them, without hesitation, although twice you paused and considered a reply, the first of which was: *Sorry. I gave your invitation to Mike Pence.* The second: *Your wife is a joke and your brilliant, genius children are, at best, mediocre.* But if you had come clean, if you had spoken the lone truths you'd never told, he would not have taken you at your word. Rather, he'd have said to Katrine something about how you are lashing out, how it's your way of coping with the humiliation. "It's sad, really," he'd say. "But she knows I'll forgive her."

You don't agonize over which black dress to wear. They're all the same, but you do sniff your armpits because you don't have time to shower. No detectable stink, but you err on the side of caution and spritz perfume on your neck.

The Weber Gallery draws a crowd. You see a few familiar faces. You smile and nod in recognition, but you're not about to stop to say so much as hello. At least not until you have a drink in hand. The bar offers a variety of wines, all of them decent and served in real wine glasses. You ask for a Merlot.

"French?" the server asks. "Or Napa?"

"Whichever," you say. "But do me a favor. Fill it to the brim. I'm one of the artists. A little nervous, you know."

At the reception, there will be a fully stocked bar.

To keep the wine from sloshing over the rim of the glass,

you drink a third of it before venturing further into the gallery, where you can't help but notice that no one is lingering in front of your work. They stop, barely look, and then move on, and as you watch this lack of interest, you come to a conclusion: your collages look like the efforts of a child, a not particularly talented child, and no one buys art to tape to their refrigerators.

You set your empty glass on a window ledge and turn to find yourself face-to-face with Isabelle Weber. "I'm sorry," you say. "But I have to go."

"You have to go? Go where?"

"There's been an accident. My husband." You grab your coat from the rack, which might not even be *your* coat, but someone else's black coat, and you run.

Your Status

Night after night, sleep eludes you, which is why you made an appointment with this doctor, not your primary care physician but a doctor you found on Zocdoc. What you want from this Zocdoc is for him to refill your prescription for Ambien. Ambien, Sonata, Lunesta, whatever will put you to sleep. It's one thing for your doctor to grill you about the frequency and consistency of your bowel movements, alcohol consumption, exposure to STDs, and then send you off to pee in a cup with instructions to give the cup filled with your warm pee to the receptionist on your way out, but your primary care physician is Leo's primary care physician, too, and she will ask about Leo, why he hasn't been in for a checkup. When it comes to invasion of privacy, the public offering of your urine sample is your limit.

The Zocdoc receptionist gives you the new-patient forms to fill out, the pen attached by a chain to the clipboard. *Insurance Carrier and Policy Number, First Name, Last Name, Address, Phone number, Age, Gender, Marital Status, Emergency Contact.*

The second and third pages of the forms cover the usual: chronic illnesses, surgeries, family histories, allergies, current medications, including vitamins, herbal remedies, and internet quack-pills or powders, and a list of vices. How much, how often.

Your signature, today's date, and then you flip back to the first page, to the questions you've yet to answer. *Emergency Contact*: Denise's name, but your phone number. If you had a medical emergency, she'd have to send Joey, in which case, as good a man as he is, you'd rather die alone.

Marital Status is presented as a multiple-choice test. Check the appropriate box: *Single, Married, Domestic Partnership, Divorced, Widowed.*

There is no appropriate box for you to check. No box for *Other.*

Indecency

Who is so rude as to call you at eight in the morning?

Not until she asks if you will be coming to see Leo today do you connect the name Joan to the person Joan. She wants a word with you and prefers it be in person, not on the phone. "I'd appreciate it if you'd stop by my office before five, assuming you get here by then."

"I'm always there before five," you say.

"Not always. But please make an effort today.

Not always? Does she keep tabs on your arrival and departure times? Does she check the sign-in book every night? Or is that happy little twit at the reception desk the Dickerson House Stasi agent?

You fall back to sleep for two hours, and then, in a panic to get there before five, you grab the jeans and sweater from the top of the pile of dirty clothes on the floor. Clothes left on the floor where the air circulates probably don't smell as bad as clothes stuffed in the hamper. If they do emit an unpleasant odor, well, that'll bring Joan some satisfaction, as if she had you pegged right all along.

When you get to the station, the train is ready for boarding. You take an aisle seat, which, unless the train is full, practically guarantees no one will sit next to you, and no one does.

Just before you reach Bridgeport, one of those nagging sensations takes hold. You forgot something, something serious, like to turn off the stove or the kitchen faucet, and your apartment will flood or explode. But you didn't forget to turn off the stove. You haven't turned it on since heating up a can of soup on Wednesday, and you didn't leave the water running because you neglected to rinse the cat-food can for recycling. You conjure disaster after disaster until the train stops at New Haven, and then you remember you left the cookies and the book on the coffee table.

When you get to South Station, you remedy your negligence. Four éclairs from one of the bakeries, and then you backtrack to the newsstand for *The Boston Globe*.

Leo is in the dining room flipping the pages of *People* magazine. "Is there nothing you won't read?" you tease him. "I got you the *Globe*."

"Thank you." He pushes the magazine aside. "This thing is tedious," and he folds the newspaper in that neat, nifty way, easily held in one hand, something that you, despite your gift for folding dollar bills into swans, never mastered.

"And look what else I brought. You open the box of éclairs, and Leo says, "Fantastic."

The same way he's got the folded newspaper in one hand, to eat an éclair is also a one-handed operation. He reads and eats, and only when he sets about licking the residue of chocolate frosting from his fingers do you ease the newspaper from his hand. "You can read later. I'm here to visit you."

To visit him, to talk with him, but about what? What did he have for lunch? Did he sleep well? Was the éclair good? What did he have for breakfast? And then Leo saves you. "I was thinking," he says, but whatever it was that he was thinking is articulated in a lingual mudslide. As if you couldn't agree more, you're nodding your head vigorously when, as if seeing the bakery box for the first time, Leo says, "Éclairs. Fantastic." This one he holds the way you'd hold a flute, two hands, poised between both sets of fingers. He leans in to take a bite, but then, as if he's had a sudden loss of appetite, he puts it back in the box. His eyes are on his roommate, who waves as he passes by. If not for his belly protruding over the waistband of his sweatpants, you'd describe him as a wiry man, no apparent muscle between skin and bone, and he is ruddy-faced. His overall appearance is that of an old drunk in a dive bar, the kind of old drunk with rancid beer breath and an edge of belligerence. Alcoholic dementia, maybe? But really, what does it matter—alcohol, hereditary factors, causes unknown—when the end result is more or less the same?

"I don't like that guy," Leo says. "He's a troublemaker," but you don't get the chance to ask why he's a troublemaker because one of the aides, the one you've never seen do anything but play video games on his phone, is there to relay a message. "Joan asked if you'd come to her office now. She's going home early."

You tell Leo that you'll be back in a minute.

"Take your time." He picks up the newspaper.

Joan gestures to the chair on the other side of her, and she clears her throat, not to dislodge the metaphoric abundance of phlegm that defines her but rather to issue something like a nonverbal command: sit up straight, look alert, pay attention. It's terrifying, yet impressive, the way she's got that whole Mother Superior thing down pat.

"Last night," she says, "there was an incident. One of the aides found Leo's roommate in his bed. They were engaged," Joan says, her vocal cords twisting like tree rope, "in an indecent act. Of a sexual nature."

Indecent acts of a sexual nature surely must be routine here, like how little kids in preschool play doctor, or when they discover how it feels really good to touch themselves "down there," to which enlightened parents say, "Honey, it's fine to do that, but only in private, in your room. Not on the playground, okay?" After all, however old these people are, they *are* like children.

"What were they doing?" you ask. "Exactly."

As if having discovered a worm in her apple, she spits out the word. "Oral." Then breath in, breath out, again, once more, and Joan has regained her composure. "Has he ever shown any proclivities in this direction before?" She says *proclivities* as if the word is defined as fucking chickens or dead people.

"With me, yes." You smile at her, your best mean-girl smile. "Could you please be more explicit?" Explicit because you suspect that *explicit*, in this context, will give her the willies. "Which of them was *performing* the *indecent* act? Was Leo standing or was he on his knees?"

"Your husband was in a reclining position. But that's irrelevant."

"It's not irrelevant, Joan. It sounds to me like Micky was engaging in predatory behavior, that he molested Leo."

"Ridiculous," she says. "Micky has been here for years. There have been no prior incidents with him. None."

"Maybe. Or maybe this is just the first time you've busted him."

"Micky has seven children and approximately twenty grandchildren. But you," she says, her implication as pointed as a needle, "you don't have children."

"There is such a thing as birth control," you say.

"Yes. I'm well aware of that." End of discussion on that subject. "The problem has been resolved, in part. We've moved Micky into a single room."

You don't bring up her promise that Leo would get the next

single room available, because you can't afford it anyway, so you say, "Well, at least for now Leo can have Micky's side of the partition." Micky's side of the partition has two windows, an armchair, and a small table with a chair that Leo could use as a desk. Leo's side of the room is a jail cell.

"No," Joan says. "That's not possible." Not possible. No explanation.

The way the last bit of the toothpaste is squeezed from the tube, you squeeze out the last of your civility. "If that's all, I have a train to catch."

But that's not all. "He can't be wandering into other people's rooms at night."

"Has he been wandering into other people's rooms at night?"

"Not yet," she says. Not *yet*, as if it is inevitable that at the stroke of midnight or 3 A.M. Leo will slip out of his room, prowling for a blowjob. "You'll have to hire a private aide to watch him at night. There isn't sufficient staff to deal with a rogue resident."

"There isn't sufficient staff?" You're already paying for unused aide time, money that should be in an escrow account.

"As long as he stays in his room, it shouldn't be for more than a couple of weeks." Joan gives you the contact information for a private agency and says, "Please don't delay calling."

A private aide costs thirty-five dollars per hour, eight hours per night, every night until their services are no longer required. Don't bother adding or multiplying the numbers. It's all subtraction now.

Seven of This, Seven of That

Google is keeping count: you have visited *this* site seventeen times, *that* one fourteen times, and the other one nineteen times, but still you keep at it, scrolling and jumping from site to site, until a different set of Seven Stages pops up: *The Seven Stages of Grief.*

The seventh stage of grief is Acceptance.

Acceptance?

No, there will never be Acceptance.

This Grief is unacceptable.

Nowhere does it mention Relief.

A Room at the Inn

It's one of those smack-yourself-on-the-head moments: Marcy. Call Marcy.

You fill her in on the recent developments. Recent. Three months. Three lifetimes.

Marcy shares your opinion of Joan. "These people," she says. "So uptight. Provincial. And the obvious favoritism and clear-cut dislike for others is unacceptable. She's in the wrong line of work."

"I've got to get him out of there."

"Yes. You do. For him, but for yourself, too. Schlepping up to Boston every week. It's too much. Give me two minutes. I'll send you a list of reputable places in the area. I'm sorry. I should've thought of that before."

"Don't apologize," you say. "It wouldn't have made a difference. It was an emergency. I had no choice. But there's one other thing I wanted to ask you. All the websites refer to the day of diagnosis, but you were the one who diagnosed him. Is that where I begin?"

"No. I would've called it when the brain scans found no cause for the hallucinations."

"I can't thank you enough," you say, and that is a fact. The best you can do is ask how much you owe her for this round of help.

"No charge," Marcy says. "Unless you're of the one percent."

"Ha! You're a good person, Marcy. The best."

True to her word, Marcy's email shows up in two minutes.

One minute and forty-four seconds to be precise. It's a lengthy list. You start at the top.

Different city, same story: They are full up. They can put you on the wait list. Yes, at some point a room *will* become available, but when? Next week? Next month? Next year? *Twenty years?*

You once read about a cat that lived in a nursing home. The cat was psychic, able to predict who was next in line to die, and in that room, the one nearest to death, the cat settled in, and there it stayed until the end, but not even a psychic cat can give you an exact, or even an approximate, date of departure, a date when there will be a room available for Leo.

By now, you're pretty well resigned to more of the same, but you go on. Next is the Hotel Jacobs. A woman answers the phone, and like a parrot with a limited vocabulary, you say, "I was wondering if you might have a room available?" You're on the verge of saying, "Thanks, anyway," when it hits you: she said yes.

"We have one that just opened up. May he rest in peace. But only the one."

You pounce. "I'll take it. Please, please, don't give it to someone else."

"Can you get here by one? Marty will need time to show you around, and it's Friday. He has to get home before sunset."

What sunset has to do with room availability, you don't know, and you don't care. You swear you'll be there by noon, but when you ask for directions, it's clear that noon is pushing it. "Twelve thirty. At the latest. But you'll hold it for me? You promise?"

"I promise," she says.

Another World

At Fulton Street, you switch to the D train. It's a new experience; not the D train, but the absurdly courteous subway conductor who, at every stop, holds the doors for passengers who are still two blocks away, made all the more infuriating because the train is moving as if the speed limit were two miles per hour. You're tapping your feet, checking your watch, snorting, and muttering, "Move, *move* already," as if that will pick up the pace. At 12:21, the subway emerges from the tunnel to run above ground on tracks made of wood, weathered and rickety. It's the telltale sign: you're in the hinterlands.

The steep metal steps leading to the street are rusted. This is not the Brooklyn of historic townhouses, hipster artisanal breweries, cozy bookstores, narrow shops selling vinyl records or overpriced vintage clothes. The avenue is dreary, soul-crushing dreary. A plumbing supply warehouse, empty lots cordoned off with chain-link fencing, a paint-chipped sign, AUTO PARTS, is fixed to a concrete wall. Not a coffee bar in sight. No people, either.

The second left off the avenue puts you on a street enlivened by a two-bit strip mall: a no-name grocery store where the shelves are sure to be dusty, the floors grimy, and each piece of fruit, wrapped individually in cellophane, is guaranteed to be mealy. A ninety-nine-cents store is flanked by an out-of-business hair salon. You walk three blocks and turn right, where you're struck by the incongruity, the juxtaposition of that hideously miserable avenue and the sorry-ass shopping center with these single-family brick houses, solidly middle-class. Although—aesthetic snob that you are—the effect of the brick houses is marred by the aluminum awnings over the doorways, and the gates are chain link, too. Cars are parked in every driveway, not dumped in front of the houses like lawn furniture. Not the newest model cars, but they're nowhere near ready to be stripped and sold to the auto-parts dealer.

There's not a person in sight, but surely come spring, when the weather is warm and the yards go from brown dirt to green grass, gardens will bloom, then there will be children playing outside and neighbors will congregate for barbecues and cocktails. Come spring, the sky will be blue.

Your destination is not heralded by a circular driveway and tall maple trees, but from the top of the building near to the ground level runs a white sign: HOTEL JACOBS. A hotel, like one of those small hotels set within walking distance from the ocean in an unfashionable resort town. But why would anyone have erected a hotel here? Neither Brighton Beach nor Coney Island is within walking distance, and even if they were, those are city beaches, not beaches where people vacation. Whatever the explanation, who cares? They have a room.

All you ask is that Leo be treated with respect, and that the interior is not as bleak as the neighborhood.

More Is Less

Two young women, one wearing a pillbox-type hat, the other wearing what looks like a wig slightly askew, are at the reception desk.

"I'm the person who called," you say. "About an hour and a half ago."

The woman with the crooked wig smiles warmly. "Have a seat. Marty will be out in a minute. Unless he's on the phone, in which case he'll be out tomorrow. He's a talker, that one."

This woman is like the anti-Joan, a good omen.

Across from where you sit is a dining room. Cavernous, and on the shabby side, but shabby grandeur, like in its day, this was the posh place for wedding receptions and golden anniversary parties. Mammoth chandeliers hang from the high ceiling, and the chairs retain some residue of gold gilt. The tables, covered with white tablecloths, are interspersed between Doric columns, and a smattering of them are occupied by people who have far exceeded actuarial life expectancy. Yet they're decidedly alive. A foursome is playing cards, bridge or poker. Women are gabbing while knitting, and one man is alone reading a book.

Marty is a short man, not fat but plump and schlubby. His shirt, not fully tucked in, isn't dirty, but it could be that he slept in it. He's wearing a yarmulke, which explains why, on a Friday, he has to be home before sunset. His face is oval shaped, like the shape of an egg or a football, but he smiles a man-in-the-moon smile. "Come," he says. "We'll talk in my office."

His office has all the charm of a storage unit, empty but for a few unwanted items left behind: a calendar tacked to the wall, a metal file cabinet, five folding chairs spaced unevenly around a Formica table. "Sit, sit," he says. "Make yourself comfortable. Can I offer you something? Tea? A soda, maybe?"

"No, thank you. I'm good."

"Let me know should you change your mind." It's not the accent of someone whose English is newly acquired, but Marty speaks with a vague intonation and slightly off-kilter diction. He takes the seat directly across from yours. "So, tell me the story," he says, and you do. Not the whole story. You leave out the juicy parts, about how Leo stabbed Joey and punched the nurse, and forget the blowjob. You tell him that the commute is taking its toll, and you conclude your saga with a coda: The people who run the place there are not very nice. To put it mildly.

"Between us," he says, "a lot of them are like that. I'm sorry. For you and for your husband, I'm sorry. So young for this. It's a tragedy." His eyes reflect the sympathy of his words. "The residents here are much older than he is, but many of them are very well-educated people. Your husband, he still reads?"

"He sure does. Nine times out of ten, he's got his nose in a book."

"A blessing. Such as there is a blessing to be found. Some of our residents get a little antsy on the Sabbath. I understand. Friday sundown to Saturday sundown with no activities except television and reading. Your husband reads, he'll be happy."

If Marty has made an assumption, one that is incorrect, you fear that if corrected, it would be a deal-breaker. You're prepared to lie, but he doesn't ask, and yet as if the truth were like a sneeze, out it comes. "We're not Jewish. We don't practice any religion." In all good faith, you don't feel it necessary to mention Christmas. It's not as if you give so much as a wink to the Jesus part.

Marty shrugs his round shoulders. "The majority of our residents are Jewish. Not all of them, but most. We do observe the Sabbath, and we keep kosher. Saturday breakfast is cornflakes and milk and for lunch, sandwiches or cold leftovers from the night before. Not especially delicious"—he shrugs again—"but nourishing."

"Is it possible for him to have vegetarian meals?" you ask.

"Absolutely," Marty says. "Many of our residents are vegetarians. It's a popular way of being kosher." Then he stands up. "Let me show you around."

The once-ritzy dining room is where they hold music recitals, play Bingo, and mingle. In the basement, they have parties and watch movies. "They like the old movies. From the forties and fifties, with popcorn and a soda." A fenced-in courtyard is replete with benches and a few picnic tables.

Marty ushers you into the elevator. "The fourth floor," he tells you, "is exclusive to the dementia residents." The other residents, Methuselah-old and bones like dry twigs but of sound mind, live on the second, third, and fifth floors.

Exclusive, as if the demented ones are an elite group, but segregation is segregation, and it stings.

It occurs to you that Joan never mentioned other floors, floors like gated communities. Maybe Dickerson House is a *compos mentis*–free zone, which makes sense because it's not as easy to treat people of sound mind as subhuman.

Directly across from the elevator is the aides' station and a freestanding birdcage, home to two parakeets, their feathers no longer bright like the rinds of lemons and limes but rather the same faded yellow and pale green of pulp. The birds sit on their perch, listless, as if they are depressed, wanting nothing more than to fall from that perch of theirs, dead.

The fourth-floor sitting area is small, cramped. Two rows of the same kind of lightly padded folding chairs as those in Marty's office are arranged in a horseshoe around the TV. The residents, those who look to be awake, are staring at the screen, seemingly as listless as the parakeets, as if the washed-out birds are both simile and mirror.

That fancy-ass dining room on the ground floor is not where the demented people eat. Their dining room is done up with all the pizzazz of a cafeteria. The space between the tables is narrow and the ceiling is low.

Marty knows what you're thinking—the fourth floor is not a happy floor—and he aims to put a spin on it. "When they're not so far along, they can spend leisure time in the dining room downstairs, should they want. They like the concerts, too. Bingo not so much. Maybe when you came in you noticed one of them there with a book. He was a professor of history. A big reader, too, like your husband. In fact, your husband will be in the room next to his. A friend for him, perhaps."

As you and Marty walk down the long corridor to what will be Leo's room, a private room—all the rooms are private rooms—you note the rectangular cardboard posters, name-plates, taped to the doors, names written in bold print with black Magic Marker, some with crude crayon drawings, squiggles, glitter sprinkled at random. Marty tells you, "They make them in arts and crafts," and he unlocks the one door without a cardboard name tag, which opens into an alcove with a narrow bed and a closet. "Should someone need to stay overnight," Marty explains.

The room beyond the alcove is Cream of Wheat bland, but

reasonably spacious. "We encourage you to decorate," Marty says. "Family photographs are always nice. We ask only that you shouldn't use nails. Tape or Velcro," he says. Adjacent to a double-size bed is a nightstand, one drawer, a shelf below, and a lamp on top. Nestled in a corner is a brown armchair. Unattractive, but well padded. A chest of drawers is flat to the wall, and a small table with two folding chairs is adjacent to the window that looks out over the street. Not exactly a scenic view, but it's a window, a big window, a vast improvement over Leo's jail cell at Dickerson House. Beneath the window ledge is a mini-fridge.

"They can keep food in the rooms?" At Dickerson House, food taken beyond the confines of the dining area is a violation for which there is hell to pay.

"People get hungry at all hours, no?" Marty says.

You return to Marty's office, where the talk turns to business. "We ask that you provide a toothbrush and an electric razor, but soap, shampoo, and toothpaste are included, and of course the room, three meals a day, snacks, activity expenses, laundry. I know some places charge for diapers, but we don't. I buy in bulk."

"He goes to the bathroom just fine." Your voice sounds snippy, and you take a moment to alter the tone before you say, "He's self-sufficient."

Marty does not belabor what you refuse to consider. "Three times a week a team of nurses come to do Wellness exams. That's what they're called now, right? A Wellness exam?" His smile is sheepish, as if, somehow, he has both embarrassed himself and is waiting for praise. "They take the blood pressure and temperature, and they clip the toenails and fingernails. We have a doctor on call, but a doctor's visit and any medication, financially speaking, is your responsibility. The same goes if, God forbid, he should need the hospital."

Now for the twenty-four million dollar question: How much? Despite the dolorific locale, and the far-from-grand fourth floor, the Hotel Jacobs, with its private rooms and free amenities, has got to be in the Dickerson House price range, or more.

As if negotiating a high-end salary or an out-of-court settlement, Marty writes a number on a piece of paper and slides it over to you. "This is the full amount? The place where he is now is twice as much. Why is that?"

"We understand the hardships. I make a good living. Not to speak ill of others, why should I gouge you? But," he says, "there is something else. From experience, I know a change of venue can be distressing. I ask that you hire a private aide. For two or three weeks. It's a comfort if he has the same person with him 24/7." Marty says *24/7* the way he said *Wellness exam*, as if unsure that this lexicon is for the likes of him.

You begin the calculation in your head, but Marty breaks in to tell you that the Hotel Jacobs covers their meals, and they reside in the alcove, but you pay their salary. "Directly," Marty says. "Eight hundred and fifty dollars per week."

For a round-the-clock job, $850 is on the unacceptably exploitive end of a paycheck, but if you mention that to Marty, he might take offense. You'll throw in a little extra to ease your conscience, such as your conscience can ever be eased.

Marty has the perfect person for you. "Larissa cared for my wife's uncle, at our house for three years, like she was his mother. He recently passed away. May he rest in peace."

Why, you wonder, didn't they move his wife's uncle into the Hotel Jacobs? Is something sinister going on behind the scenes? Or is his wife one of those Message Board people?

"She's still at our house for now. She's made her plans to move home. To Jamaica," he says. "But a few weeks' work before she goes would be a gift. If this is agreeable to you, let me call her now."

Marty doesn't have her on speakerphone, but you listen to his side of the conversation. "I'm not sure exactly," he says. "But very soon. Good?" He hangs up, and then he asks you when you'd like to move Leo in here. "It can't be tomorrow. The Sabbath. But any day after then is fine. Between nine and five."

"Sunday," you say.

"Sunday it is. And if that's not possible, just let us know. I ask for two months up front." But when you take out your credit card, Marty apologizes. "I don't take credit cards. They charge a fee. If you don't have a check with you, it's okay to bring it when you move him in. Just promise me it won't bounce."

"It won't, I promise." A promise you can make with impunity because you haven't yet sent this month's check to Dickerson House, nor will you. Stiffing Joan for the few days is something like giving her the finger.

It's because of his yarmulke that you resist the urge to kiss Marty. Not a *kiss* kiss, just a peck on the cheek, but you do froth expressions of gratitude, until Marty says, "You're welcome. You're welcome. Enough already. Go home. Rest easy."

Pass Go

You're not two steps from the entrance to the Hotel Jacobs before you get Denise on the phone. "I've found a great place for Leo, but I have to move him in on Sunday. Do you think Joey will be able to pick him up then and drive to Brooklyn?"

"Absolutely. Hang on. You can give him the details."

You instruct Joey not to tell anyone at Dickerson House that Leo is leaving for good. "Just say that you're taking him out for the day. Don't take anything. I'll bring everything he'll need."

"Sort of like breaking him outta jail," Joey says.

"Exactly like breaking him out of jail. I'll call you when I get home with directions and whatever. It's a long drive," you warn him. "Longer than to our place."

He snort-laughs. "Don't worry. I'll tell my mother to wake me up early," and you say, "Joey, thank you. Really, I can't thank you enough."

"You don't have to thank me. Leo's my uncle. I love him."

"He loves you, too." And then you add, "So do I."

This is good, you tell yourself, all good, and if it weren't a cold day in winter, if you didn't have to shop and pack for Leo, you might have walked all the way to Brighton Beach, but you head to the subway. This *is* good, although the streets are no less bleak.

Something Like Home

Marty is waiting in the lobby to introduce you to Larissa. She is a strikingly beautiful woman. Early to mid-thirties, cocoa-colored skin, smooth without a wrinkle or a blemish. Her hair is pulled into a tight bun near the top of her head. She's wearing jeans, a sweatshirt, and gold hoop earrings. Her excess weight is Rubenesque.

"You should forgive me," Marty says, "but work is calling."

"Hold on," you say, and you give him the envelope, the one containing the check. He folds it in half, slips it into his shirt pocket, and heads to his office, which is when it hits you. The bank. You forgot to go to the bank. You don't have the cash to pay Larissa. "I'm so sorry," you apologize. "I forgot. I'll have it for you tomorrow."

"Not tomorrow. I get paid at the end of the week. You have to think. Suppose I took your money now and tomorrow I disappear?"

You laugh and say, "Good point."

She doesn't laugh and says, "Yes."

Larissa isn't cold the same way Joan is cold, but it's the same insofar as you're getting the distinct impression that she doesn't much like you, if at all, which compels you to blather nonstop. You tell her about how Leo is self-sufficient. "He dresses, showers, uses the bathroom, eats, all that with no help. He understands everything you say, but not everything he says makes sense. His speech is often garbled, and he sees and hears things that aren't there. Sometimes, he gets confused. The main thing is he doesn't seem to be aware of where he is or what's happening to him. But otherwise he's fine, and he's a nice guy."

Not even when you tell her that you are going to pay her more than $850 do you get a rise out of her. You'd have thought, if nothing else, she'd ask how much more, but she doesn't, which is for the best because you haven't yet figured out what you can afford.

Finally, finally, although earlier than you'd expected, Leo and Joey come through the door. You dash over to Leo, and you hug as if months or years have gone by, not days, and you've missed each other desperately. When you break apart, Joey asks where Leo's room is, and he reaches for the suitcase next to your chair, but Larissa beats him to it. "I've got it," she says, and Joey doesn't argue.

"Okay, I should get going anyway. Sunday traffic, you know." He extends his hand toward Leo for a handshake, but Leo looks puzzled, unsure of what's expected of him. Joey gives him a hug. Not like your hug, more like a clap on the back. "I'll see you soon, Uncle Leo," and you say, "Joey, you're a good man."

Larissa lifts the suitcase as if it were light enough to carry with her pinkie finger. "Wait," you say to her. "Where are your things? Your coat? Your suitcase?"

"Upstairs," she says. "I unpacked before you got here."

The three of you walk to the elevator and when you get off on the fourth floor, you and Leo trail behind Larissa like a pair of ducklings until you get to his room. There, Leo heads straight for the armchair. Larissa puts his suitcase on the table and opens it.

"No, no," you say. "You don't have to do that."

"It's better if I unpack for him," she says. "I need to know what is where."

You're left to stand there, between the bed and the armchair, until Larissa sets the two books on the nightstand, and then, as if you were a shoplifter, you make a quick grab for them and bring them to Leo.

"Books," he says. "Thank you." But when he looks at them, *Discovering the Gene* and Leibniz's *Philosophical Essays*, he says, "I've already read these. This one"—he holds up the Leibniz—"I read in college."

This is not the time to tell him to go fuck himself. Instead, you tell him, "I'll bring you more tomorrow," and seemingly satisfied, he puts the Leibniz on the floor, and sets out rediscovering the gene.

Leo's reading, Larissa's hanging his coat and shirts in the closet, and rather than standing there with your thumb up your ass, you say, "I'm going to take a walk around. See what's doing out there. I'll be right back."

What's doing out there? Not a damn thing. You pace the halls twice, sit for a couple of minutes with the demented people watching a soccer game on television, and then go back to Leo's room, where you find him now sitting at the little table across from Larissa.

"He's telling me about his job," she says. "Such a smart man."

The dinner bell rings. You'll be having your dinner at your apartment, but you go with them to the dining room, such as it is one. There, you tell Larissa that Leo doesn't eat meat. You can't decipher if she is puzzled or disapproving. "We're vegetarians."

"Whatever you say." It seems as if she disapproves of your diet. Then she tells you that there's no reason for you to stick around, that you can leave now, leaving you relatively certain that her disapproval is not limited to what you eat. It's you.

In your entirety, but you're hardly going to argue when it's an argument you don't want to win. But then, for no reason you can determine, she warms up to you. "Go home," she says. "Get some rest. You've had a long day. He and I are getting along just fine. Isn't that right, Leo?"

It could be that he is only echoing Larissa when he says, "Go home, Addie. Get some rest."

But no. He said *Addie*, which sounds like a new word to your ears. When did he last call you by name?

You start to button your coat, but then Leo stops you. "Addie, wait." *Addie*. Again *Addie*. "Do you have any cash?"

Why he needs, wants cash, is a mystery, but you give him what you have. Seven singles. That's it. "Here you go, Leo. Spend it wisely."

Leo. Addie.

Leo and Addie.

Monday, Day Two, Week One

The plan was to be at the Hotel Jacobs by noon, but by the time you wake up, feed Roberta and Howie, shower, wash and dry your hair, dress, pack a bag of books, gather together a few photographs, and then stop at the bank for cash and the bodega for six Peppermint Patties, you're four hours late.

Leo and Larissa are grouped in with all the others gathered around the television, except for the aides who are huddled together in a far corner. None of the residents are actually watching *The Price Is Right*. They are either staring at the screen, eyes glazed as if they have cataracts, or else they're looking down at their feet, or resting their chins on their chests, asleep, drugged up, possibly dead. Leo and Larissa, deep in conversation, are not watching the game show, either.

"Hey, there," you interrupt them, and Leo gets up to give you a hug.

Because you can't, won't, sit here in this sea of woe, you take Leo's hand. "Let's go to your room. Have a proper visit."

Now, taped to his door is the ubiquitous cardboard name tag: *Leo* written in black marker edged with silver glitter, crayon drawings of cats that are recognizable as cats, and a woman's face colored brown, a big emoji-style pink mouth, brown hair pulled into a bun. Diagonally across from the rendering of what must be Larissa is another woman's face: same smile, but bright red lips and long black hair. You.

"Leo," you ask, "did you make this yourself?"

His mouth spreads into an emoji-style smile, too, and he nods.

"We had Arts and Crafts this morning," Larissa tells you, and you say to Leo, "I didn't know you were a such a good artist. You were keeping a secret from me."

"Yes," he says, "I am," and he opens the door to his room and, as if you were a guest and he were the host, he tells you to make yourself comfortable.

There, you take the books from the bag and set them on the table. Leo picks them up one by one, pronouncing each to be an excellent choice. Then he stacks them on the nightstand shelf, in size order.

"There's more," you say. "Not books. Pictures." You spread out the photographs: The two of you together in front of City Hall the day you got married. Neither of you looks all that different, except for Leo's hair, which was brown; a copy of your professional headshot; Roberta; Denise; and an old photograph of his parents.

First, he points to Roberta's picture and tells Larissa, "This is my cat."

My cat? "Leo," you chide, "Roberta is *our* cat."

"Right," and he moves on to the next one in line. "My parents, and that's my sister. My mother died when she was young. But my father died just last year."

You don't correct him. His father did not die *last* year, but he knows that his father is dead, and that is good enough.

Larissa gathers the photographs into a sheaf. "Let me put these somewhere safe. We'll hang them up tomorrow."

"Look what else I got for you." You put the Peppermint Patties in two stacks of three on the table where the pictures were before Larissa put them away in the drawer, sliding them underneath Leo's sweaters, which you noticed were folded in the way sweaters are folded in shops, professional folding.

Larissa warns him not to eat more than one now. "You don't want to ruin your appetite for dinner."

"I don't know about that," Leo says. "The food here isn't all that good."

Larissa lets out a laugh that doesn't quit, but when she does pull herself together, she says to you, "He's right. It's not very good. Breakfast was okay, scrambled eggs, but the lunch . . ." She scrunches her nose.

You give her the five twenty-dollar bills from the bank, from *the money machine.* "If you want to buy food or whatever else."

Leo takes his wallet from his back pocket and opens it to show you that it is empty. "I need some cash, too."

"What did you do with the money I gave you yesterday?"

"Oh, you won't believe this." Larissa is laughing again. "He tipped the women in the dining room. I told him no, but he wouldn't listen."

"Oh, I believe it. You always tip big, don't you, Leo?"

He says something, but it's incomprehensible.

You give him the change from the Peppermint Patties: five singles, but the fifty cents, two quarters, you keep for yourself.

Teetering

Make coffee, feed the cats, get dressed, put two books in your tote bag, only two because one, a textbook, *Anatomy and Physiology*, weighs almost as much as you do, and when you're halfway to the subway, your phone rings. You look at the caller ID: Isabelle Weber.

Incredulous, except true. You'd forgotten all about the show, which closed last night. "One sold," Isabelle Weber tells you.

"One?" Are you crushed that only one sold? Or, because you were expecting none to sell, are you elated?

You know where Leo would've landed, on the upside of the seesaw.

You're teetering. One sale isn't going to skyrocket your career, that's for sure, but one is better than none, if only because of the money. With the demise of Leo's salary looming, some money is better than no money.

In her inimitable way, Isabelle Weber gives you explicit instructions: you're to come to the gallery within the week to retrieve the rejects. She doesn't actually say *the rejects*. She says *the others*, but you know she's thinking *the rejects*.

You lack the spunk to tell her that you can't be bothered to pick them up, that she should just go ahead and drop them in the garbage along with everything else in your life.

Then, just before she hangs up, Isabelle Weber says to you, "Perhaps Sheila will want them," which is her way of letting you know that you're a Sandstone artist, respectable but not Weber Gallery caliber.

You go back home and call Larissa. "I'm really sorry, but something unexpected came up. I'm not going to be able to get there today. Will you be okay without me?"

"Don't you worry. We're doing great."

"I'll be there tomorrow," you promise, and then desperate for comfort that Leo can no longer provide, you get the fanciful idea that one of the cats will lick your wound the way they lick their paws to wash their faces. You find them in your bed, cuddled up together, sleeping.

Transformation

The subway car windows are grimy with soot, and although the station is above ground, it's nonetheless tunnel-dark inside. Not until you're out on the street do you see that the clouds have dispersed, but the sun, this winter sun, directly overhead and white bright, is not enough to melt the patina of desolation. Did you really believe that, somehow, beams of sunshine would transform this gray Kansas-in-Brooklyn landscape into Technicolor Oz or a Jane Jacobs vision of urban utopia? The reality is that this neighborhood is a sad place. It was built sad, and it will always be sad, and if it were ever razed to the ground, the ground would be sad.

But then, as if the cardboard nameplate on Leo's door were the first note to a song, a song that heralds a transformation, his room has morphed from institutional-drab into one that pops with color. From moth to butterfly. Two Crayola-red throw pillows liven up the brown armchair. Centered on the table is a yellow vase filled with yellow flowers, plastic but cheerful. A small red-and-black plaid rug is at the foot of the bed. The beige lampshade has been replaced with one that is a soft blue, and the photographs in sky-blue frames are artfully arranged on the wall.

"Wow. This is amazing. It looks fantastic." Granted, it's not the way you'd have spruced up the room, but *you* didn't take the trouble to spruce it up. "Really, fabulous."

Leo smiles as wide as arms stretched out for a hug, but that's it. He takes a book from the night table shelf and sits in the armchair.

"We went shopping yesterday," Larissa tells you, "to that ninety-nine-cents store. Would you believe almost nothing there costs ninety-nine cents? He picked the vase and the pillows himself. They were three seventy-nine. Each."

"Really? That's a bargain."

"No," Larissa says. "Ninety-nine cents would've been a bargain."

"Touché." You laugh, and Leo laughs, too, and then he asks Larissa if he can have a glass of orange juice.

"Of course you can." She's got two glasses, two plates, and silverware stashed in her suitcase. "So the cleaning people don't find them," she says. "After the ninety-nine-cents store, we went food shopping. He insisted on pushing the cart *and* carrying *all* of the bags back. He wouldn't let me carry even one bag." With a note of pride, she adds, "Your husband is a real gentleman."

"Sometimes," you say, "but clearly you bring out the best in him."

The mini-fridge is stocked: orange juice, apples, pears, a six-pack of Coke, a loaf of bread, peanut butter, strawberry jelly, and an Entenmann's crumb cake. Larissa pours the orange juice, gives the glass to Leo, and tells you, "We used all the spending money you gave me."

"That's okay. Everything you've done is wonderful, but I'm sorry. I don't have much cash with me. Maybe ten dollars. But I'll bring more tomorrow."

Leo twists in his chair to look at you. "Don't forget money for me, too."

"I won't. But look what I have for you now." You take the books from your bag.

Leo and his books.

He is particularly delighted with *Anatomy and Physiology*, the 7th edition. "I was hoping for this one," he says. "I need more textbooks here. Next time, could you bring the one on cellular respiration?"

Cellular respiration?

"Do you want anything else?"

"*Brock Biology of Microorganisms*," he says. "And money."

Larissa asks if you could bring more pictures. "One or two more of you, and another one of the cat, and his parents. He talks about his father a lot. Not so much his mother."

"I didn't like her," Leo says.

"Your mother?" Larissa is aghast. "Leo, how could you not love your mother?"

"Because she died."

The sound of the dinner bell is, for you, like the school bell at the end of the day. You can run home now, but when you get to the ground floor, you pause at the fancy-ass dining room. As if you were the Little Match Girl peering through the window at a rich family chowing down on a bountiful feast, you get a pang. Not a hunger pang, but a pang of wanting, all the same. Leo should be there, at a table with a tablecloth, dining under the chandeliers. A man who selects red pillows, yellow flowers, who knows to tip the servers when they bring him food, who asks for a textbook on microorganisms, should not be sentenced to take his meals in a room under a low ceiling of soundproof tiles with people who can only babble or cry or put spoons in their ears because they don't remember the anatomy of a face.

Until Death Do Us Part

L eo and Larissa are not in Leo's room or anywhere on the fourth floor. You ask one of the aides if she knows where they went, and she says, "No."

That's it. No. Fuck you, too.

Two weeks and two days, that's how long Leo has been at the Hotel Jacobs. Marty had arranged for Larissa to stay with Leo for three weeks. After that, she is leaving, going home to Jamaica. Then what? The aides at the Hotel Jacobs are on a par with the aides at Dickerson House, both set on two speeds of operation: indifferent or cruel. When one of the no-marbles women slipped from her chair, seemingly oblivious that to be half on the ground is not a comfortable position, you watched the aide take her sweet time helping the woman up, and then she pulled the woman's arms with enough force to yank them out of their sockets, ignoring Larissa, who told her, "Not like that. From behind, you slip your hands under her armpits and gently, gently, slide her up." Although, officially, Larissa is responsible only for Leo's care, she pushed the aide out of the way and eased the woman back into her chair. And when that poor, pathetic man's robe fell open, his shriveled dick on display, and the aides nearly busted their collective guts pointing and laughing, Larissa closed the man's robe, and she confronted the aides. "Which one of you dressed him this morning? You don't put the man's underwear on? Do it now."

Maybe Leo and Larissa are downstairs in the normal people's dining room, or maybe they went out to buy food or browse around the ninety-nine-cents store. At the reception desk, the woman with the wig tells you that they're outside on the patio.

Bundled up in their coats, Leo and Larissa are sitting at one of the picnic tables huddled together over a book, the *Anatomy and Physiology* textbook, open to a color plate of the skeletal bones of the hand. Because they are seemingly unaware that you are standing behind them, you clear your throat. Larissa glances in your direction and says to Leo, "Look who's here."

Leo doesn't look away from the book, and Larissa tells you, "He's showing me all the body parts. He says I should be a nurse or a doctor." She laughs, as if the idea were preposterous.

"He's right," you say, adding, "It's cold out here."

"I know," Larissa says, "but the sun is good for him."

"*You're* good for him." You sit down, and Leo is now book-ended between the woman who loves him and the woman who cares for him.

The sun shifts, and the air turns colder. It's time to go indoors.

Larissa carries the textbook, and you and Leo hold hands until you get to his room, where you take off your coat and Larissa helps Leo out of his, and when her coat is off, she holds out her arm to show you the bracelet on her wrist: her name spelled out with red, white, and black plastic beads strung on elastic thread, the ends tied into a knot. "He made it in Arts and Crafts. He made one for you, too. Leo," she asks, "where did you put the bracelet you made for Addie?"

"I don't know."

Larissa locates your bracelet under one of the red pillows. You slip it on. A-D-D-I-S-O-N. Addison. *Addison.* Not Addie.

As if the plastic name bracelet, your name but not your name, were the same as the opal bangle or the garnet-encrusted one or any of the many bracelets he gave you back when he was still Leo, you say, "It's beautiful. I love it."

He seems pleased with himself, as if he'd chosen well. "I thought you'd like it."

Larissa tells Leo that she'll be right back, she's just going to the bathroom, but the very second that she is no longer in his line of vision, Leo cranes his neck, looking like a dog tied up outside the grocery store, straining at his leash, whimpering from fear of abandonment. Whenever you encounter a frightened dog like that tied up outside a store, you don't care whether you're perceived as a humane person or a crazy one, you barge into the store and call out, "Who left their dog outside?"

The dog's owner, either miffed or ashamed, invariably says, "It's only for a minute," to which you say, "Guess what? Dogs can't tell time."

Back from the bathroom, Larissa settles into the armchair. Leo, now visibly relaxed, shifts his gaze and says to you, "I have to tell you something."

"What is it? What do you have to tell me?"

"I still like you, but"—he points to Larissa—"but I'm with her now."

Larissa laughs, and you say, "Well, I'm glad you still like me."
But I'm with her now.

You ask Larissa if you can have a word with her alone, alone but where Leo can still see you, see her. If it sounds as if you are pleading, it's because you *are* pleading. "Is there is any way you would consider staying on longer? I'll give you a raise. A good raise. Anything. Whatever you want."

"Okay," Larissa says.

"I can't leave him here with them." You don't have to tell her who them is.

"I said okay. He's a good man. I'll stay for as long as you want."

"Really? How about forever?"

Larissa will stay, and you can leave. You kiss Leo goodbye, kiss him on the cheek, as you would kiss a little boy, and as if he were indeed a little boy and you were some overly perfumed distant relative, he crinkles his nose and recoils in the way that would prompt the little boy's mother to say, "He's shy."

I'm with her now.

Accounting

Although the Hotel Jacobs is a bargain compared to the Dickerson House of Horrors, when you include what you are paying Larissa now—$850 plus the extra $150 per week you threw in to ease your over-burdened conscience—the bargain turns out to be like one of those ten-percent-off sales. Not exactly a bargain basement bargain, and now you've promised Larissa a raise. But here's the rub: it was a promise predicated on Leo's paycheck coming in, and it's only a matter of months until Leo's paycheck becomes something for the history books. After that, your income will amount to his disability checks and his radically reduced pension, and you've already cut your personal expenses down to the necessities.

Even if you could afford it, there is no one with whom you'd go out to dinner, and you don't order takeout because you don't care what you eat. Everything tastes like nothing. You've located a wine shop that offers deep discounts if you buy by the case. There's no point to buying new clothes when you no longer go to parties or gallery openings or the theater (the one loss that's a win, sparing you Katrine's shit-on-the-stage plays). Other than to run errands and visit Leo, it's like you're under house arrest. All streaming services, magazine subscriptions, and Leo's phone service have been canceled. You've got enough art supplies to last you twelve decades. That leaves the maintenance on your apartment, Con Ed, Wi-Fi, your phone, minimum payments on the credit card bills, and food, litter, and toys for Roberta and Howie. You can deprive yourself, but how do you explain to cats why you have no treats to give them?

How much of a raise can you afford to give Larissa?

You open your computer to the calculator app.

Fifty dollars?

You imagine having this conversation with Leo. "I think maybe I could manage fifty dollars?"

He'd give you the fisheye. "Fifty dollars? That's nothing."

"It's two hundred dollars a month."

Again, you'd get the fisheye. "What does she deserve?"

To pay Larissa what she deserves would require that you have a Jeff Bezos-level of income, although Jeff Bezos would never pay her what she deserves. If she worked for Jeff Bezos, he wouldn't even give her a bathroom break.

And then you would remind him, "You promised to take care of me, Leo. You promised that you would always take care of me."

A pause, a cute, sheepish smile, and he'd say, "I accept your apology."

What he would not say to you, but what you say to yourself, is that you are a grown-ass woman, and regardless of your lack of marketable skills, a grown-ass woman should be able to figure out how to support herself.

It was Leo's idea that you quit waiting tables and devote yourself full-time to your art. "It's not like I'd be working a second job to support you. My salary is plenty for the two of us."

"But what if I don't succeed?"

"We can look at it like an investment. Some pay off, some don't."

"Cute," you said. "Very cute. But really, Leo. It's the art world."

Then he put it another way. "If the situation were reversed, wouldn't you want me to pursue what makes me happy?"

"Of course," you said, but it *wasn't* the other way around.

You promised to take care of me, Leo. You promised that you would always take care of me.

One Little Pill

When you left your apartment, it was a cool sixty-four degrees out, but now, regardless that it's too warm for your denim jacket, you don't take it off, just as despite the pure blue sky and sharp sunlight, you don't put on your sunglasses. Why wear sunglasses here in this land of perpetual winter, winter in Scandinavia at dusk?

At the Hotel Jacobs, you greet the women at the reception desk, as you always do, with a smile and a wave. The one wearing the hat says hello. The other one you don't recognize. She gives you a curt head nod.

On the fourth floor, the yellow parakeet is alone on its perch. You don't have to ask about the green one to know that it died. Lucky bird.

Excessive sleeping is another Lewy body symptom that supposedly shows up in Stage 2; another one that Leo has yet to exhibit, but now it's early afternoon, and he is in bed, snoring lightly.

Larissa is at the table moving around the pieces of the jigsaw puzzle, something you bought because all the websites highly recommended jigsaw puzzles for people with dementia. Leo showed fuck-all interest in the jigsaw puzzle, and Larissa wasn't exactly reeling with excitement over it, either, but you assume with Leo napping, it's a way for her to occupy her time.

"He fell asleep right after breakfast," Larissa tells you. "All morning he slept, and I couldn't get him to wake up for lunch."

"Is he sick?"

"No." Larissa's jaw is set in what looks like anger. "He's not sick. But we need to talk. I am very upset."

Upset? Larissa is upset?

You feel sick.

What has upset Larissa began yesterday when Leo had his Wellness exam. Because only family members are permitted in the examining room, Larissa waited in the hallway. There, she took out her phone, and while responding to a text from her sister, the door opened, and the nurse stepped out.

"You can't come in," she said to Larissa, "but would you take a look at him?"

Leo was sitting upright on the examining table, his legs dangling over the side, his hands and arms going as if he were swatting at a storm of gnats.

The nurse wanted to know, "Is he always this agitated?"

"No, not at all. He gets nervous when he can't see me," Larissa explained, "but as soon as I'm back, he's fine. He's happy."

"Okay," the nurse said. "Thanks." She closed the door, and a minute later, Leo was back with Larissa. Back with Larissa, fine and happy.

Fine and happy until this morning, at breakfast, when the aide who dispenses medication stopped at their table with a pill in a paper cup for Leo.

"You're making a mistake," Larissa told her. "He doesn't get any medicine."

"He does now," the aide said. "It's right here on the chart. Seroquel."

Larissa said no, the aide said yes, and the no and the yes went like a volley in a tennis match until the aide slam-dunked the ball, and here is where Larissa squints at you, as if you're not to be trusted. "This aide told me Management said you approved, but I'm telling you, he doesn't need Seroquel."

"They said I approved? I most certainly did *not* approve. How could I have approved when I wasn't asked?"

You go off to have a word with Management.

Marty is away until Thursday, and the woman whom you didn't recognize when you came in tells you that she is the supervisor. "Can I help you with something?"

"I sure hope so," you say.

She steps out from behind the desk. You give her the once-over: frumpy, built like a sumo wrestler. The buttons of her white blouse strain against her triple-D breasts.

After you've finished outlining the problem, she says, "Larissa must have been confused. Leo was not prescribed Seroquel. Dementia patients sleep a lot."

You caught her implication and, in no uncertain terms, you let her know that Larissa does not lie.

"I didn't say she lied. I said she was confused. We'd never dispense medication without your permission."

Be careful. Adjust your tone of voice. You need the Hotel Jacobs far more than they need you, and that's your pill to swallow. "Perhaps you could call the nurse or check the records yourself. I just want to clear this up."

"I'll see what's on the computer, although I'm sure Larissa misunderstood." But lo and behold, there it is. The nurse *did* prescribe Seroquel for Leo, and you say, "No more. You didn't ask my permission, and Larissa says he doesn't need it. I trust Larissa." You both know what was left unsaid.

Leo has yet to wake up, but Larissa has made progress on the puzzle. "What did they say?" she asks.

"They made a mistake. He won't be getting Seroquel again."

"Thank you, because sleeping all day like this is not good."

"Unless you're a cat," you say, and you wonder if that Zocdoc who gave you the Ambien would write you a prescription for Seroquel.

PART FIVE

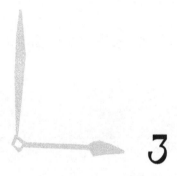

3

The Sunny Side of the Street

I t could be the psychological contrast between *there* and *here*, or maybe the glare of the late-afternoon sun is that much more blinding, but when you emerge from the subway, you put on your sunglasses and, instead of going straight home, meander around your neighborhood.

Four blocks up and one avenue east of your apartment, a red sign dangles from a chain hooked to the fire escape on one of those soft-gray brick buildings. The white print reads: APARTMENT FOR RENT, and below, on a white strip and written sloppily, is a phone number.

It's not the same kind of inspiration that inspires art; it's a life-altering inspiration, like an epiphany, except of practical value.

You whip out your phone. It's near to the end of the workday, but on the third ring, a man answers. "Larsen Realty. John Larsen speaking. What can I do for you?"

"The apartment on Twenty-First Street," you say. "Is it still available?"

If you can wait forty-five minutes to an hour, he'll show it to you today. If not, then tomorrow.

You'll wait.

The lobby is more like a truncated hallway, but it's clean. The apartment is on the third floor. The only window in the decidedly not-spacious living room faces the wall of the adjacent building. No more than one person can fit in the kitchen, but it's got a dishwasher sandwiched between the sink and the stove. The fixtures in the decent-size bathroom look to be new, and the square footage of the bedroom is more or less the same as your bedroom—*your* bedroom, *your* apartment, *your* cats, all of it *yours*, not *ours*—with a big window that faces out onto Twenty-First Street, a relatively quiet block.

Mr. Larsen tells you that there's a laundry room in the basement. Four washers and dryers.

It's the kind of apartment often referred to as a starter apartment, a place rented by recent college graduates or young couples determined to live in Manhattan, never mind that they could get a whole lot more bang for their buck in Brooklyn or Queens. The rent, although not outrageous, is New York steep, but it's less than half the price of the Hotel Jacobs, excluding Larissa's salary.

"I'll take it," you say.

The realtor's office is nearby. There, you show him your ID, and he does a quick credit check, which is momentarily worrisome. Your credit score could well be in the toilet, but the only thing that gives him pause is that you already own an apartment in this neighborhood.

"Why do you want this one?" he asks. "We don't allow sublets."

"My husband and I are separating," you say, which is not a full-fledged lie. "He's with someone else now."

"I'm sorry. That's tough."

As to be expected, he wants first and last months' rent, plus a security deposit. You ask him to put it on two credit cards, and then you sign two copies of a three-year lease, and he does the same.

"It's almost the end of the month. If you want to move in now, you can have the week, no charge." He gives you two sets of keys.

One set of keys for you, and one set for Larissa.

Larissa. You didn't stop to think about Larissa. What if she doesn't want to move to Manhattan? She might not want to be a caretaker *and* a housekeeper because, excluding Denise, who wants to clean the bathroom, mop the floors, and do laundry?

You'll have to give her another raise.

You forgot to factor in utilities, food, household expenses.

Add it all up. Roughly speaking, it still comes to a little bit less than the Hotel Jacobs. Or maybe a little more, but still, it's a steal.

A Better Place

Leo gets up from the armchair to give you a quick hug before going back to his reading. Perhaps it is inconsiderate, or worse, but you make no attempt to include him in the conversation. He's given no indication that he even knows or cares where he's living, and if he has any recollection that six months ago his home was on a tree-lined street in Manhattan, his home with you and Roberta, he hasn't mentioned it.

With Larissa, you start with the plus column: the desirable neighborhood, safe, lively, lots of cute shops, cafés, restaurants, restaurants that deliver, well-stocked grocery stores, the parks. It's handy to the subway, and the building is clean, and you live only a few blocks away. "And you can fix it up however you want," you say.

But you're not going to bullshit her, either. "It's not huge. The kitchen is kind of cramped, but it has a dishwasher and both rooms are bigger than these. There's plenty of closet space. The bedroom gets direct sunlight. You can have that room for yourself. We can set up a bed for Leo in the living room. Maybe get one of those daybeds, the kind that can double as a couch. I know it means extra work for you, but of course I'll give you a raise. Three hundred dollars a week more."

"No," Larissa says.

"No?"

"No," Larissa repeats. "No. Leo gets the bedroom."

"But you're okay with moving? Really?"

Larissa says, "That's a crazy question. Yes, of course I want to move. Oh my God. I'm so happy, and Leo will be so happy."

Larissa is happy.

Leo will be happy.

For you, *happy* is like a childhood memory, something like going faster and faster and higher and higher on a backyard swing, something you can recall but never relive. No, you can't say that you are happy, but if nothing else, you'll be spared the walk along those sad streets to the Hotel Jacobs where, on the fourth floor, a parakeet sits alone on its perch.

Home Is Where the Heart Is

Two beds, a console, a TV, a small bookcase, and a drop leaf table with four chairs were delivered yesterday. At a discount store on Fourteenth Street, you bought pillows, white sheets, white towels, and a coffeemaker. Dishes, glasses, silverware, a frying pan, and a pot, you brought from home.

This morning you stocked the kitchen with the staples: milk, cereal, bread, eggs, peanut butter, paper towels, dishwasher detergent. Then you went to Rite Aid for toilet paper, soap, toothpaste, and two toothbrushes.

The previous tenants left behind a broom and dustpan.

Outside, standing in front of the building, you watch the cars go by until the prearranged and prepaid minivan pulls up. The driver unloads the two suitcases, a large carton, and an industrial-size black plastic trash bag. Leo's got both suitcases, and Larissa insists on carrying the carton of books because she is strong and you, she says, are a weakling. "Those skinny arms of yours. You can take that." She nods at the black plastic bag. "It's the things we bought for his room before."

You unlock the door to the apartment and hold it open for Leo and Larissa. Leo puts the suitcases down alongside the entryway to the bathroom. Larissa slides the too-heavy-for-your-skinny-arms carton onto the table and tells you to leave the black plastic bag on the floor. "Right there, next to the chair." While she's inspecting the kitchen, you guide Leo to the bedroom, where he goes straight to the window. You stand alongside him and ask, "So, what do you think? Do you like this place?"

He responds with a nod of his head and an outpouring of mishmash that communicates nothing, but a nod is a yes, isn't it?

For a minute or so, the both of you just standing there at the window like you used to do when he was seeing swans and ponies and Gandhi on the street at night, and then Leo says, "This direct sunlight is terrific, and the view is nice."

You leave Leo standing at the window and find Larissa unpacking her suitcase. She looks up at you and says, "I love this place. I have all kinds of ideas how to decorate."

"This is *your* home. You do what you want with it."

"Even from the car, I saw so many stores. After I unpack, I'll take him grocery shopping."

"I got a few things. I put them in the fridge."

"Yes. I saw, but that's not food. One other thing," she says. "I noticed a Best Buy near here. Do you mind if I get another television? One for each room. In case we want to watch different shows."

"Sure," you say. "Of course you can." You give her a credit card to buy food and a television and whatever else she needs, along with fifty-seven dollars in cash. "Now that the weather is nice, you'll probably go out a lot, and if you want an ice cream or a soda or something, the guys with the carts don't take cards." Then you give her a set of keys and say, "I'll let you get settled in. I just want to say goodbye to Leo first."

Leo is where you left him, looking out the window, and you tell him, "I'm happy that you like your new home."

And then you leave, you go home, to *your* home, which has come to be more and more like a haunted house.

So Many Nice Things

Leo is sitting upright in bed, his knees bent, a book, open, rests against his thighs, and his back is bolstered by one of those big pillows shaped like the back of a comfortable chair. It's made of the same red corduroy as the bedspread. The red throw pillows from the more-than-ninety-nine-cents store are wedged into the adjacent corner. He puts the book aside, face down, and when he gets up, he points at the big pillow and says, "This thing is terrific. I should've gotten one years ago."

Larissa tells you that she thought the pillow would suffice until they can get something better, like a reclining chair. "I saw a pair on sale for a good price. Fake leather," she adds, "but it looked real and the fake is easier to keep clean."

You don't ask what constitutes a good price. It's not as if she's going to be furnishing the place every month. It's a one-time thing, so suck it up.

"Maybe later this afternoon, if I have the energy, we'll go back to that store. I don't know how long the sale will be. After you left yesterday, we shopped till we dropped, didn't we, Leo?"

"You bet. Look at all the nice things we got." As if he were one of those game show hosts, he sweeps an arm over the display of all the prizes you could win: the particle board chest of drawers, the same approximation of oak as the night table, a brass lamp with a red-and-blue plaid shade, the same blue as the curtains. "Did you see the . . . ?" The words that followed fell off a cliff, but he's pointing at the two plants soaking up the brilliant afternoon sunlight.

"Do you believe it?" Larissa says. "We got them at that big supermarket. Whole Foods. They sell flowers *and* plants. First, he wanted a cactus, but I said no. Because of the needles. So, he picked these instead."

The needles? You refrain from saying he's not a child or a dog, he's not going to eat the needles off a cactus because, for all you know, he might.

On top of the chest of drawers, the framed photographs from the Hotel Jacobs are stacked in a neat pile. "I didn't hang them yet," Larissa tells you, "because I forgot to get a hammer and nails. Leo, did you put the hammer on the list?"

"Yes." He sounds like a dutiful husband. "And the bath . . ." And whatever else is on the list gets garbled and swallowed.

"I have a hammer and nails at home," you say. "I can bring them over tomorrow."

Maybe she didn't hear you or maybe she wants her own hammer and nails. Whichever, Larissa doesn't respond. Instead, she asks Leo if he's ready for lunch.

He wants to know if there's any egg salad left.

"No. You ate all of it. But I'll make more now."

"Thank you. You're very nice."

"Last night," Larissa tells you, "I was too tired to cook dinner. So, I made egg salad sandwiches. He ate two, *two*, of them and then another one later for a snack."

Egg salad. Sometimes, before, on Sunday mornings, you and Leo would go out for egg salad sandwiches on bagels, egg salad on a poppy seed for himself and egg salad on a sesame seed for you.

"He's wild for egg salad," you say. "Me, too."

Leo returns to his bed and his book. Larissa goes to the kitchen, and you sit at the table. Propped up against the wall is a print of a cityscape, the Empire State Building predominant, that Larissa bought from a street vendor.

Arranged like a small studio apartment, at the far end of the room, away from the "living area" and kitchen, Larissa has set up her bed, which is covered with a pink floral spread and pink throw pillows. Her night table is white, a garland of small pink rosettes painted on the drawer. The white ceramic lamp is topped with a pink shade.

After setting a pot of water on the stove, Larissa takes a carton of eggs, a mammoth jar of mayonnaise, scallions, and a loaf of packaged bread from the refrigerator. Standing on her toes, she reaches into the middle cabinet for salt and pepper, which are in cut glass shakers.

"You've really turned this place into a home," you say.

"It's getting there." Using a big spoon, Larissa eases the twelve eggs, one by one, into the boiling water. "It's better if the yolks are a little bit soft. Too hard and they lose flavor." On a marble cutting board, she's chopping the scallions with a knife that looks like a hatchet, but the scallions are not scallions. "Chives," Larissa corrects you.

"Chives," you repeat, with awe. "That sounds delicious."

"It is." Larissa cools the eggs under a steady stream of cold water, and then she conks herself on the head. "Mustard." The mustard, coarse grain, is in the refrigerator. "Two teaspoons."

"You make a mean egg salad," you say.

After she's peeled and chopped the eggs, added the mayonnaise, chives, salt, and the measured amount of mustard into the bowl, she mixes it all together until your arms ache just watching her. She then brings a dollop to her mouth for a taste test. Two slices of bread pop up from the toaster. "Leo," she calls to him, "lunch is ready."

A glass of sparkling water, two paper towels, and on the plate is the sandwich, thick with egg salad. Leo takes a big bite, but before he goes in for the next big bite, he says to Larissa, "This is fantastic."

She pats him on the head and turns to you. "The minute he finishes this one, you'll see, he'll want another."

"Who could blame him for that?" You wait. Nothing. You give it one more shot. "I should get home. Make myself some lunch. Maybe I'll make egg salad, too," and Larissa reminds you, "Don't forget the mustard."

What with Everything

First, you say hello to Leo, who is sitting on his new recliner, which is not in the reclining position, but the footrest is up. He's reading, and you touch his shoulder. "I don't want to interrupt you. I just wanted you to know I'm here."

"Good," he says.

You're not sure if he means good that you're here or good that you don't want to interrupt him, but he's back into his book, and you go to talk to Larissa, who is sitting on her bed folding laundry.

Yes, you are broke, but you still know the difference between a relatively decent person and one who believes that with privilege comes license to be despicable, as if upward mobility were social Darwinism in reverse.

You pull up a chair to be nearer to her, and you apologize. "What with everything going on, I completely forgot, but we need to figure out what to do about your days off, weekends or whatever, and vacation time. Do you know anyone, a friend or a relative, who might cover for you when you're off?"

There's no good reason that you could not fill in for her, except you can't. Not *won't* but *can't*. You'd be too afraid; afraid of nothing specific but something intangible, something you can't point to or name, something like night terrors.

"I don't want days off," she says.

"But you'll need time to yourself. Go to a movie or something?"

"A movie? Alone? No thanks. Anything I want to do, I can

do with Leo. I'd rather you pay me what you'd pay someone else to stay with him. And at the end of a year, you can give me three thousand dollars instead of a vacation."

Although, from your perspective, this is the best possible scenario, the prospect of her working every day, all day, all night is fundamentally wrong. "But you might change your mind," you say.

"If I do, I'll call my aunt. She lives in the Bronx. She's done this kind work before."

You then raise the subject of the other expense you forgot to include in your budget. Health insurance. "We need to get you health insurance."

"Ha," she laughs. "I've never been sick a day in my life. And if I did need a doctor, I'd go to one of those walk-in clinics. All my family here swears by them."

"Okay, but *if* you do ever need to see a doctor, I'm paying for it."

Leo's health insurance is covered by his disability insurance, but that is not a family plan. If you get sick, you'll have to go to a walk-in clinic, too.

Then, as if you were visiting someone you barely know, you ask Larissa's permission to use the bathroom. There, three red towels are neatly folded on the rack. Why did she buy a new set of towels? You get your answer when you dry your hands. These towels are soft, much softer than the towels you bought for her and Leo, and incomparably softer than your towels at home. Your towels are old. You should explain to Larissa that money is tight, but not today when she's turned down health insurance. It would be too chintzy to ask her not to splurge on things like a set of soft towels. Instead, when you emerge from the bathroom, you say only,

"I need to get going. I've got to do some work," which is the same thing you tell Leo.

He looks up from his book and nods his head. "That's good."

You don't know if he means that it's good that you're going to do work or if it's good that you're leaving, but what difference does it make? You kiss him on his cheek. "I'll see you tomorrow."

At home, you open a bottle of wine and your computer to calculate: Is there any way that you can buy a set of new towels for yourself?

Avoidance

It's the same sensation as a high-anxiety dream, like the one in which you've skipped school for you don't know how long—time in dreams is vague—only to realize that you've been absent to the point where it's too late to go back now, but if you don't go back now, you'll fail all your classes. You'll be a high school dropout.

You're not a high school dropout, but if you don't go back to work, you won't be anything.

If you don't get back to work, you won't be anything, except that much closer to destitute. The way your cash flow is flowing out is like the exsanguination of blood from a body, and with each passing day, another vein opens.

You take a deep breath, cross the threshold, survey your studio, and when the anxiety subsides, you reach for a brush and coat a 12 × 16 inch canvas board in a deep, cold ultramarine blue.

As if having painted the entirety of a 12 × 16 inch canvas board with background color were an indication that you are on a roll, you call Sheila.

"I was just thinking about you," she says. "It's time for another solo."

"What a coincidence. I was calling you for the same reason. The sooner, the better."

Sheila asks you to hold on. "Let me get the schedule."

You hold on, holding on barely, and you won't be able to hold on for much longer.

"I could do early next June," she says, "if you can swear to me that you'll have eighteen pieces ready by December, the first week of January, at the very, very latest. Six months should give you plenty of time. You've been working, right?"

Although undoubtedly Sheila went to the exhibit at the Weber Gallery, it's unlikely she'll remember what was there. You have the four that garnered not so much as a flicker of interest, and you managed to resist trashing the stink-bombs Isabelle Weber rejected right off the bat.

"I've got ten done," you tell her.

"Excellent," Sheila says. "You're already more than halfway there."

Halfway there.

Homing Pigeon

Plenty of time, it turns out, is not forever. Day after day, and no matter what you try, your work winds up seeming derivative, as if you were imitating yourself. What you need to do is get outside your comfort zone, venture into a space unknown.

And so you are in a space unknown. A grocery store, a fifteen-minute walk from home, where you've never before shopped, but although the layout is unfamiliar, you can't say it's generating inspiration. However, it's a lot cheaper than Whole Foods. You load up on cat food, almond milk, veggie burgers, broccoli, a wedge of cheddar cheese, potato chips, bread, and because it's the start of apple season, you take three Macintoshes from the Macintosh-pyramid. Honeycrisps are expensive.

At the checkout counter, you ask the cashier for two bags. "To balance the weight," you explain. "Makes it easier to carry."

One bag in each hand does lighten the load, but a lighter load isn't exactly a *light* load. You're counting the number of blocks to go before you reach Seventeenth Street, but once there, when you turn the corner, you stop, a split-second full stop. If you had been riding a bicycle and hit the brakes in that way, you'd have pitched forward and cracked your head wide open. You could pivot and run, but it's too late. Larissa and Leo, coming from the opposite direction, are waving at you.

The bags slap against your thighs as you gallop toward them, to head them off at the pass before they reach your building. What if Larissa is curious to see your apartment? How could you say no? You'd have to invite them in, and then what would you do if Leo were to sit on the couch, if Roberta were to curl up on his lap? What if he went to the bedroom and fell asleep? What if he were happy, so happy to be home? How could you take that away from him again? And worse, what if you were happy, so happy to have him there with you, only to lose him, again?

"Fancy meeting you here." You rest your bags on the sidewalk.

Larissa explains that they were walking back from Hudson Park, but when they got to their building, Leo refused to go inside. He said that this was not his apartment. He would show her where he lived.

"Come on, Leo," you say. "I'll walk home with you."

Leo picks up your grocery bags, and as she so often does, Larissa marvels, "He is such a gentleman. I can't get over him. Do you know he doesn't swear? Not once has he ever said a curse word to me."

Unlike you, Leo has never relied on expletives to express himself, but he was fond of *shithead*, albeit more as a term of endearment, like how he would say to Roberta, "Sit with me, you little shithead." It could be that he still does say *shithead*, but if the words come out garbled, how would Larissa know that he's calling her a little shithead?

You put your arm around his waist to steer him around. "This way."

"No," he says. "I live here."

"No. You moved. Don't you remember?"

Maybe he does remember, or maybe he understands that you

remember what he does not, or maybe he's just humoring you, but whichever it is, you walk to Twenty-First Street, where he unpacks your bags. Milk, broccoli, and apples in the refrigerator, the bread on the countertop, and he stacks the cans of cat food in the cabinet above the sink.

With everything in its place, he wants to watch the news. He sits in his recliner chair, Larissa turns on CNN for him, and you put your groceries back in the bags. Without saying goodbye to Leo, you go home. Home to your home, where Leo does not live, where you live alone.

Who Says You Can't Buy Love?

Although payments are not yet due, you dial up your bank statements. The balances on credit cards you use reflect those of a person who almost always pays with cash, which you don't. It's that other than the bottom-line necessities, you buy nothing.

The cost associated with moving into the apartment on Twenty-First Street was, or should have been, a one-shot deal, but Larissa is on the freewheeling side when it comes to forking over your credit card. You brace yourself to run down the itemized expenses: DoorDash (eleven charges). You don't begrudge that she takes a break from cooking dinner every night, but whatever she's ordering in, it's not pizza. Barney's Butcher Shop—free-range, grass fed—does provide the cow with a cow's life, pre-slaughter, as opposed to the life of cows tortured by agribusiness, which is in keeping with your philosophy, but moral decency doesn't come cheap. HBO. Netflix. Hulu. Bubble tea (seven). *What is bubble tea?* When she told you that she needed to get a bigger skillet, you asked, "What's a skillet?" Then you said, "Sure. Get what you need."

She bought a new skillet. That's okay, but Williams-Sonoma?

You should let her know about the discount store on Fourteenth Street. You should explain your dire financial circumstance to her, explain that she can't spend your money with impunity, but you can't. What if she took offense? Larissa is irreplaceable. You have no choice but to swallow what she spends, even if it means you don't eat. Although you could mention the discount store.

Tracking Time

Today, according to what the calendar claims, is the fall equinox, but the leaves on the trees outside your window have not yet begun to turn from green to the yellow, orange, and reds of fire.

Your colors, conversely, the colors you've been trying out, have undergone a radical change. A conscious and deliberate decision to go from your signature midnight blue, burgundy, ink-black, plum purple, gloomy greens, and sulfur yellow to an alarming palette of robin's-egg and baby-blanket blues, colors of the bright rinds of lemons, limes, and oranges, and maraschino-cherry red. A radical departure, although your rate of success is status quo.

You play around with your color wheel. Three parts translucent white, two parts vermilion red, a dot of lavender purple, and another dot of orange gives you Pepto-Bismol pink. Instead of wood or canvas board, you paint the backdrop on a sheet of shatterproof glass, and then slide three boxes out from your stacks: postcards, galaxies, and houses, but before you get a chance to look through any of them, the phone rings. Ever since you set up Spam Block your phone rarely rings but when it does, you react the way Howie does whenever anything louder than a pencil falls on the floor, a gravity-defying jump, all four paws mid-air, and then he scrambles to hide under the bed.

Although earlier in the week, Citibank did get through the Spam Block to let you know that your account was hacked. You don't have an account with Citibank, and the week before,

the Policemen's Benevolent Association called soliciting donations, to which you said, "Fat chance." Now that you've waved
toodle-oo to Twitter, adios to Instagram, fuck off to Facebook,
your communication is pretty much limited to Larissa and Leo,
such as your interactions with Leo *are* communication. Denise,
who calls Leo three times a week, calls you routinely on Sunday
afternoons. Periodically, when you're bored out of your skull,
you check your email which, aside from spam, consists mostly
of announcements for upcoming gallery exhibits, the rare invitation to an opening, for which the chances of your attending
are .0002 percent which, statistically speaking, falls within the
range of a bird growing teeth.

It's been nine months, give or take, since you've heard from
Z. Prior to that, he must've called you a dozen times, asking if
you wanted to meet for a drink. On the second to last call, you
said, "There's something I never told you before."

"What's that?" he asked.

"Your wife. Her plays are stupid and tedious."

"No shit," Z said. "You think I don't know that?"

And it came over you, why you loved him, and for the
briefest of moments, you loved him again, but you couldn't love
him because you'll never forgive him.

The next time he called, you asked, "How do you say 'No, not
a fucking chance' in German?" *That* he understood.

Four or five months ago, Miriam asked if you would have
dinner with her. "Just the two of us. A girl's night out. Come on,
it will do you some good."

"No," you said. "It would not do me some good."

"Addie," she asked, "did I do something to offend you?"

"Me? No. You didn't do anything to offend *me*, but you did
plenty to offend Leo. Treating him like he was a leper or dead."

One thing in Miriam's favor, she didn't argue the point. All she said was, "Well, if you change your mind, I'm here."

"*Now* you're here?"

To whatever degree you like or don't like Sheila as a person, your relationship is strictly business, which is why you answer the phone now, and why when she asks, "How's it going?" you know that the *it* to which she's referring is your art.

"It's coming along," you say.

"How many have you got thus far?"

"Thirteen."

"Wow. You've been a busy bee. You can send me JPEGs, if you want."

"No. It's better to see them all at once. There's movement from the earlier ones, a progression, like time."

"I like that," she says. "Maybe we could go in that direction for the title of the show. Something with *evolution*. It works with all those climate change images you use. No later than the first week of January, remember?"

Despite Larissa's preference for texting, more often you call her so as to be able to say hello to Leo once she and you are done talking. Now, you call her to let her know that you won't be coming over today. "I'm on a tight deadline," you say.

"No problem. You come when you can. To tell you the truth, he hasn't been following time so good. Last night, I called him to dinner, and he said he just ate breakfast five minutes ago. Then ten minutes later, he asked when we were having dinner. I made salmon, and he said, 'Again? We had that last night.' I hadn't made salmon in over a week."

"Anything else weird going on? Aside from everything?"

You've often asked Larissa to keep you apprised when there are any notable changes with him, but now, as always, Larissa laughs and says, "Every day there's something. Minute to minute, but then he goes back. Like a couple of days ago, he told me his mother was here, but she just left. He said it was a shame I didn't get to meet her. All perfect words. I asked him what his mother had to say, and he looked at me like I was crazy. Did I forget his mother died when he was seven? But he's doing great. Don't worry. Go do what you have to do."

The leaves haven't changed color, but the sun is shifting, the minutes are ticking by, and you are all too well aware of time passing.

Food Is Love

It's a few days shy of one year, one year since Leo stabbed Joey. One year, one cycle of seasons, is, supposedly, the official close to the period of mourning. But that is applicable only when you are mourning the dead.

You ring the doorbell, and Larissa calls out, "Just a minute."

Although you have a set of keys, a set of keys does not give you license to let yourself in as if you live here. Even if you are the one paying the rent, it's not your apartment, and you have to wait until Larissa unlocks the door. You hear the bolt turn, but Larissa leaves the door ajar because, as if something were burning, she dashes back to the kitchen.

But nothing is burning.

What you smell smells like paradise.

Larissa is preparing a Thanksgiving feast: curry chicken, yams, plantains, coconut shrimp, empanadas, stew peas, and callaloo, which she tells you is a leafy vegetable with tomato, garlic, onions, and thyme.

At least twice a week, if not more, Larissa makes curry chicken. She's determined that it's Leo's favorite because, invariably, he eats two servings and licks the plate clean. You never did remind Larissa that Leo doesn't, or rather, didn't eat meat or fish or fowl. The world won't end because Leo's eating chicken. Not even the chicken's world will come to an end because the chicken's world came to its end well before it landed in Larissa's pot. And when push comes to shove, if this curry chicken tastes half as good as the scent of the spices wafting from the kitchen, you're not so sure that you could resist licking the plate, either.

Larissa's family—her brother, his wife, their children, her two sisters with a slew of kids between them, and her aunt who lives in the Bronx—is coming for Thanksgiving dinner. "If it's okay with you. My brother invited us to his place, but his wife can't cook like me," she said, "and I don't think it's a good idea to take Leo so far away to the Bronx."

"This is your home, not mine. But how will you fit so many people in such a small apartment? Where will they sit?"

Larissa got a kick out of your question. "You don't know Jamaicans. Trust me."

You are not invited to this Thanksgiving dinner. You are not family. Larissa refers to you as her boss. When you corrected her, when you said, "Larissa, I'm not your *boss*," she said, "No? Who pays my salary?"

Standing at the stove, Larissa dips the long wooden spoon into each of the four pots and stirs, each timed as if she were a juggler spinning plates on the handle of a broomstick. She lowers the flames to simmer and tells you that Leo is napping. "He fell asleep just a few minutes ago, but I'll wake him. He napped in the morning, too."

"No. Let him sleep."

Excessive sleeping without Seroquel? Now? Where, oh where, is Leo situated on the moving-target Stages of Decline?

"Too much sleep is not good," Larissa says. "He should be awake and keeping busy."

Larissa wants him to live his life as if he were Leo, but he is not Leo, and this is his life in name only. Let him sleep.

Dipping the spoon into one of the pots, Larissa brings it

to her mouth to taste, and you suggest that she should open a restaurant.

"Cook like this every day? No way."

With Leo sleeping and Larissa as busy as she is in the kitchen, you're only in the way. You wish her a happy holiday, and she says, "You, too. Happy Thanksgiving."

On the Next Noel

The way Denise's world has shrunk is different but still comparable to the way the lights in Leo's world have dimmed. A wool scarf isn't much of a gift for someone who is now a full-fledged agoraphobic. You tried to think of something else to buy her, but surely she already has a lifetime supply of carpet cleanser and ditto with Brillo pads. You got Joey a high-end bottle opener. Red cashmere gloves for Larissa, and you'll write her a check, too. But for how much? You can, reasonably, afford to give her five dollars, but even five hundred dollars would be insulting. Because you are not remiss about paying the monthly minimum on your Visa bills, a few thousand dollars of credit remain before you max out. It's the right thing to do, and, moreover, no matter if Larissa thinks of you as her boss, she's the closest thing to a friend you've got.

As if cats know Christmas from Jupiter, you nonetheless jostle your way through the crowds at Petland for a package of six catnip mice.

That leaves Leo.

A gift for Leo.

What do you buy for a man who has lost everything?

What the Angels Did and Did Not Say

Tonight, on the twenty-third of December, is when you're celebrating Christmas with Leo and Larissa. A silver wreath is tacked to the door, and the apartment is festooned with little white lights woven through silver garland. Three elf dolls are perched on the console, eliciting not the jolly Christmas spirit but irritation: *How much did all this shit cost?* On a red string that runs end to end across one wall, Christmas cards are hung like socks on a drying rack.

"I didn't get a tree," Larissa tells you. "They take up too much room."

"And they're crazy expensive, too," you say.

You transfer the gifts from your shopping bag onto the table. All of them, excluding the carrot cake you got for Leo but including the card with the money inside for Larissa, are wrapped in green paper tied with red ribbon.

Leo comes out of his room, and you rush to give him an extra-large hug. "Merry Christmas," you say.

"Today is Christmas? I didn't know that."

"Today is Christmas with me, and the day after tomorrow, you'll have Christmas again with Larissa and her family. Two Christmases for you."

Larissa sits in the chair, the one with easy access to the kitchen. "Remember when they came on Thanksgiving? All that fun you had playing Nerf ball with the kids and dancing with everyone. And you know Aunt Jasmine." The few times that Larissa has taken a day off, which is never a full day because she insists there's nothing she wants to do, or it's too cold out, or it's supposed to rain, her aunt stays with Leo. "You like Jasmine, don't you?"

He nods his head, and a big grin beams across his face, a grin reflecting either the recollection of Aunt Jasmine or Nerf ball or dancing or it's just random fragments of neural activity.

Leo? Dancing? Really?

He never used to dance in public, but at home, you'd put on music, pull him up from the couch, cajole him into dancing with you for a few minutes. Leo danced the way you imagine Frankenstein's monster would dance. Leo's dancing was good for a laugh.

First, you give him the book *Field Guide to the Neighborhood Birds of New York City*, but because he makes no move to unwrap it, you tear off the paper and untie the ribbon for him. He looks at the cover and then at the first few pages. "This is fantastic," he says.

"Wait until you see what else I got for you." You break the cord tied around the bakery box.

As if he were wearing a pair of gag-gift eyeglasses, the kind where the eyeballs are attached to the frame by wire coils, Leo's eyes practically spring from their sockets—boing!—and then he swipes the frosting with his index finger, popping the glob into his mouth.

"Leo, where are your manners?" Larissa whisks the cake off the table and carries it to the kitchen, where she cuts not a slice but a slab of carrot cake. A spoon rests on the plate. "It's better for him to use a spoon." She doesn't say why, and you don't ask, but you do ask Leo if you can have a bite.

He swallows what's in his mouth and says, "No. But there's more in the kitchen. You can have a piece."

"Let me get it for you," Larissa says, and you tell her, "Just a sliver."

A sliver is what you get. It continues to baffle you how Larissa never offers you food or even a glass of water. Is food reserved for family alone? Leo is family, but you are not family. You are Larissa's boss.

"Aren't you having any?" you ask.

"No. I don't like sweets."

Now you can add *petty* to the list of your crappy attributes: *You don't like sweets, but when I bring Leo a bag of jelly donuts, you always have one. Or two.*

This is what you're thinking, but what you say is, "This is for you. From me."

She tries on the gloves, remarking on how soft they are and how red is her favorite color, but the red gloves pale in comparison to the gift from Leo. Such as it is from Leo. The crisp ten one-hundred-dollar bills tucked in the *Merry Christmas* card, the card that you signed *With all my love, Leo.* She thanks you effusively and kisses Leo on the cheek.

Now that Leo has polished off the mountain of cake on his plate, you open the box of hand-dipped chocolate-covered mints, which you splurged on despite knowing he'd have been equally pleased with Peppermint Patties. After he eats two, he asks you and Larissa if you'd like one. Neither of you wants a chocolate-covered mint, but, as ridiculous as it is, you are overwhelmed with gratitude that he offered to share his food with you.

You and Leo always share.

Two wrapped packages remain on the table. Larissa tells you that she's saving her gifts for Leo until Christmas. "So he'll have things to open along with everyone else here." She taps a cube-shaped box wrapped in candy cane–print paper. "This one," she says, "is from me."

It's a coffee mug featuring a cat wearing a Santa hat. Sweet and thoughtful. "This is so cute," you gush. "I love it."

You're not only petty. You're an ingrate. And mean-spirited. Such ugly thoughts you're thinking: *This is headed to the thrift store where it'll be crammed on a shelf along with all the other like-minded coffee mugs.*

"Leo," Larissa says, "give Addie the present you got for her." She points to the only gift that is still wrapped. "This one."

It's a photograph, one that Larissa took of him standing next to a tree outside their building. He looks happy, and it hits you like a whomp on your head: Leo *is* happy, a whole lot happier than you are, and why wouldn't he be? He doesn't know what's happened to him, he doesn't remember who he was, what's been taken from him, he doesn't worry about paying the bills, he's not alone, he won't be alone on Christmas.

"He picked out the frame," Larissa tells you. The frame is gold-colored metal stamped with curlicues.

The same as Larissa did, you kiss Leo on the cheek. "How did you know? This is just what I wanted. And I know exactly where I am going to put it."

You're going to put it in the back of your closet and try to forget it's there, along with everything else you try to forget but can't.

"It's getting late," you say. You kiss Leo's cheek again, wish them both a Merry Christmas, and you go home.

Feed the cats, fill your glass with wine, and open the box from Amazon, your Christmas gift from Denise and Joey. A bathrobe, yellow and splashed with daisies. One more thing to donate to the thrift store.

Other than the catnip mice for the cats, you have no more gifts yet to give. It's ridiculous to wait. You get the package of six mice from the kitchen cabinet and toss one to Roberta and one to Howie.

No more gifts to give and none for you to open.

The box in the Cerulean blue bag? No. Not this year, either.

As you could've predicted, Roberta has confiscated Howie's mouse. Two for her. Zero for Wee-Wee. You toss another catnip mouse to him despite knowing perfectly well she's only going to take that one away from him, too.

Muscle Memory

It's not as if you're eager to visit Leo, but you walk at a brisk pace because it's freezing out here, and the apartment will be homey and toasty warm.

All in one move, Larissa opens the door for you and swoops the basket of laundry up from the floor. "I was just on my way to the basement. I'll be right back."

Leo, seated at the table, hunched over an open book, seems unaware of your presence. It's something like a sweet calm that descends over you as you watch him read, no different from the way he's always read: his index finger raised a hair above the page as if it were a Torah pointer, as if the book were sacred, not to be sullied by the touch of sticky hands as they traverse the lines of text. It's similar to the way children read, except children get tripped up by words like *cloud* or *friend* or stymied by the illogically spelled *laugh*, whereas for Leo, *ginglymoarthrodial* and *patellapexy* are words no more complicated than *Look, Jane. See Dick.*

You unwind your scarf, stuff your gloves into your coat pocket, and drape your things over the back of the chair, the one nearest to the door. Still, he doesn't look up, not until you say, "Hey, there. Hello." Your voice has the tenor of the chirp of a newly hatched chick, but the words are words, as opposed to Leo's marbles-in-his-mouth response. Maybe he said hello or maybe he was telling you that he's too busy for idle chit-chat right now. Whatever it was, he's gone back to his reading.

The incalculable distance that separates you cannot be

bridged, but you close the measurable gap between you by walking over to stand alongside his chair, where you bend slightly to kiss the top of his head. If what is on his head, full thick hair, were a reflection of what's inside, by all rights he should be going bald.

The book he is reading is upside down.

You turn away as fast and as absolutely as if you'd walked in on a stranger sitting on the toilet, as if you've invaded his privacy, seen something you were never meant to see, or uncovered an indecent secret: the words are meaningless squiggles on paper, and reading is nothing more than the muscle memory of his index finger on the page, gliding left to right.

Confidentially Speaking

L eo sets his glass of milk on the table next to a plate of cookie crumbs, but he stays seated.

"Don't I get a hug?" you ask.

"Not now. I'm drinking m . . ."

Larissa admonishes him. "Leo, give your wife a hug," and begrudgingly he gets up.

You get your hug, but that's it. He tells Larissa that he wants to watch television, and she says to you, "I have to turn it on for him. He doesn't know how to use the remote control."

How do you turn this thing on?

Voices, a talk show, and then you hear Larissa ask if he wants anything else, and Leo says, "No, thank you."

Once again, Larissa remarks on Leo's good manners. "Always so polite. But this morning, he refused to get dressed. That's why he's still in his bathrobe."

His bathrobe, and he's wearing slippers that are not exactly slippers but rather the rubber beach shoes generally favored by old men. "Well, it's not like he's going out," you say.

"Not in this cold. But I don't like it. It's not good to stay all day in a bathrobe. It's better for him to put on clothes."

You don't put on clothes unless you're going out, but you keep that to yourself.

"Sit down. Relax," she says. "So, do you have plans for tonight?"

It's New Year's Eve.

"No. I have work to do."

"I'm going to make salmon for dinner. He loves my salmon. If we can stay awake, we'll watch the ball drop on TV. Tomorrow, we'll take down the Christmas decorations. When I was young, I went out on New Year's Eve, but to tell you the truth, it was never any fun. All those drunk people out everywhere." Larissa disapproves of people who drink.

There is a growing list of things about yourself that you will never tell Larissa. Not that your bad habits are any of her concern, but you want, you crave, her approval. "Leo and I never went out on New Year's Eve."

"He's a good man. Really, it's a pleasure to take care of him. Some of the people I took care of, you wouldn't believe."

"He obviously adores you. I can't begin to tell you how grateful I am."

"It's my job," she says.

"Yeah, but no one is better at it than you."

"I do my best," she says.

"Your best is miles above anyone else's best. You know, back when he told you that you should go to nursing school, he was right. You should. But not now. Please." You laugh. "Please not now."

"We'll cross that bridge when we get to it. As long as he is with us, I'm taking care of him." Then, after a pause, she says, "I couldn't go to nursing school, anyway. I didn't finish high school."

You're not sure if it's that you're surprised Larissa didn't finish high school or if you're surprised that she's confided in you, but it's the latter that allows you to venture forth. "You can always get your GED. You can even do that now."

"Now? Now, I'm busy."

You don't push it.

Larissa checks her watch. "I should get dinner started. The salmon only takes a few minutes, but I am going to make baked potatoes and a tahini sauce for the cauliflower."

"Sounds delicious. I need to get to work, too." Perhaps now you are risking her disapproval, but she confided in you, which allows you to confide in her. "My work isn't going well. I'm really worried I won't have everything ready in time."

"Yes, you will. Stop worrying."

"You sound like Leo," you tell her. "I miss him, Larissa. I miss him so much it hurts. All over, it hurts."

"Go kiss him goodbye," she says. "Get back to your work. We'll see you tomorrow."

Dropping Off

Straighten up your studio. Do laundry. Turn on the TV. Pace. You met your deadline, but when you got to the gallery, Sheila wasn't there. The intern told you she had an emergency and won't be back until tomorrow. "I'll put them in her office. I'm sure she'll call you first thing in the morning. She's very excited."

But it's well past first thing in the morning. Six minutes ago, it was noon. Now it's eighteen minutes past noon. At eleven minutes before two, finally, Sheila calls, and she says, "You've got to be kidding me?"

"About what?"

"Addie, I can't show these. Maybe a couple of them are okay, but uninspired. Nowhere near your best work. And those things with the Day-Glo colors, what were you thinking? I'm sorry, but I have to take you off the schedule. I can't believe this. I don't know what I'm going to do."

She doesn't know what *she's* going to do?

This Is What You Do

You kick a stack of your boxes. You kick hard, the force of pent-up rage released, and the boxes tumble, the contents taking flight in all directions. And you kick another stack and another until there are no more stacks to kick. Some have landed on their sides, others fully upside down. All of them have lost their lids the way a house loses its roof when a tornado hits, and you stand there like one of those people you've seen on the news or in a documentary. People who, after a natural disaster, return home to find their lawns littered with their belongings, things that were irreplaceable destroyed, scattered, wondering what, if any of it, is salvageable.

When you call Larissa to tell her that you won't be coming by today because you're not feeling well, she says, "It sounds like you've got a cold. A stuffy nose. You stay home. We're fine. But you, juice, soup, and rest. More than anything, you need to rest."

You don't have a cold, and no, rest is not what you need more than anything; not even close.

After the Big Bang

Those people whose homes are destroyed by hurricanes, tornadoes, earthquakes, fires, bombs dropping from the sky, they pick through the rubble of their lives, trying to make some semblance of order from the chaos, rescue that which can be saved.

Flipping the boxes upright, you lay them out in a row: *Photographs. Fabric & Lace. Letters. Animals. Miscellaneous* landed under your table, empty of its contents except for a three-inch powder-blue plastic baby's crib, dollhouse furniture turned on its side. It's missing a leg, but you would not have bought it had it been intact. You set the box on the table and lean the three-legged crib against the far side, and then return to grope for whatever else might be under there: a beat-to-shit Matchbox car, a metal shoe from an old Monopoly game, and one of those paper umbrellas, a yellow one, the kind they used to use to gussy up cocktails. There's a hole in it, what looks like a burn hole, and you twirl the little paper umbrella between the tips of your fingers. You twirl it, and then you sprint to the bedroom, where you shake out the blanket to find your phone.

You google: *dollhouse furniture shopping near me.*

The Upper East Side is not exactly near you. The 1 train to Times Square, then the shuttle to Grand Central Station, where you catch the 6 train to Seventy-Second Street, and then you have to walk for ten minutes, during which time you text Larissa: *Not so congested, but have a fever. Will stay home for another day or two.*

The shop, as befits its merchandise, is small, but the shelves offer a Macy's warehouse assortment of miniatures. You fill your basket with tiny tables, a couch with matching tufted chairs, a rocking chair, a canopy bed, a hospital bed, and a bed with a wooden headboard painted white, a floor lamp, a chandelier, two pots no bigger than dimes, a matchbook-size packet filled with flatware, itty-bitty books with actual words printed on the pages, a grandfather clock, a lace tablecloth, three Persian carpets smaller than index cards, two homey-type braided rugs, two bicycles, a handful of plastic trees, a few rubber farm animals, a dozen rubber people—children and adults—and a couple of Disney characters reduced to the size of bugs.

Your mind is racing, your adrenaline level is on overdrive, you're itching to get home, but you've already shelled out a bundle of money. A cab would be overly indulgent, which is not what Leo would have said. He would've asked you, "What's more important? Time or money?" The correct answer, when Leo was Leo, was time, but Leo isn't Leo and time saved taking a cab is measured in minutes, not years. Years of time lost are more like the wristwatch you lost, the watch Leo bought for you, an anniversary gift, one year married, and one week later, it slipped off your wrist, maybe on the subway or while walking a circuitous route home. All you knew for sure was that it was gone, and there was no getting it back. Leo said, "I'll get you another watch," but another watch was not *that* watch, and a new watch would not have made that one less lost.

Years lost cannot be recovered, not in minutes or decades, and you've just spent a week's worth of food money to buy dollhouse furniture. You walk to the subway.

After you empty the bag of miniatures onto your worktable, you spread them out, spaced evenly, and take a few charmed minutes to consider them before you isolate your preliminary selections. Those remaining you return to the bag, and then surveying the essentially empty boxes on the floor, you pick one. A white one, a few inches longer and wider than a shoebox, made of sturdy, thick cardboard. Beneath the box is a tattered remnant of terre verde velvet, which you take to be a good omen. You drop it into the box along with your home furnishings.

As a precautionary measure, lest your apartment go up in flames, you take the box with the Lilliputian furniture to the bathroom and set it down in the tub.

The box of kitchen matches is in the drawer next to where you keep the silverware, and you bring it to the bathroom. You shut the door to keep the cats out, and then you kneel on the floor, strike a match, lean over the tub, and set the little couch on fire. You let it burn until a significant portion of the upholstery, along with the cotton padding underneath, goes crispy, like a toasted marshmallow. The coffee table, apparently, is fire-resistant, but the corners char nicely. The velvet, which you will use for curtains, burns just as you imagined it would. The bottom is ragged and you put a few black-rimmed holes in the middle because it's aesthetically pleasing. If this were a real house, the real people would have no choice but to bring the Persian carpet to the city dump.

Because cardboard, even thick cardboard, could go up in flames and burn to ash in no time at all, you're extra careful when you singe the top and the edges of the box.

The cats are scratching at the door. Cats hate it when a door is closed, but it's safe now to let them in and you pass them by on your way out.

The wallpaper sample you wanted is in plain view, having come to rest on top of a sewing pattern. You decide against putting a match to the wallpaper. Instead, you glue it to the walls of the box. Generous smudges of black and gray eye shadow make for an excellent approximation of soot. Because what's a house fire without a broken window, you take a hammer to a 4 × 6 inch pane of glass and sweep the smallest shards into an envelope, which you put aside for later, to scatter around the floor. The window wants a view. Yours gets a bowl of goldfish.

Not until Roberta and Wee-Wee are there at your feet, yowling, do you realize how late it is. You feed them, fill their bowls with fresh water, and make yourself a cheese sandwich. Tomorrow will be the first morning in years that you're almost looking forward to waking up, that you might, in fact, want to get out of bed.

Up and Down

The velvet curtains go up, the Persian rug goes down, and one by one, you line up each piece of furniture at the edge of the box and flick, fixing them where they land. A chandelier dangles from the ceiling by two of six wires, and the teeny rubber Tinker Bell dangles from the chandelier. To prevent warping and to give it a yellow tinge, you coat the outside of the box, the top and the three walls, not the bottom, with polyurethane, which will take hours to dry. The fumes are noxious. On your way out, you shut the door to keep the cats from coming in to sniff the polyurethane or swat at Tinker Bell.

You text Larissa: *I've fully recovered. I'll be over soon in an hour or so.*

Along the way, you stop at the bodega to get a bag of Pepperidge Farm oatmeal raisin cookies for Leo. Most days, he decidedly recognizes you, or at least recognizes your face as one that is familiar, that you are the woman who brings cookies and candy for him. Other days, like today, he is aware of your presence the way a mannequin is aware of whomever is checking out their outfit. Eyes open, expression blank, no one is home. Only when you shake the bag of cookies do you get his attention. Or maybe it's the cookies, not you, he sees.

"Look what I got for you. Oatmeal raisin cookies," you say, and he says who the fuck knows what.

But before you can give him the bag, Larissa takes it from you. "Last night he tried to open a bag of potato chips. You should've seen it. Chips flying all over the place." Larissa is amused by the flying potato chips, as if it were something cute, like those YouTube videos of dogs getting into the garbage. She puts two cookies on a plate.

He's munching away, and you say to him, "They're good, aren't they?"

Again, you can't determine if there are coherent thoughts connected to the sounds he makes, thoughts trapped in the left hemisphere of his brain, Broca's area, with no means of escape. Or has his ability to process language gone the way of his speaking in words? Stroke victims have been known to bang their fists in frustration and anger when their words don't come to fruition, but Leo exhibits no frustration, no anger. Does he think he's saying what he wants to say? Or is it that the sounds he emits are like what happens when a dog barks and then every other dog in the vicinity starts barking? The group barking isn't an in-depth roundtable debate but rather an auto-response: You're making noise, so I'll make noise, too. But when Larissa asks if he'd like a glass of milk with his cookies, he nods.

You trail after Larissa to the kitchen because, really, no matter what the circumstances, when you talk about a person, you should at least have the decency to do it behind their back. She reaches for a glass from the cabinet, and you ask, "Does he understand what we say?"

"I don't think he follows much of a conversation, but when I tell him it's time for dinner, in a flash, he's at the table, or like now, he knew I asked if he wanted milk."

Dogs, too, understand when you tell them to sit, when you pat them on the head—good boy!—and when you ask if they want to go for a ride, they run to the door, tails wagging.

Whatever it is he's saying now, it's directed at Larissa, who either intuits what he's saying, or maybe she's learned how to translate babble into English.

"More cookies?" she asks him, and again, he nods. "Leo, I don't know how you can eat so much and not gain weight."

He shrugs, which could mean he does understand, or else it could be nothing but a coincidental twitch.

Larissa puts two more cookies on his plate, and when he finishes eating and his glass is empty, she wipes away the milk mustache on his upper lip.

You slide your chair over to sit close to him, and you open your phone. "Look," you say. *Look. Look, Jane.* But he doesn't look until you put the phone under his nose. "You know Roberta, right? And that's Howie with her. Wee-Wee. Remember, I told you about him. Aren't they cute?"

Leo nods, and the conversation, such as it is, comes to its end.

Creation / Destruction

You can't compare it to the six days it took to create the universe, but in six weeks, excluding the time spent with Leo, running errands, and the two crucial shopping sprees at the dollhouse store, you've completed four boxes: The fire, then a tornado in which, among the cacophony of ruins, are downed trees, a mangled bicycle, the broken powder-blue crib, the broken pottery, and a cow flying across the backdrop of a green sky. The funnel constructed from cotton balls is off in the distance. After that was the hospital room, a little rubber man glued to the bed and covered with a white sheet except for his feet peeking out, not bare feet but feet wearing brown shoes. Three aspirin tablets, a vitamin D gel tablet, and two blue fluoxetine capsules rest on the floor. On the night-stand is one of the tiny books with a bookmark protruding near to the end. You reduced the EKG monitor you brought up on Google Images to 1.5 × 1 inch and cut a frame for it from gold foil paper. The monitor you printed is flatlined. On the wall opposite the foot of the bed, you glued a picture of a television, one of those 1960s televisions that look like the helmets astronauts wear. It wasn't easy, but you managed to sew a pair of doctors' scrubs for Goofy. Last night you finished the fourth one. A polluted river. Rubber cement glue mixed with brewed tea got you murky water. The surrounding foliage is gray. Turquoise frogs and polka-dotted birds hang like Christmas ornaments from the little dollhouse trees that you painted hot pink and neon green. The finishing touch: the smallest of the rubber people, one inch in length, a little girl, floats face-down in the river, dead.

You take a slew of pictures, select the best of each, and convert them into JPEGs. Then, after you've done your best to buck up your confidence, you swallow what remains of your pride and compose a brief message to Sheila. You attach the four JPEGs to the email and hit Send.

Moving Right Along

Four days go by, and you're about ready to give up on Sheila, as you've concluded she's given up on you, when, late in the afternoon, she calls. As if her mouth and mind are out of sync, she's talking too fast for you to follow what she's saying, although you do catch a few words: incredible, fabulous, mind-blowing.

Or was that mind-bending?

After she pulls herself together, she asks, "How many more do you have?"

"Nothing finished, but sketches, ideas for some others."

"Okay, okay. I know you're going to need time, and these can't be part of a group show. Any chance you can have ten more in nine months? I don't want to rush you, but these will command good money, very good money. I swear to you, we're going to cha-ching big. You can bank on it."

Cha-ching?

You lean back in your chair, and another kind of idea comes to you. It's a long shot, but if Sheila is banking on a big cha-ching from a show at the Sandstone, is it possible that a bigger cha-ching might be out there? You send the four JPEGs to Isabelle Weber.

What Remains

There is little variation to your days. Feed the cats, work, grocery shop, and either late in the afternoon or after they've had their early-bird dinner, you visit Leo and Larissa, which does come with the occasional surprise, like Leo is alert and seems to enjoy your company, and last week you learned that Larissa's father walked out on her family and then went and had another family. "I never met any of them," she told you, "and I don't want to." You opened up to her about your father, how he was an alcoholic, how you wished he would've walked out.

"Leo would have been such a good father," she said—*the child you denied him*—and she asked why you didn't have children.

You shrugged. "We talked about it, but we decided we liked our lives as they were. Our cats were our babies. And oh my God, how he spoiled them. Bringing them smoked salmon, and one time he came home with a book, one of those picture books that teach little kids how to spell, for our first cat. Elaine. Of course, he knew that cats are incapable of spelling. They don't even understand one word you say. Maybe they know their names, but he insisted Elaine was far more intelligent than other cats. After a few days trying, he finally admitted that to buy a spelling book for her, for any cat, was an insane thing to do."

Larissa was laughing to the point where she begged you to stop. "Please. My belly is hurting."

At home, alone, at night, you watch the news, movies, and documentaries or read, and on Wednesdays you log into your bank account, which brings its own predictability. The numbers have continued to dwindle, except for your credit card debt, which rises with alarming regularity.

Whatever the *cha-ching* Sheila predicts your new work will bring, that amount is *not* predictable, and however much it turns out to be, it's too far off in the future to do you any good when you need it now. There was a time when you could've asked Z for help, but you need money, not pity. If pity could pay the bills, you could pity yourself out of the hole. You'd be a billionaire.

Your brother? He'd let you starve.

That leaves Denise.

"I really hate to ask," you say, "and honestly, I'll totally understand if you can't, but I'm having some financial problems . . ."

"How much? Just tell me what you need, and you've got it. Unless you're talking millions." Then, after a snort, she adds, "That I don't have."

"If it's doable, fifteen thousand would be a game-changer. I'll pay you back. I have a solo show scheduled, but it's a long way off."

"You don't have to pay me back, Addie. He's my brother. All you're doing for him. Some other woman would've dumped him off somewhere and walked away."

Dumped him off somewhere and walked away. How is that different from what you've done?

The Mind / Body Problem

Predictable variations might be an oxymoron, but that's how it's been with Leo. His cognition, lucidity, and abilities continue to fluctuate. Some deterioration or other, erratically and irrationally, will roll backwards, albeit briefly. With greater regularity, yet no easier to predict, are the new developments. New, not new and improved. Although you've continued to ask, off-handedly ask, still Larissa does not keep you apprised of the day-to-day slips and slides, or if there were any interludes in the opposite direction. Only when you witnessed her cutting his meat into bite-size pieces did she tell you he is no longer able to manipulate the knife in tandem with the fork. Occasionally, something would come up in casual conversation, like how he watered the plant with orange juice. She really should tell you these things as they occur, but be honest with yourself. Do you really want to know that he ate toothpaste?

Leo is in the living room, relaxing in Larissa's recliner, watching some idiot show on TV. He likes to be near to her.

You angle your seat at the table so that only a small corner of the TV screen is visible. It's not the case, but it seems to you that, from Leo's vantage point, the entirety of your being is *in*visible.

Now that she's done cleaning up in the kitchen, Larissa sits across from you. "Yesterday, after you left, we had such fun. The weather was so nice out. This time of year, you never know. We went all the way to Union Square Park."

"You just reminded me. I found a lightweight jacket of his at home. With the tags still on it. I'll bring it next time."

"He didn't even need a jacket yesterday. His sweater was enough. I'm hoping it will be warm like that again tomorrow. He had such a good time with the music, and there was a man walking on stilts and all the kids with the skateboards."

"Are you kidding? A man on stilts? Did Leo say anything about that?"

"No. He was more interested in some kids flying a kite." She turns to Leo and says, "If the weather is nice tomorrow, we'll go to the park again, but you'll have to let me wash your hair first, okay?" Larissa laughs and Leo laughs, and she says, "Oh, now you think it's funny."

"I must've missed something," you say. "What was funny?"

"Him. He put up such a fuss. He doesn't always like it when I wash his hair. You know, he'll pull away. But today, I tried three times in the morning to get him in the shower, and twice in the afternoon, but he just kept on shaking his head, kicking and waving his arms around, making all kinds of noises, even some words like *no, go away, never*."

"You wash his hair? In the shower?"

"Of course. He can't go around with dirty hair."

A flash of something rises up in you, something that feels like the jealousy that would come if you'd discovered that your husband has a mistress, that some other woman is as intimately familiar with his body as you are—correction; as you *were*—but Larissa is not just some other woman, *I'm with her now*, and how could it be otherwise?

What feels something like jealousy *is* jealousy. You're jealous of their intimacy, and you're jealous of all the other secrets they share, secrets kept, secrets stolen away, from you.

"It's nothing to worry about," Larissa says. "We've been through this before. I know not to fight with him. Tomorrow, he'll want to take a shower. He's a sweetheart."

"Yes," you say. "He is a sweetheart. My sweetheart. Let me know when you go to the park. I'll try to meet you there."

"He would love that," Larissa says.

"Maybe," you say, and maybe he would, because now when you get up to leave, Leo stands up, too, and he holds his arms out for a hug.

You go to him, and you hug him, and then he wraps his arms around you, tight, like before, like when you and he were intimate, when you had secrets that were kept between the two of you alone, and you hug him tighter, *your* sweetheart, you don't want to let go of him, you don't want to let go of this moment, so familiar, you want him to hold you, and you want to hold him, you want to keep him with you, but the moment ends when the picture shows up in your head, the picture of Leo in the shower, Larissa lathering soap in her hands, washing his naked body. With that, your longing for your husband is subsumed by something like revulsion. Your arms fall away, you take a step back, you let him go.

Phoenix Rising

The avenue is crowded, but your street is deserted. The townhouse opposite your building is undergoing renovation. You scoot across the street and take a peek under the tarp. A quick look around, and with no one in sight, you pilfer a brick.

Roberta and Howie greet you at the door. They're hungry.

While they're scarfing up their stinky meals, you bring the brick to your studio and then go looking for your hammer, which is not in your toolbox. It's in the closet where you keep your linens, and you grab a pillowcase to spread out over your worktable.

Because greater distance creates greater force—that might not actually be accurate, but it seems like it should be—standing up, you raise the hammer high over your head and bring it down hard on the brick. Again and again and again you pound the brick until all that remains is dust and rubble; the rubble, reduced to scale, of a building that was bombed to smithereens.

Your shoulder is sore, and you rub it until that particular ache is gone.

You don't yet know what, but something will come of this.

Au Revoir

Denise does not trust online financial transactions. She's mailed you a check, a check for $15,000. Or, that's what you were expecting to find in the envelope, but the check from Denise is written out for $25,000, which is like a winning lottery ticket, and who uses money won in the lottery to pay Con Edison?

You could go away. A vacation. Before the hallucinations started, you and Leo spent ten days in Paris. After that, it was back and forth to Boston, hardly a holiday getaway. The excursions to the Hotel Jacobs were like strolling through a sinkhole, and your dream trip to the Serengeti has vaporized into dream mist.

You're not so foolish as to blow the full jackpot, but $3,000? With the exception of beach and ski resorts where you'd never go regardless, the end of March is off-season for travel. Plane fares are practically free.

New Orleans isn't Paris, but you can stay in the French Quarter.

You book a flight, four nights in a hotel, ask Caroline, your neighbor, to cat-sit, for which, this time, you'll pay her, and then you go to visit Leo with an offering of three Peppermint Patties. While he's off in Candyland, you tell Larissa, "I have to go out of town. For work. I don't want to go, but I have to. Work is work. I'll be gone for a week."

"It'll be good for you," Larissa says. "You've been through a lot."

If Leo has no sense of time, and, if he recognizes you only as the woman who brings him candy and cookies and asks for nothing but a hug in return, why not tack on an extra day at each end? But still, you ask Larissa, "Do you think he'll forget who I am?"

But instead of reassuring you, saying that of course he will remember you, Larissa is up in a flash. With one hand, thumb and forefinger spread wide, she's squeezing Leo's cheeks, forcing his mouth to open, and with her free hand, she runs two fingers along his gums and under his tongue. "Leo," she says, "did you eat the candy paper?" She sits back down and says, "He's been doing this lately."

In addition to the toothpaste, Larissa ticks off the other non-food groups Leo has eaten or tried to eat: paper towels, corners of book pages, a clump of stuffing he pulled from the hole he made picking at the armrest of his recliner, a banana peel, a popsicle stick. "He bit it in half. Good thing I was right there. He could've gotten splinters. It's like he's always hungry. Last night he had three helpings of dinner. And all three times, he licked the plate. Even after it was all clean, he kept licking it."

"Look at the bright side," you say. "At least he didn't try to eat the plate."

"Not yet." Larissa laughs, and you might have laughed, too, if you weren't thinking about Leo biting into a plate, his mouth and tongue cut and bloody, and what if from New Orleans you were to bring him something like barbeque sauce in a jar?

Au revoir.

Make New Friends, But Keep the Old

Four and a half days of exploring the streets, eating scrumptious food at little holes-in-the-wall, listening to music, walking through the aboveground cemeteries, and all the while your conscience has been gnawing at you like the persistent nibbling of a mouse making its way into a box of cereal.

Every night you called Larissa, and each night she told you, "Everything is good." Everything is good, except when Larissa would tell him you wanted to say hello, he'd refuse to take the phone. According to Larissa, this isn't something you should take personally. "I don't think he understands what the phone is for. It happens sometimes when Denise calls, too."

Yesterday, you went to the super-touristy voodoo store looking at magic candles and potions, but they didn't carry the kind of magic you need. You did buy an oil that promises Luck and Prosperity for Larissa, and from a street vendor you picked up a T-shirt for her, *The Big Easy*, which is ironic, and for Leo you got *I Heart New Orleans*. Although he's illiterate, he might recognize the pictogram. But whether or not he can differentiate between a picture of a heart and one of a hat, food is guaranteed to get a rise out of him. Beignets are pretty much the same as donuts. He likes donuts. On your way over to that big beignet-for-rubes place, you came upon a bakery where, displayed in the window case, were macarons. French macarons. French macarons, which might well be the same as the Pepperidge Farm oatmeal raisin cookies as far as Leo is concerned, but you know the difference. The macarons are as expensive as saffron, but you bought him a box of twelve because of how lousy you'd feel if you didn't.

Like everything else that was good, your trip to New Orleans is over. Now, after a day at home, showering the cats with affection, unpacking your suitcase, and doing a load of laundry, you put the gifts for Leo and Larissa in a tote bag and off you go to the place of obligation.

When you ask Leo if he missed you, he responds with his verbal equivalent of mashed potatoes. Words that are words are becoming more and more like the black rhinoceros, rare and nearing extinction, but he does have his way of communicating. When you hold up the *I Heart New Orleans* T-shirt, he rolls his eyes and shakes his head. A flicker of his former self. Leo never wore T-shirts, and one with an embossment, heart or no heart, not in eighteen million years, but because Larissa appears to be delighted by *The Big Easy* T-shirt, you tell her she can have that one, as well. "I got you something else, too."

Larissa unscrews the bottle cap and inhales the Luck and Prosperity oil. "This smells nice. Like perfume."

In direct opposition to his disgust for the T-shirt, the macarons elicit expressions of ecstasy, along with a perfectly articulated "Delicious." After he devours a second one, he goes to his room, taking the box with him.

Larissa asks about New Orleans, what you did there, and you shrug. "Not much. Mostly work. Some people I had to meet. How about you? How'd the week go?"

"Leo was fine, but oh, I had such a fight with my brother's wife. They want to go away and asked if their kids could stay here. I take care of Leo. I can't be taking care of her children."

"Did she at least offer to pay you?"

"Ha! Fat chance." Larissa laughs, and you wonder what it is

that allows her to laugh so easily, how is it that she's not cra-
bapple sour, just as you wonder if she ever thinks about having
a love life. Larissa is a beautiful woman. But these are questions
you can't ask. Instead, you ask, "Do you think he's finished all
the macarons yet?"

"Probably. I don't know how he eats so much and never gains
weight. Not like me." Again, she laughs. "I should go check that
he's not eating the box."

"No, no. You relax. I'll go."

Leo is not in his recliner, and he's not munching away on
the box or licking the crumbs from the corners, either. He's
standing at the full-length mirror, the one that's fixed to the
closet door, with the box in one hand, his arm extended. Five
macarons remain. Two pink, three green, and he says, in words,
but not to you, "Have one." He's offering a macaron to his reflection. By means of encouragement, Leo gives the box a jiggle.
"Really, they're excellent," he insists. Leo waits for the man in
the mirror to reach out, to help himself to a macaron, but when
that doesn't happen, Leo jiggles the box again. "Are you . . ."
he garbles something unintelligible, and then comes back with,
"for me, then." Leo laughs, and the man in the mirror laughs,
the two of them practically rolling in the aisles, and you ask,
"Can I have one?" to which Leo says, "No. I don't have enough.
I'm sorry."

No Turning Back

As if you could extract truth from the deception that you went to New Orleans to work, you're constructing, or trying to construct, a Category 5 hurricane. The wind has got you stymied. Maybe one of those small handheld fans? You go online to investigate the choices available. But first, you ought to check your email because it's been weeks since you last deleted your inbox. And now you do: delete, delete, delete, and then you stop short. Four days ago, while you were boarding the plane for your flight home, Isabelle Weber sent you an email. The subject line reads: *Call me.*

Other than her phone number, that was the whole of it. Not even the prescribed hours to call.

It's not like you forgot that you'd sent her the JPEGs, but you had quit fantasizing that you might hear from her, and even back when you were indulging the fantasy, you'd tell yourself to cut it out, get real. Now you need to tell yourself to calm down, don't wet your pants, it's probably about nothing.

Except now you *can* wet your pants because Isabelle Weber is apologizing to *you*. "My apologies for the delayed response. As you know, I'm not keen on JPEGs. I forwarded them to my assistant. She then insisted I take a look, but I had a terrific backlog of work." Then, as if she'd told herself to get a grip on it, she says, "To my point, these are quite special. Cornell-influenced, but with a woman's perspective. How many have you done, thus far?"

"Seven. Well, six and a half, really."

"I'd like to show twenty of them. A solo. Your debut," she says.

You bristle at *debut*, but you're not about to quibble over it.

"I don't want to rush you, but I've got a slot open at the end of May. Not this coming May. May of next year," she says, almost as if she's teasing, reminding you of your having asked that question. "I'll use these for the advance publicity. Then fourteen more by mid-January? Is that possible?"

A quick count on your fingers. Ten months. One every three weeks. "Yes," you say. "I can do that."

Yes. You're confident that you can do that, or as confident as is possible for you, but you have to tell her the other thing.

"Good. I'll send my movers over to pick up the six of them. Does Friday afternoon work for you?"

Tell her.

"We'll keep in touch, then. Is there anything else you need for now?"

Now. To delay won't alter the inevitable. Tell her now.

"Actually, there is a problem. Kind of a big problem. You know, I'm represented by the Sandstone. Sheila has already scheduled a show."

The problem is not a problem in Isabelle Weber's world. "You're no longer represented by the Sandstone. I'll deal with Sheila." Isabelle Weber is like a female praying mantis, done with her mate and biting his head off for food or fun. It's that easy. "Problem solved."

Problem solved. A solo at the Weber. Here is your excuse to be happy, elated, to dance around your apartment, but you can't dance alone.

You go to the mirror and extend your hand as if to invite your reflection to dance with you. But that isn't what you're doing. You're just standing there looking at your mirror image: *It's not the same, it'll never be the same. If you want to dance, you'll have to dance alone, solo.*

You stand on the tips of your toes and twirl.

Mixed Messages

There's a text from Larissa: *Don't come today. He's sick.*

Sick? Leo is sick? You call her, and she tells you, "Oh, it's nothing. Just a summer cold. He woke up this morning congested, and he's been sneezing, coughing a little. I ran to the store and got Tiger Balm and Mucinex. I'm making chicken soup. He'll be fine, but I want him to rest."

"Sounds right," you say. "Let me know if anything changes. I'll call you later."

When a person with Lewy body disease gets a cold, there's a high risk of it turning into pneumonia, and pneumonia is the predominant cause of death for people with Lewy body disease. *Life Expectancy: 3 to 5 years, 5 to 8, 5 to 12, cases of up to 20 years!* Pneumonia, but a lot of them starve to death because they've forgotten how to swallow. You'd thought that swallowing was like breathing, sneezing, smiling, crying. Not something you could forget, but part of the package of simply being alive. Leo might not be able to cut his food with a knife and fork, but he sure can eat. He swallows. Starving to death is not a good way to die. Pneumonia has got to be preferable.

Don't get ahead of yourself. He has a cold, but still you count. Not from day of diagnosis. You start with the halos, the angels on the rooftops. Three years? More? Four years?

Even if it is just a summer cold, a common cold that will not turn into pneumonia, you're glad that Leo is sick. You have things to do. Things you need to do, want to do.

When you were in the fourth grade, for your science project, with help from your grandfather, you built a volcano. A volcano that spewed lava. Not *real* lava, but two tablespoons of bicarbonate of soda, and then standing in front of the class, you added vinegar, and the volcano erupted. It wowed the fuck out of everyone.

The volcano itself is a snap to construct, a plastic bottle covered with papier-mâché, painted, and clay for form and texture. Now, the question is how to get it to erupt without you there to add the vinegar, how to get it to erupt without human intervention.

Before Leo got sick, your grandfather's death was the pinnacle of your pain, but unlike Leo, your grandfather died only once.

A water pump! A water pump with a timer to release the vinegar at regular intervals.

At Petland, in the tropical fish aisle, you buy two different pumps, a small fish tank, two bags of aquarium sand to absorb any spillage, six packets of multi-colored gravel, a plastic scuba diver, a faux coral formation, and a plastic fish.

You wonder if a plastic fish is meant to be a stand-in companion for a living fish, and if so, is the fish fooled into thinking it has a friend?

Clarity

A common cold generally resolves itself in five to seven days, but under Larissa's care, it took a mere four days for Leo to recover.

"He's strong as a bull," she tells you. "If you want to come tonight, that would be good. He'll be happy to see you." It's one of those things Larissa says, that Leo will be happy to see you. Maybe he will be happy to see you. Maybe not.

"I'll be by after you have dinner."

"Could you pick up a pint of ice cream for him on your way over? Häagen-Dazs. Vanilla. With the vanilla bean. It's his favorite."

Häagen-Dazs vanilla bean was Leo's favorite ice cream, but now does he really know Häagen-Dazs from Breyers? Or is it Larissa's penchant for top-dollar brands? You did try, more than once, to extol the virtues of generic products, telling her how Tylenol and acetaminophen are the exact same compound, that it's the label that jacks up the price, but Larissa has faith in advertising. You can't argue that Häagen-Dazs isn't superior to Breyers, nor that Larissa wants only the best for your husband, and you've become, more or less, inured to the sticker shock of the credit card bills.

Larissa takes the bag with the ice cream from you and then returns from the kitchen with a hefty portion in a bowl, along with a spoon and a wad of paper towels.

At home, Leo no longer wears shoes. Instead, like now, he's wearing socks and the old-man beach slippers, but his shirt is pressed and his jeans, although not recently purchased, look as if they are because Larissa washes them in cold water to keep them from fading. All that's missing are his eyeglasses. "He broke them," Larissa tells you. "This time, it was on purpose. Yesterday. He just snapped them in half."

This makes the fifth pair of eyeglasses he's broken, but the previous four broke when he sat on them or when he fell asleep with them on and rolled over. "I'll get him another pair tomorrow."

"I don't think you should bother," Larissa says. "He doesn't seem to need them anymore. A lot of times when I put them on him, he's been taking them off, even when he watches television. I don't notice any difference."

It makes sense. Glasses or no glasses, there's no clarity for Leo. Although he does see the ice cream and holds out his hands to take the bowl.

Larissa turns on the television because it's time for Anderson Cooper, and then sits on the arm of the chair to blot the ice cream that dribbles down Leo's chin. She is gaga for Anderson Cooper, and as she often does when he's on the screen spewing his middle-of-the-road commentary, Larissa remarks, "Leo looks just like him."

True, both Leo and Anderson Cooper have thick and prematurely white hair and blue eyes, and Leo's eyeglasses were similar in style, but you don't see the resemblance.

"Your husband is a handsome man," Larissa says.

She washes his body and his hair, towels him dry, brushes his teeth, buttons his shirts, zips his pants, ties his shoes when they are going out, cuts his food into bite-size pieces, and yet she looks at him and sees Anderson Cooper. Maybe she needs glasses, too.

Not Fast Enough

Larissa sends you the link for the wheelchair she wants to get for Leo. It's not the most expensive wheelchair, but it's sturdy, and it has a basket to hold snacks and drinks when they go to the park. The most expensive wheelchairs are motorized, the ones operated by gears as complicated as those of a car with a stick shift. Motorized wheelchairs are for people whose legs don't work but whose minds are fully functioning.

Leo's legs have not gone the way of his brain. Larissa said that although he doesn't actually need the wheelchair, it would be useful to have one when they go out, especially when they go for long walks. She explained that sometimes he gets stubborn and refuses to walk or he gets tired and goes too slow. A couple of times, he was determined to go in the opposite direction.

"Is he shuffling?" you asked.

"A little bit, but not so much."

Symptoms that resemble those of Parkinson's disease.

"Are you sure that when he doesn't want to walk, it's because he's being stubborn? Is it possible that his legs froze up?"

"I'm sure." Larissa laughed. "Because all I have to say is we're going for ice cream, and he gets moving fast."

You order the wheelchair.

Because your preference is to work without interruption, you've been visiting Leo after you're done for the day, after Leo and Larissa have finished their dinner. It's a few minutes after seven. Music is coming from the apartment. The music that Larissa calls *The Golden Oldies.* You have to ring twice before she opens the door, slightly out of breath, and there's a sheen of perspiration on her brow. "We've been dancing. He exhausts me."

As if he were oblivious to Larissa's having bowed out, or to the fact that you are watching him, Leo dances on. *Solo.* His arms are bent at the elbows, his hands are doing some kind of Bob Fosse wave, he's twisting his torso, and his feet move two steps left, two steps right, one foot forward and back. You knew that dancing to disco music is something that Larissa and Leo do, together, often, but you've never before seen it for yourself.

Wiping her forehead, Larissa says, "He sure can boogie."

Walking is learned, but dancing, you conclude, is primal.

Hide and Go Seek

If you'd been Marcel Proust triggered back in time by the whiff of a madeleine, you'd have sprayed pine-scented air freshener up your nostrils. Your aim is to ward off remembrances of times past, but now you have to buck up, venture to the last place you want to go. Five new boxes completed to your satisfaction, and you've got three that are close to done, but you've set them aside because they are lacking something. Something, but what? The flea market is your only option.

There ought to be something like horse blinders for memory banks, flaps attached to the neocortex to block out intrusive thoughts.

You do make a concerted effort, with a degree of success, to see nothing, or nothing that registers, until on a table in the middle of the second row, you spy two cartons: $1, or 5 for $3. This vendor is deluded. One dollar for an empty travel-size aerosol canister of deodorant? Nonetheless, you continue to poke through the box, setting aside a root beer bottle cap, a small ball of tangled wire, the inner workings of a watch, and four fishing lures with wooden fish dangling from sharp hooks.

The vendor says, "Those are three dollars each."

"Then why are they in the dollar box?"

"A mistake. But I'll let you have everything you've got there for ten bucks."

She asks if you want a bag.

You don't want a bag, but because of the hooks, you ask if

she would wrap the lures in paper. While you wait for her to do that, you scan the length of her table, and as if she had nothing else, literally nothing else, on display, you see only the amber glass apothecary bottle. The label is worn thin, but it's legible: HEMLOCK

As sure as if he were standing there at your side, you can hear Leo say, "This is fantastic." The price tag is taped to the bottom of the bottle, but you don't look to see how much it costs. Instead, as if you've been cast under a spell, you bring the bottle to your mouth, and only when you're near to pressing the rim against your lips do you snap out of it, out of danger, danger not from the possibility of residual poison but from the overwhelming urge to kiss the amber bottle as if it were something like a mouth or fingertips, and the vendor says, "I can do twenty on that, if you're interested."

You give her two tens.

As if it were an imposition, she asks if you want the bottle wrapped, too.

"No, don't bother." You put everything into your bag and hurry to the exit, where you collide with a young woman coming in. Her hair is dyed purple. Her nose and lower lip are pierced. The young man with her has matching hair. His forearms are heavily tattooed. As if they had knocked you to the ground and stepped on your face, the both of them go overboard with the apologies.

"No, no," you say. "It was my fault. No need to apologize. But, wait. Hang on a second." Taking the amber bottle from your bag, you hold it out for them to see the hemlock label. "I just bought this, kind of by mistake. Would you like it? As a gift."

The girl takes it from your hand and asks, "Are you kidding?"

"You mean, you're just giving this away? It's so cool." *So cool,* with extra *o*'s, *soooo coool.*

"Yeah, I don't want it. Please, take it."

She passes the bottle to her boyfriend, who says, "This is fantastic."

Fantastic.

Out of the Mouths of Babes

I t's late in the game Stages, but it's here now: a distinct tremor. To prevent his milk and juice from spilling or jumping from the glass, Larissa got him a sippy cup, the plastic kind with a straw poking out from the hole in the lid.

A sippy cup? What's next? A rubber-nippled bottle?

It's not just the milk and juice. His food sometimes catapults off the fork, or his soup spoon does a backflip, which is why Larissa is now scooping a forkful of sweet potato from the skin. Leo opens his mouth as if he were a baby bird, and Larissa feeds him not as if he were a baby bird but a baby all the same, a baby in a high chair, until she says, "All done." After wiping his lips and chin clean with a paper towel, she carries the dirty dishes to the kitchen.

You're sitting there smiling at Leo like an imbecile while he babbles wind-swept torrents of gurgling garble, but when Larissa returns, he stops. Nothing. Not a *glub*, a *ler*, or an *ewwha*, not any kind of sound, but, as if he's accusing you of a crime, he's pointing his finger right at you.

He's pointing at you, but he's looking at Larissa, and then he says, he *says*, "Did you know that she is an artist?"

Larissa gasps. "Leo, you talked."

Did you know that she is an artist?

The words were crisp, clean-edged, and his thought was clearly defined, but the same can't be said of your thoughts. You make a mad dash to the bathroom, where you sit on the floor. Your thoughts are muddled. You have no words, and to cry is the same as to babble.

A Blink and a Nod

This year, the same as Christmas last year, you celebrated the holiday—such as the word *celebrate* is the appropriate word to suit the occasion, which it's not—with Leo and Larissa on the twenty-third. The apartment was again festive, but you were relieved to see that Larissa reused the decorations from the previous Christmas, with only a few new additions: a sprig of holly and a cardboard snowman taped to the door.

Instead of buying a book for Leo, you wrapped up an old issue of *National Geographic*, which he seemed to like just as much as last year's book, and again, you got him the pricey chocolate-covered mints and a carrot cake. You bought a sweater for Larissa, a red one, but a cashmere and wool blend because a 100 percent cashmere sweater exceeded your budget, and you wrote her a check for the same amount as last year. Maybe next year, if there is a next year, you can be more generous.

Larissa got you a scarf, black with one pink stripe running from end to end. It's pretty, and a vast improvement over the mug. The gift ostensibly from Leo was perfume in a blue bottle. A brand you'd never heard of. You unscrewed the cap and took a whiff. "That smells so good," you said, and you kissed Leo on the cheek. "Thank you, Leo."

He blinked at you. That was it. A blink. Supposedly, a blink is a cat's way of saying "I love you."

This year, you're spending Christmas in your studio.

Next year, maybe next year, you'll take the Cerulean blue bag down from the shelf and open the box inside.

Over and Out

The movers have collected the last of your boxes. You clean up your studio, everything in its place, but now what? Now, what do you do with yourself?

Play with the cats. Have lunch. Make a grocery list. Visit Leo.

If the three of you were a right triangle, you would be the hypotenuse, the greater distance between the two points. Leo is as well-informed as a tadpole, but nonetheless, he's sitting comfortably in the armchair watching the news.

Larissa on the edge of her bed, is hemming a skirt, and the two of you are talking about your families. "I had no idea that you had a brother," she says. "You never mentioned him."

"We're not close. We haven't spoken in years."

"I love my brother," she says. "But his wife, I've told you about . . ." Larissa stops mid-sentence, and she sniffs as if she's detected an odor. She puts down her sewing and goes to Leo's chair, where she slips one hand behind his back and tells you, "He pooped."

He pooped?

She takes hold of his hand. "Come. We'll change your diaper."

His diaper?

If Costco purchases were itemized, you might've known that, along with everything else Larissa buys in bulk—paper towels and toilet paper, twenty-four rolls to the carton, tuna fish by the case—now there's this, *this* has been added to the tally of life's expenses. But Larissa didn't tell you, it didn't come up in conversation, and unlike when she tells you not to come over because he's sick, she obviously doesn't consider this to be deadly the way you do.

Larissa helps Leo up from the chair and says, "It takes only a minute. He doesn't fuss."

For Larissa, it is what it is and this is how it goes. Leo doesn't fuss, but you are about to fuss up a storm, scream and howl, kick and pummel the walls and bang your head on the floor. You have to get out of here. Now.

More of What You Do Not Need

What you need is a drink. A martini, a vodka martini, just a splash of vermouth, but instead of lemon or lime, you're thinking of olives, three olives. A new place opened up near to your apartment. Chez Marie Pierre. The food must be good. Every seat at every table is taken, but at the bar, which is at the far end of the restaurant, vacant stools are plentiful.

The maître d', a young woman who succeeds at being both arrogant and friendly all in one ball, asks if you have a reservation.

"No," you say. "I'm just here for a drink."

It's like an obstacle course to get to the bar, the way you have to weave your way around the tables with only inches between them. The near-deafening decibel level, which you appreciate because it's loud enough so as not to hear yourself think, but not so loud that you don't hear someone, someone at the table you're trying to squeeze past, call out your name. Not just someone. It's Miriam, who says, "Addie." Perhaps in greeting or, more likely, as a warning to her three dinner companions that you've been spotted in the vicinity of their table. Patrick, Z, and Katrine. Since when did they become all buddy-buddy? When, how, and why?

You could easily pretend that you neither heard nor saw them, but for some perverse reason, you don't.

"How terrific to run into you," Miriam says.

"Oh, come on now." You smile like you've got a knife clenched between your teeth. "You're just being polite."

They all laugh. Except Z. He knows you're not joking, and

you know he's cringing when Katrine asks, "Why don't you join us? We'll have them pull up an extra chair."

"I wouldn't dream of it," you say.

"You wouldn't be intruding," Miriam assures you.

"Really," Patrick insists, "we'd love for you to join us."

Z, who's been staring at his plate as if divine intervention were hiding between the leaves of baby lettuce, looks up, not at you but at his compatriots. "Stop it. She doesn't want to join us. Let it go."

"Well if you won't join us," Miriam says, "at least tell us what you've been up to, how you are doing."

You could tell them about the Weber Gallery, but because any success you might be having, any possibility that your life might not be entirely wretched, would let them off the hook, you say, "Me? I've been busy with the humiliation thing."

The three of them nod, as if you'd said only, "I'm good. And you?"

But you don't walk off, not just yet. "I am curious," you say, "since when did you all get to be such good friends? You know, considering how you felt about each other before, all those nasty things you used to say."

You're hardly going to wait around for an answer, but you're not about to have a drink here, either. On your way home, you buy a bottle of vodka. Just vodka. You don't need the splash of vermouth, and forget the olives. You're not hungry.

Artificial Intelligence

You wouldn't be surprised if, instead of showing you how many times you have visited this site, Google tells you, *"Enough already."*

Places to Go

The days and months have gone by the way in old movies the pages of a calendar flip to let you know time has passed, fast with nothing of note to distinguish one from the next until now. Tonight is your opening at the Weber Gallery.

You pop a Xanax and say to the cats, "Wish me luck." Needless to say, they don't, although Howie yawns.

Just before you reach the gallery, you pop another Xanax and let it dissolve under your tongue because that speeds up the rate of absorption.

Isabelle Weber beelines over to you. "You're almost twenty minutes late."

You mumble an apology, something about traffic, as opposed to the truth, which is that you tried on seven different black dresses, which was pointless because the difference between the one you're wearing and those you rejected is discernible only to you.

Your bullshit excuse is not met with skepticism. On the contrary, Isabelle Weber commiserates. "Why this city doesn't ban cars is a mystery to me," and then she switches gears and compliments your necklace. "It's lovely." The necklace, a cascade of rubies, was a gift from Leo. Everything lovely you own was a gift from Leo. Unlike other people, Isabelle Weber doesn't ask where you got it or if it's a family heirloom. Instead, she asks, "Are you ready?"

"Give me a second," you say. "I want to get a drink."

Three of your boxes sold in preview. "In preview," Isabelle

Weber emphasizes. "And two more before you arrived. I'm confident that another five or six, at a minimum, will go tonight. There's a buzz in the air. Now, come. There are some collectors you need to meet."

It's a one-eighty from the previous show at the Weber Gallery. The very well-heeled attendees are gathered around your work, too many people gathered around for you to see which of them are sporting the small red-dot stickers, the red-dot stickers: Sold.

Isabelle Weber leads you over to a woman who is studying your polluted river. She is tall, with excellent posture. Her gray hair, cut in a chic angle, brushes her shoulders. She is cloaked in an emerald green robe-type thing, which you compliment profusely and with sincerity.

"Your boxes," she says, "are tragic, alarming, stunningly beautiful, and yet there's a touch of whimsy to them. Have you lived through any such horror?"

"It depends how we look at it," you say. "I mean, we all know the effects of climate change, and I suppose one specific tragedy could be metaphor for some other kind of tragedy."

Then, as if you'd said something wrong or foolish, which isn't impossible, Isabelle Weber lets out a mammoth gasp. "Oh, dear God," she says, and she's off in a flash. You and the woman in the green robe follow her to the reception desk, where a man is poised to grab a handful of the Frosted Mini-Wheats from the crystal punch bowl. In the nick of time, Isabelle Weber plucks his hand away from what is not a snack but an artfully arranged breakfast cereal coated with synthetic preservatives and mixed with glitter, from her permanent collection.

The man slinks off, and Isabelle Weber whispers to you, "Philistine." Then she asks, "He's not a friend of yours, is he?"

"No." You don't mention that you don't have any friends here, that except for Larissa, who wouldn't have come even if you had invited her, you don't have any friends anywhere. For one thing, it's safe to say that Isabelle Weber wouldn't give a flying fuck if you have friends or not, and also, the woman in the green robe might look for a connection between no friends and whimsical tragedy.

By the time the night is over, an additional six boxes have sold.

"You've arrived," Isabelle Weber tells you. "You're a some-body."

It's not like you've been catapulted into Basquiat or Holzer or Walker territory, but you've arrived. You're a somebody.

You're a somebody.

A somebody with nobody.

Pride Before the Fall

I t's late when you get home, but you're not tired. You feed the cats, get undressed, and open your computer. Although Isabelle Weber is confident that others will sell before the show closes, you add up only the prices of what's sold thus far, and then you calculate the gallery's hefty commission and the chunk you'll need for taxes.

Even with the subtractions, it's a healthy amount of money. Not rich people's money, but you'll be able to pay off your credit card debt with enough left over to carry you through for a while. Maybe even for as long as one year.

Five to eight to twelve years, and . . .

There's really no way to know for sure.

A Day in the Park

Larissa texts you: *We're in Washington Square Park. So much fun. Come meet us if you're not busy.*

Washington Square Park, in your estimation, is a rather unpleasant place; chaotic and KEEP OFF THE GRASS signs are posted on the small patches of tufts of greenery, and although they do have a bathroom, it's got to be filthy, not one you'd ever use. What if Leo were to poop in his pants? You know that Larissa wouldn't step foot in that bathroom. Would you have to sit there with your husband and his soiled diaper? You could text back that unfortunately you are busy, and you *are* working, that's true, but it's not as if you're under a deadline, and it is a beautiful day, and you'd feel like poop if you refused.

You find them sitting on a bench between the Dog Run and the fountain. The wheelchair is parked at the edge of the bench, alongside Leo. He and Larissa are wearing matching New York Yankees baseball caps. You'd wear a plastic bag on your head before you'd wear a baseball cap, and Leo? A baseball cap? Never in a million years, so it turns out, is today.

"I got it to keep the sun out of his eyes," Larissa tells you, "and one for me because it makes me feel like a real New Yorker." She laughs. Leo laughs. You can't laugh, but you manage to smile. Larissa slides over so you can sit next to Leo, who looks like he's having the time of his life.

Nearby, a group of men are singing doo-wop, "Duke of Earl," and Leo starts bopping his head, offbeat, to the music. When you hear the sound of the bells coming from the Mister Softee truck as it pulls up to the edge of the park, you ask, "How about some ice cream?" Leo is listening to the music, not to you, but Larissa says, "He'd like some. None for me."

Because you don't want Larissa to be feeding Leo in public, and you're not about to feed him, either, you buy a large cone of Mister Softee vanilla, not a cup with a spoon. You grab a wad of napkins and walk back to the bench, where you have to sit next to Leo and hope he doesn't get ice cream all over his face.

It seems that the concept of licking ice cream when it's in a cone has been lost to him. He's eating it in bites, which is better because the faster he eats it, the less it will drip.

A big dog pulling the woman on the other end of the leash rushes over to you. "Don't worry," the woman says. "She's super friendly. A big honey bear."

The dog is wagging her tail, and Leo, giggling with delight, holds out the ice-cream cone to offer her a bite. But the dog doesn't take a bite. She takes the whole thing, what was left of it, and Leo couldn't be happier; that is, until she's licking the residue off his fingers, and then Leo is happier, like this is the happiest moment of his life, one he'll never forget. But, of course, he will forget. You, however, will not.

The Humane Thing to Do

Other countries, civilized places, like the Netherlands and Canada, they put people out of their misery the way beloved pets are put to sleep. No humane person wants their dog or cat or horse to suffer. Here, in a handful of states, including New Jersey, assisted suicide is legal, but with assisted suicide only the person who would be better off dead, as opposed to the person who is writhing in agony, can green-light their exit.

5 to 8 years, 8 to 12, and cases of . . .

It could be that a trip to Canada or the Netherlands to euthanize a loved one is like how people go to Argentina for cosmetic surgery, which is something that Argentina encourages. It's a lucrative part of their tourist industry. You would take Leo to the Netherlands. You would fly first class. It is more comfortable, and if he were to soil his diaper, there would be a chance the flight attendant would help you out with that because you get what you pay for. On the return trip, you would fly coach.

The Netherlands sounds like Neverland. Not Michael Jackson's creepy child-molesting Neverland but Peter Pan's Neverland, *the second star to the right and straight on 'til morning,* which is why you'd give Leo the window seat, to look out and see nothing but sky, to be above the clouds. Even when Leo was perfectly Leo, he preferred the window seat. Children, too, go bananas over the window seat. But children also get agitated on planes. You'd put a hefty dose of Xanax in a Peppermint Pattie, as if a Peppermint Pattie were a pill pocket, the pill pockets used to trick dogs into taking their medication without your having to pry open their jaws and then hold their snouts shut. Dogs fall for the pill pockets. Cats don't. Leo is more like a dog, sweet, obedient, eager to please. Within a half hour of devouring the Peppermint Pattie, he'd conk out, and while Leo slept, you'd watch every crap movie on the menu, because you'd want to be the kind of brain-dead that would ward off thinking of what you're about to do.

Leo would not wake until the sunrise, *straight on 'til morning*, when he'd press his face to the window, agog all over again at finding himself in the sky. And it would be in the morning when the plane would land. You'd have no luggage.

You would take a walk, stroll the streets holding hands, the way you did when you traveled and when you were at home, too, and then you'd sit in a café and have ice cream, vanilla with vanilla beans for Leo. You'd order a second serving of ice cream for him, and you'd watch the clock, one of those big clocks on the spires of some eighteenth-century buildings that are ubiquitous to all European cities. You'd watch the minutes go by, the way you imagine a condemned man watches the clock throughout the night, the night before the morning of his execution. Your opposition to the death penalty is vehement and absolute. How is killing a person, a physically healthy, fully cognizant person, not a cruel and unusual punishment, made all the worse by watching the minutes tick, tick, tick? But this, this would be not at all like punishment. This would be a gift. The only question is who would be giving the gift, and who would be on the receiving end?

Leo would finish his second serving of vanilla ice cream with vanilla beans, and then it would be time to go, time to go to the place, the *place*, which you envision as a newly constructed building. White, all white, inside and out.

While you filled out the requisite forms, a nurse would escort Leo to the room, all white, and after you were done signing and dating all the pages that required your signature, you'd meet with the doctor, who would outline the procedure for you. The *procedure*, which likely is not the correct terminology, but it is the word you choose, like *disease*, not *dementia*, because it is the word you'd want it to be, the word that is used for things like colonoscopies or having a boil lanced.

You'd be sitting on the edge of the bed, where Leo would be stretched out, serene and waiting to die, only he wouldn't know about the dying part. You'd take his hand and hold it to your chest. You'd want him to feel your heartbeat. He'd be smiling, the big, stupid grin of an imbecile, interrupted only once for a quick wince of the needle injected into his brachial artery at the crook of his elbow; the needle that connects to the tube that connects to the bag of saline solution laced with morphine. The nurse would ask if you are ready, and you'd say, "No. Yes. No," and then you'd nod your head yes.

The morphine would drip, drip, drip from the bag and run through the tube, and Leo's eyelids would flutter. You'd bring his hand from your chest to your mouth, too late to change your mind.

The Little Girl You Invited
Over and Then Lost

The doll is a Google recommendation. Not an action figure or a Barbie. A doll along the lines of a Cabbage Patch Kid, but, unlike a Cabbage Patch Kid, these dolls are alarmingly realistic.

If it weren't a doll, a toy, but a person, it would be not yet a toddler but not an infant, either. No, not *it*. She. A girl doll dressed in a pink skirt and a white blouse patterned with pink flowers. You chose this one because her face is set in laughter, and her skin is the same shade of brown as Larissa's skin. When you lift her from the box, you squeeze her arm, which feels not dissimilar to flesh on bone. The doll is made of the same variant of plastic—vinyl or silicone—as lifelike sex dolls. Not the kind you blow up as you would a beach ball.

The doll comes with accoutrements: a plastic baby bottle, a pad like a pee pad for toilet-training small dogs, a four-inch pink hairbrush, and a white teddy bear dressed in a tutu that is just the right size to be the doll's toy. The adoption certificate says her name is Marlene. You leave all the extras in the box, except the diaper, which you bury in the trash, and, gently, you put Marlene in a large shopping bag.

The Saddest Day Ever, Thus Far

Larissa answers the door with the broom in one hand, which she leans against the wall. You take off your coat, and she wants to know if it's very cold out.

"No. A little chilly. But not cold."

"I hope we get a few more nice days. He gets such a kick out those parks."

"I got something for him. It was recommended." You take Marlene from the bag. "I thought he'd like her better than he would a white one."

Larissa laughs, an echo of the laughter coming from the TV in Leo's room.

Comfortable on Larissa's recliner, Leo is engrossed in an episode of *Three's Company*. Even in the early 1980s, when you were six, seven years old and it aired during prime time, you knew that *Three's Company* was six steps behind stupid. One of the actors, the blond woman, in an attempt to remain relevant, wrote a book of poetry reported to be astoundingly dreadful. It's not the plot that draws Leo to *Three's Company*. He can't follow the plot. He's in it for the soundtrack, the call-and-response of canned laughter. Laughing is like dancing; a primal, pre-language expression of delight.

You wait for a commercial break before you say, "Well, hello there." If a Hostess Twinkie could talk, it would sound like you. Artificial sugar that leaves a cloying aftertaste. There are days when it could be that he recognizes your face as a familiar one, a friend, someone nice enough. Today is not one of those days.

Today, he looks at you warily as if whoever you are, you're not to be trusted, and he watches you as if what you are taking from the shopping bag were a miniature Trojan horse.

"Look," you say. "A little girl has come to visit you. Her name is Marlene."

He takes the doll by one leg so that her head, torso, and arms hang upside down over the arm of the chair. It could be that he thinks Marlene is a sock. You pry her leg from his fingers and sit her on his lap, but his eyes are riveted to the television. He cracks up laughing along with the soundtrack laughter. You place your hand on his forearm. To be touched is essential to our emotional well-being, which is why these dolls are recommended, why you bought him the doll to hug, to cozy up with when he watches television, to cradle while he sleeps. You rarely touch him now.

It had crossed your mind that he might get pervy with the doll, slip his hand under her little skirt, stroke the part of her where there would be genitalia were she a sex doll. It crossed your mind but was dismissed because if there is anything to be said for Lewy body disease, it's that, unlike the unfortunates with Alzheimer's, the unfortunates with Lewy body are not boob-and-ass grabbers, they don't sexually harass their caregivers or anyone else, or—fuck you, Joan from Dickerson House—go prowling for blowjobs. They might play with themselves, vaguely and without purpose, but that's the whole of it.

You leave Leo with the doll, limp on his lap, just there, like a piece of lint. Larissa is now, as she so often is, folding laundry. Diapers aren't foolproof.

"He doesn't seem to like the doll," you say.

"You never know with him," she says. "Hour to hour, he's different. The last few mornings, he's been wobbly on his feet.

I have to hold him. But then later, he's walking okay. Slow, but ..." She stops mid-sentence when her phone rings. She looks at the caller ID and says, "I'm sorry. I should take this. My aunt."

"That's fine." You get up to say goodbye to Leo, to tell him that you'll see him tomorrow, which is no different from saying, "I'll meet you napkin."

Maybe you should take Marlene home with you. *Touch is essential.* Cats, when they are in the mood, will sit on your lap or snuggle with you in bed, but if you try to hug them, hug them tight, they let you know that you've crossed the line. You don't take it personally. Cats are cats. *But touch . . .*

Now, *The Brady Bunch* is on, and, the same as *Three's Company*, *The Brady Bunch* commands Leo's attention, but not his full attention. Leo's got the doll snuggled in the crook of his arm. Together, he and Marlene are watching *The Brady Bunch*. At the sound of the canned laughter, Leo laughs and then looks down at Marlene as if to see if she, too, finds this hilarious. Her laughter is without sound, but her expression says yes, yes, this is hilarious, and in that way, the laughter is shared.

You go home.

You sit on the couch and toss a small plastic ball with a bell inside to Roberta. She rushes after it. Howie watches her, as if he's confused.

Cats can be highly amusing, but they don't laugh.

Yes, You're Sure

Larissa sends you a text with three attachments, three pictures of Leo and Marlene. They are inseparable, and while it's good to know that they've hit it off so well, the only pictures that could cut a deeper wound would be pictures of Leo wearing nothing but a diaper. Larissa is fond of saying, "Once a man, twice a child," which is not something you are fond of hearing. The diaper thing, for her, is nothing more than a stage of life. *Stage 4? Stage 5? Stage 6?*

Larissa is big on taking pictures, and in the many she has sent to you—Leo pushing a shopping cart, Leo at the park, Leo eating pizza—his eyes are sparkling, and if he's not grinning, he's laughing. He's laughing probably at nothing, and when you look at these pictures what jumps out at you most is that Leo is demented, and for you to look at them is like looking directly at a solar eclipse. To look will cause irreparable harm.

The pictures that Larissa has shared with you today are essentially identical: Leo is sleeping, on his side, his hair sleep-disheveled, his cheeks sleep-pink, and his arm is curled around Marlene, hugging her, keeping her close. His chin rests on the doll's head.

Select messages.

Delete message? The question mark is asking you to reconsider: Are you *sure* you want to do this?

Delete.

PART SIX

2

PART SIX

Fire Drill

This text is without an attachment: *Don't come today. He's sick.*

You call and ask, "What is it?"

"He has a fever. Not so high, but he's coughing a lot. It's just a bad cold," she says. "Maybe a flu. I made chicken soup. He's had two cups of tea with honey and lemon. A few minutes ago, I gave him Mucinex and rubbed him down with Tiger Balm. Right away, he fell asleep. A couple of days and he'll be fine."

You want to tell her to skip the chicken soup, skip the tea, forget the Tiger Balm, forget the Mucinex, let him go, *pneumonia*, but Larissa is more like a parent who, understandably, will go to great extremes to keep their child alive because if their child pulls through, there will be a future, a life, a life with promise.

"Don't you worry," Larissa says. "He'll be fine. Four days. Maybe five."

5 to 8 years, 8 to 12, and cases of . . .

For three days running, it's been the same. Mornings, his fever is down. Nights, his fever is up. That's how it goes with fevers. Chicken soup for lunch and dinner. Plenty of orange juice. He's still coughing, but he's sitting up, watching television, and drinking tea with honey and lemon. Tiger Balm, Mucinex. Aspirin.

This morning, Larissa texted that he had orange juice, tea, and toast for breakfast, and now he's taking a nap. No text in the afternoon, but early in the evening, she calls. "Leo won't wake up. He slept through lunch, and dinner, too. He's not even opening his eyes." Her voice trembles, so much as to seem like your phone is on vibrate. "His fever is high. Over one hundred three."

Ten minutes later, you're there, gently shaking his shoulder. "Leo?"

It's like he's in a coma. You scramble through your bag for your phone, but you must've left it at home, which could be one of those Freudian things, or not.

Larissa calls 911.

In the minutes while you wait for the ambulance to arrive, you say to Larissa, "What would I have done without you?"

"It's my job."

Her job, but it's not in her job description to gaze at his face with such love. "He is a good man," she says. *Is.* Present tense.

"Not perfect," you say, "but, yes, he was a good man. A very good man." *Was.* Past tense.

No Kind of Life

The paramedics lift Leo onto the gurney and slide him into the back of the ambulance, where you and Larissa sit on metal seats that drop from the side, like fold-out shelves. It's a wild ride to the hospital, racing through the red lights, taking sharp turns, weaving in and out of the traffic, and still, Leo is out cold, as cold as a corpse, except that when Larissa places the palm of her hand on his forehead, she says, "He's burning up."

From ambulance to emergency room to a bed on wheels and into the elevator, to the fifth floor, to room 521, where two orderlies lift him into another bed. A nurse checks his vital signs—temperature, blood pressure, pulse rate—and then she covers his nose and mouth with a mask hooked up to an oxygen tank. She jabs a needle into his vein, tapes the portal in place, hooks up the IV, and Leo reacts to this flurry of activity as if he were a man made of rags.

An hour goes by, if not more, before a doctor shows up. He listens to Leo's chest. "His lungs are filled with fluid. We'll do a chest X-ray just to be sure."

"Sure of what?"

"Pneumonia," he says.

Most often the cause of death.

Larissa stays with Leo, holding his hand, and you follow the doctor out into the corridor. There's no point to a chest X-ray. You relay Leo's wishes: *Do Not Resuscitate. No Artificial Means of Life Support.*

Let him go.

"You're his health care proxy?" the doctor asks.

"Yes. I'm his wife. It's in his will. I don't have the documents with me, but I can go home and get them. He has Lewy body disease."

The doctor gets a pen from his pocket and makes a note on Leo's chart. "I'll inform the nursing staff," he says.

Let him go.

Let me go.

Now What

When your mother died, your brother took charge, soup to nuts, of all the funeral arrangements because he thinks he's the Chairman of the Board of Everything. As much as his shoving you out of the way pissed you off, you appreciated it. You weren't with Leo then, and had it been left up to you, your mother would still be in the morgue. All you had to do was show up. "And don't be late," your brother said.

He made all the arrangements for your father's funeral, too, but you RSVP'd *NO* on that one.

You haven't spoken to your brother in years, which is why you have to google: *What to do when someone dies.*

You Need to Make Plans

Google advises: *Whenever possible, funeral arrangements should be made in advance.*

Although unlike his explicit and notarized *Do Not Resuscitate* and *No Artificial Means of Life Support* directives, Leo did not, in writing, document post-death instructions. On the few occasions when you attended a funeral or watched one on TV or on a movie screen, he'd say that you should hire an orchestra to perform "Ride of the Valkyries," the version from *Apocalypse Now,* and get a mime there to officiate. But to make certain that there was no ambiguity, he'd add, "Really, just put me in a dumpster."

Now, even if Leo *had* wanted a funeral, you wouldn't survive it. If Leo had died from a heart attack or been hit by a car, it would've been a different story. This story, as it is, isn't so much a story as it is a song, a Beatles song that was released before you were born. Your mother was a Beatles fan. Her favorite songs were of the *Yeah, Yeah, Yeah* variety, songs with a good beat and flimsy lyrics. The other songs she played less often; songs you didn't remember that you'd remembered, but like the way chicken pox lies dormant for years, one day you wake up with shingles, and from what you've heard, shingles, like "Eleanor Rigby," bring about a sharp and inarticulate pain.

It wouldn't be exactly like Eleanor Rigby's funeral, no one but the priest at her grave. You would be there, and Larissa. Not Denise because agoraphobia is the same as house arrest. Joey would show up. Drunk, but there.

Three people.

One night, long, long ago, you and Leo attended—ever-loyal, how could you not—yet another of Katrine's abysmal plays. It was closing night of a two-week run, and you were two of the four people in the audience, and one of them was the usher. The person who was not the usher left ten minutes after the curtain went up. At intermission, you asked Leo if it would be kinder to leave now and spare the actors the excruciation of going on with the second act for three people or if it would be too demoralizing to lose the audience entirely. Leo thought you should ask the usher, and she said, "Either way, it sucks, but it would probably be better if you took off. At least that way, we can all go home. Two, three people in the audience . . ." She shook her head. "It's pathetic. Worse than none."

Nobody came.

No one was saved.

Cry Wolf

I t must be protocol not to break the news by phone. Someone will be there waiting, to head you off at the pass, to
spare you from finding an empty bed or the curtain pulled all
the way around as if dead people want their privacy, but no one
is there waiting for you because Leo isn't dead. He's bushy-
tailed awake, sitting up, and the oxygen mask over his nose and
mouth isn't enough to conceal the idiot grin.

Larissa rushes to him, kisses his cheek, and then excuses
herself to go to the bathroom. "I've had to pee since we left the
apartment."

Your hug is light, as if he were fragile, although he appears
strong and robust. It could be that his pink cheeks are indicative of a fever, but it could be the pink of good health. You place
your palm flat on his forehead, which feels warm, a tad warm,
and you keep your hand there, flat against his forehead as if you
were a faith healer commanding the fever to Be Gone!

Or are you more like a reverse faith healer, willing the fever
upon him? Might that be why, when Larissa comes back from
the bathroom, you jump back, as if, instead of your palm flat on
Leo's forehead, you were holding a pillow over his face?

It's your turn to excuse yourself, not to go to the bathroom, but
to talk with a doctor or a nurse, someone who can answer your
question: Doesn't *Do Not Resuscitate* mean *Do Not Resuscitate*?

"This is a hospital," the nurse tells you. "Short of the stated
extreme measures, it's our obligation to do whatever we can to
make him well."

Apparently, a *Do Not Resuscitate* order does not include antibiotics, and an oxygen mask is not an Artificial Means of Life Support.

Had you known in advance that, short of extreme measures, they were obligated to save his life, such that this is a life, would you have called for an ambulance?

A Break

As far as Larissa is concerned, this hospital has been derelict in its duty and it's a dump. Four days, and they changed the sheets only twice. The soup they fed him was broth from a can, and they totally ignored her explicit instructions to rub his chest with Tiger Balm at night. She's not wrong about this hospital, but his temperature is down, he is lively, babbling and laughing whenever you and Larissa laugh, and he is being discharged today.

When you sign the papers, the administrator tells you that an ambulance will bring him home later this afternoon. "After hospice care is done setting up."

"Hospice care?" You're confused. "I thought he wasn't sick anymore."

"The doctor didn't speak with you?" The administrator is obviously annoyed with the doctor, but she shifts into a mode of compassion when she says, "There's nothing else we can do for him here."

Hospice care is a package deal, three months, all inclusive: a hospital bed at home, an oxygen tank, whatever medications are prescribed. The hospice nurse comes three times per week, but you can always call her, and five days a week, four hours each day, an aide comes to lend a hand and keep an eye on him when you go out. "To give you a break," she says. "Everyone needs a break. It's crucial for your well-being, and his, for you to have time to yourself."

You don't tell her that you have nothing but time to yourself.

You don't tell her that this isn't the kind of break you need.

Nothing Solid

The hospital bed, per Larissa's instructions, is set up perpendicular to the foot of her bed. She will not move into Leo's room. "Here I can watch over him all night," she says.

Maybe this was one of those clerical errors, and some other patient, not Leo but someone who is actually dying, was slated to go home with hospice care. It wouldn't surprise you if the hospice nurse took one look at him and said, "Are you people for real?" And then the bed and the oxygen tank would get carted out like furniture being repossessed.

Having raised the top half of the bed for Leo to sit up, Larissa turns on the TV to a show about two people introduced for the first time one week before their wedding: The bride-to-be is an aspiring screenwriter living in Los Angeles. Her fiancé is a survivalist militia freak whose idea of a fashion accessory is an Uzi.

Again, you wonder if Larissa longs for a love life, a life with a future, a future that is unlike the present. She is smart and kind, laughs on a dime, and she either hit the genetic jackpot or uses some kind of secret miracle moisturizer that keeps her skin baby soft and smooth.

The prospective bride and groom are in a screaming match, and Larissa says, "No way she's going through with this," but you'll never find out because the hospice nurse is here. She's in her mid-forties, has strawberry blonde hair cut in a bob, and you like her eyeglasses, round and green. She apologizes for being late, and you say, "Ten minutes late is not late." You don't catch her name, but you offer to hang up her jacket. She tells you not to bother, and she drapes it over a chair, which is when you see she did not come alone. Half-hidden in the corner near the door is a much younger woman, twenty, twenty-two tops, dressed in tan corduroy jeans and a brown sweater, a plain-looking little thing whose physiognomy puts you in mind of a Peanuts character, minus the Peanuts charisma. Although there's not a shred of resemblance between them, you conclude that she is the nurse's socially awkward daughter.

"Please," you say, "have a seat," and, as if to compensate for her absence of splash, she displays the same obedience as that of a teacher's pet in the third grade. She sits, back straight, hands folded on the table.

Larissa hovers behind the hospice nurse, who first unwinds a narrow two-pronged tube attached to the oxygen tank and then inserts one prong into each of Leo's nostrils. "This is more comfortable than a mask," she says.

Really? A pair of tubes jammed up his nose is more comfortable? But Leo doesn't pull them out. You would've pulled them out.

The hospice nurse demonstrates for Larissa, and ostensibly for you, too, how to adjust the settings to increase and decrease the oxygen flow. Then she wraps the blood pressure cuff around Leo's upper arm. As it inflates, he giggles.

His fever is slightly elevated. There's fluid in his lungs, but because he's not coughing, the hospice nurse prescribes an expectorant to loosen the mucus, to bring it up and out. The other prescriptions she phones in are for sleeping pills, antibiotics, and a super-powered aspirin to bring down his fever if it spikes.

"No solid food," the hospice nurse says. "Liquids only." She recommends Ensure. Nutrient-infused puke flavor in a can. Larissa pulls a face and asks if he can have homemade soup, chicken soup with pureed sweet potatoes.

"He loves my cooking," she says, and the hospice nurse tells her, "Provided it's fully liquefied. No bits or pieces of anything solid."

While she packs up her gear, she tells you that the agency will call you tonight to make arrangements for an aide. They will call *you*. And *you* can always call them should there be problems with equipment or if she is needed. *You* have to call them, not Larissa, which makes for a step once removed. "Only family or the legal guardian." She snaps her satchel shut, and the plain-looking girl rises from her seat, but instead of latching onto her mother, she asks you if you'd like to talk.

"Talk? About what?"

"About how you are feeling, what you are going through, things like that." She holds out a business card.

You take the card, glance at it. She's a social worker. "Thank you," you say, "but no."

"Well, my number is there. So, any time you want to talk, or if you need advice."

You walk them to the door, where you ask the nurse, "How much longer?"

"Two to three weeks is average. But he's young and his vitals are strong, so who knows? It could be months."

As soon as they're gone, you tear the social worker's card in half, drop it in the trash can, and you ask Larissa, "Did you catch her name? The hospice nurse."

"Yes. But I can't remember it now."

"Me, either. We're a pair. Next time she comes, would you ask her?"

But you and Larissa are not a pair. Larissa does everything you don't do, everything you won't do, even the simplest of things like say to the hospice nurse, "I'm sorry. I forgot your name."

One Week with Help

The soup is creamy white. Pureed potatoes and cauliflower served lukewarm, and after each spoonful, Larissa blots what's dribbled on Leo's chin with a paper towel.

"Where's the aide?" you ask.

"I fired her. Yesterday. She fed the soup into his mouth with a big spoon and so fast he almost choked. She doesn't know how to care for people."

Leo turns his head away, the signal that he is done eating, and with that, he drops off to sleep. Larissa says he's exhausted from laughing. "All morning, we watched television. *I Love Lucy* and *The Andy Griffith Show*. I never saw those shows before. We laughed and laughed." It goes without saying that Leo was not laughing at Barney Fife. He was laughing because Larissa was laughing, but he was laughing, and to laugh, no matter at what, is far nicer than not laughing, even if you don't know why you are laughing, or at what.

While Larissa is rinsing out the soup bowl and teaspoon, you call the agency to request a new aide, and then you sit and talk, mostly about Leo. She clings to the hope, the belief in the miraculous, that somehow Leo will pull through. You categorically do not hope Leo will pull through. Your only hope is that death comes without pain, and that it comes soon.

Larissa gets up to feel Leo's forehead. "I think his fever has come down," she says, but when the hospice nurse arrives, she tells you that his fever has not come down nor has it gone up.

Like a broken clock, the dial has stopped at an unimpressive 101.2, and his heart continues to beat as a healthy heart should beat.

You'd like to ask the hospice nurse if there's any correlation between the health of the heart and the progression of pneumonia, but, despite the fact that Larissa had asked and then told you, you've again forgotten her name. You try to catch her eye, but she's busy listening to Leo's lungs.

"No change there, either," she says.

Larissa wants to know if no change means he's getting better. *Please say no.*

"Given his condition, he's doing great." She turns to you and adds, "You're taking very good care of him."

"Not me." You're not about to take credit that is decidedly not yours to take. "It's all Larissa. She's the best."

"I can see that." Then she gives Larissa a tube of ointment. "For bedsores. Because he can't move, can't turn over, the skin will get irritated and inflamed."

But it is Larissa who gets irritated and inflamed. "I turn him over on a regular basis," she says. "And I put pillows under his legs and back. Twice a day I help him out of bed, and we walk a few steps."

"Wow." The hospice nurse is impressed. "You really are super," and you, not the least bit super, ask, "So, it's her care that is keeping him alive?"

"Not just alive. Alive *and* comfortable."

Alive and comfortable and better off dead.

"But he's still dying, right?"

You can't be the first family member she's encountered for whom a prolonged life is not the desirable outcome, but she responds as if you, like Larissa, harbor hope that he'll bounce back. "He's doing really well," she repeats. "But no, I'm sorry. He's not going to recover."

And what about you? Will you recover? And if so, is there any way to predict when?

Crank Calls

As of late, you've been taking calls from numbers you don't recognize, because they could be Leo related: a doctor, the hospice agency, the pharmacy. But how many times do you have to Block Spam and register with the Do Not Call list, which must keep its own list: The Vulnerable. It's not yet noon and already, some rip-you-off supplemental health insurance company called and then, as a preferred Walmart shopper, you were offered a free gift card. Preferred Walmart shopper? Nice try. As if you would ever shop at Walmart, a shit chain of stores whose full-time employees need food stamps to survive.

Now, it's the social worker.

"Really," you say. "There's nothing I want to talk about." With her, you wouldn't even want to talk about the weather.

As if she thinks your reluctance to pour out your heart to a girl, one whose most agonizing life experience was a zit cluster on her chin, is that you suspect she's going to blab about you all over town, she assures you that whatever you say will be kept confidential.

"I know that," you say, except you don't know that, not for sure. She's a kid. Kids blab. "You gave me your card for *me* to call *you*, which I have not done, so why are you calling me?"

"Yes, but some people are embarrassed to ask for help. I feel it's my professional responsibility to reach out."

"You can't help me."

"But . . ."

"But nothing."

Block Number.

Hospice Care by Half

The agency sent a new aide, but when Larissa asked her to do the laundry, she said that she doesn't do laundry, and Larissa told her that if she doesn't want to work, she should leave.

Aide number three showed up at ten this morning. "Right away," Larissa tells you, "I didn't like the looks of her. And I was right. First, she sits down and drinks her coffee. Okay, I let that go, but when I asked her to roll Leo onto his side for me to apply the ointment, she shoved him. *Shoved* him. I showed her the door."

You tell Larissa that you fired the social worker, and the two of you have a good yuk over that one.

"They're all good for nothing," she says.

"True, but you really should have some help. I'll call the agency."

"No. Don't. I have enough to do watching over him. I don't have time to be watching over an aide, too. They're useless."

"I'm useless, too," you say.

"You're not useless. You pay the bills."

"I mean, I don't help you here. I can at least do the washing."

"Thank you. That would be helpful. I need to make fresh soup."

You take a basket of dirty laundry to the basement, where, after loading the washing machine, you sit on the floor and watch as the towels and the sheets spin, as if the water were splashing against the porthole of a ship, and the lather of the soap were sea-foam, and you were going somewhere far away.

Marking Time

Birthdays, anniversaries, Valentine's Day, the first day of a new year, Thanksgiving, which is the holiday when there was no turning back, but Christmas is your holiday marker. This year is Leo's third Christmas with Larissa, but this year her family won't be here. "Not with Leo like this," she says, "and with the hospital bed, it would be too crowded, even for Jamaicans." Is she poking fun at you or at her family? You'd like it if it were at you, friends teasing each other. "It's fine," she says. "My brother and his wife are having everyone to their house."

"If you want to spend the day with them, I can stay with Leo." You offer, but you pray she says no, and yet again, Larissa answers your prayers.

"No," she says. "Thank you, but no. I want to stay with Leo. Besides, I told you my sister-in-law is a terrible cook."

This year, the three of you can be together on Christmas. Larissa wouldn't have to cook. You could bring food from one of those places that prepare holiday dinners for takeout, but you don't know if you should suggest it because the truth is that being alone on Christmas lets you at least try to forget what day it is. Larissa either senses this or else she feels the same way.

"But we'll do like we always do," she says. "Come on the twenty-third. We can exchange gifts. You can bring ice cream for Leo. He can eat it when it's all melted. I have something for you, and something for you from Leo. I ordered from Amazon. I couldn't leave him to go shopping."

"You didn't have to do that," you say, and she shrugs, then says, "It's Christmas."

Dreaming

Leo's temperature is up, not alarmingly up, but up, and there's more fluid in his lungs. Nonetheless, on her way out, the hospice nurse says, as she always does, that he's doing great, that the level of care he's getting is remarkable, incomparable. Larissa beams, and as if she were casting a warm light over Leo, he falls asleep.

You ask Larissa to help you lower the bed rail. It's not a complicated maneuver, but still, you've yet to get the hang of it. You sit on the edge, close to him, but not so close as to be touching.

Larissa's at the opposite side of the bed, where she tucks the Marlene doll under his arm.

As if Leo's hair has flopped over his face, which it hasn't, as if it were in his eyes, which it isn't, you smooth his hair back, running your hand from his brow up along his forehead.

He sleeps as if he hasn't a care in the world, which he probably doesn't considering there's not a thought in his head, but like the way a bulb pops from light to dark, just like that, his lips twitch, his chin quivers, he whimpers, and then his mouth opens in the shape of a scream.

You panic, but Larissa says to you, "It's okay. He's just having a nightmare."

A nightmare?

The kind of nightmare in which your scream is like a silent-movie scream, the scream of a Murnau film, when terror has rendered you mute. You've experienced those silent screams in nightmares, and when you're awake, too.

You've watched your cats dream. Paws running in place, emitting sounds that are neither growl nor meow. It's impossible to know if they are running from a pack of wolves or if they are chasing mice or if it's only the reflex responses to neurons firing at random, just as you can't know if Leo is dreaming of being chased by a zombie, or is it a giant eagle with talons like the tines of a pitchfork swooping down to carry him off for dinner, or is it something even more terrifying? Do dreams bring clarity?

Poor Yorick

Even if there were such a thing as a brain transplant, no one even half in their right mind would want to be on the receiving end of Leo's brain, but it's got to be top-shelf for research.

Given his profession, when he had a profession, Leo would've been all-in with donating his brain, what's left of it, to science. "Good thinking," he would've said.

To donate a brain can't be like donating clothing to a thrift store, where you put your castoffs in a shopping bag and leave it at the counter, but how do you go about donating this kind of castoff? One thing you won't do is hand it over to Leo's former place of employment. You google *Medical School + Research + Organ Donation + New York City* because, however irrational, you don't want his brain transported to some other city, to travel stashed in an overhead compartment as if it were carry-on luggage or, even worse, as check-in baggage, where all too often a suitcase destined for Minneapolis winds up looping the carousel in Cleveland. Seven schools pop up. You click on the first one and scroll until you find Anatomy Bequest Office of Research.

You launch into a quasi-prepared spiel about how your husband has Lewy body disease. "He's not going to live much longer. I'd like to donate his brain. For research."

The man who answered the phone sounds young, maybe a graduate student and answering the phone is his work-study job. He has a few questions to ask before you can proceed. "Has he given explicit directions that his body go to science research?"

"No," you say. "He gave explicit directions that I drop his body in a dumpster. But that was just a joke. Before he got sick, he did medical research, and he's got the heart sticker on his driver's license." The heart sticker on the driver's license gives permission to grab whatever organs are viable for transplant, while they're still warm.

Brains are not organs viable for transplant, and dying at home is not the same as getting killed in a car wreck.

"He can sign off on explicit directions now," the graduate student says, "before he passes."

"That's not happening. He wouldn't know a pen from a lollipop. I'm his health care proxy, and the sole beneficiary of his will. I have power of attorney."

"If he didn't sign off on the donation," he says, "we can't accept his remains."

If they can't accept his remains without his written permission, where do they get the thousands upon thousands of cadavers on slabs hacked to ribbons by first-year medical students? And all the dogs, cats, monkeys, and rats casually tortured in the name of science? You can bet they didn't sign on the dotted line.

Again, he tells you that he is sorry, but the regulations are non-negotiable, and it's no different anywhere else you might try.

Such is the state of Leo's brain, you can't even give the damn thing away.

Lifetime

The sheets on his bed are wet. "Not pee," Larissa tells you. "Sweat. His fever is high. It's bad."

His forehead is hot, very hot, and clammy.

You call the hospice nurse, who says she will be there within the hour. Larissa has a washcloth soaking in a bowl of ice water. A cold compress that she's been changing every five minutes when the ice water gets warm.

Although she changed the sheets only an hour ago, now she wants to put fresh sheets on his bed again, but you say, "Don't bother. Let him sleep."

To die in your sleep. Isn't that what everyone wants?

You check the time.

You check the time again.

The first thing the hospice nurse does is take his temperature. She listens to the beat of his heart and the rumble of his lungs. She tells you that the end is near.

"Today?" you ask.

"No," she says. "More like two days. Possibly three. His heart is strong. But if you haven't already, you should make arrangements."

His heart is strong, but yours is weak and tired.

Options

What distinguishes the funeral home lobby from the lobby of a hotel is that this lobby is quiet, deathly quiet, but still, the woman seated behind a cherrywood desk might well be mistaken for a concierge.

"Can I help you?" she asks, and you think, *No. It's way too late for that*, but you tell her that your husband is dying. "Soon. A day or two, at most. I'm told it's best to make arrangements now, before."

"Yes. Of course. Have a seat. One of our directors will be with you shortly."

To be put on hold at a funeral home is nothing like a Suicide Hotline putting you on hold. You're not waiting on a matter of *life* or death, but if the funeral directors are busy helping other customers, you wouldn't mind knowing how many are in line ahead of you. What is the approximate wait-time? You didn't think to bring a book. There are no brochures fanned out on the coffee table, and because it would be unseemly to dial up cute animal videos on your phone, you stare at the wall, and you wait.

One thing about stereotyping is how often you're proven wrong. The funeral director isn't some creepy, lugubrious man like Vincent Price in *The House on Haunted Hill*. This man looks less like a mortician and more like a mortgage broker.

The chairs in his office are the same as the comfortable chairs in a boardroom, and his desk is also cherrywood, polished to a high sheen. He takes a sheaf of papers from the drawer. "Are you thinking about a casket and full funeral service?"

"No," you say. "Just a cremation."

Maintaining neutral facial expressions must be a mandatory course in funeral-salesmen training school. If he is disappointed that you're going low-end, he's keeping it well under wraps.

"Do you have a particular style of urn in mind?" he asks.

"A Grecian urn would be nice," you say.

"Let's take a look at what we have." He comes out from behind his desk and escorts you to the Urn Showroom, where, in glass cases, myriad urns are on display. None of them are Grecian urns. Only two of them are not appallingly ugly. One of the not appallingly ugly ones is white porcelain decorated with bluebirds, bluebirds with yellow-tipped wings, an urn that could be mistaken for a tea canister, but Leo liked birds. The one made of wood looks like a jewelry box. If the price stickers are affixed, they're not placed where you can see them. You don't want to pick out the cheapest one. Leo would've told you to go with a ziplock baggie, but you could never put your husband's ashes in a ziplock baggie, and you don't want him in some bargain basement urn, either. The funeral director quotes the price for each. They must turn a pretty profit on these urns. The porcelain one is slightly more expensive, but porcelain is easily broken. What would you do if Leo's ashes got strewn across the floor? What if the cats thought ashes on the floor were something like a sandbox? Would you have no choice but to grab the broom and sweep Leo's remains into the dustpan?

You go with the jewelry box.

Back in his office, the funeral salesman has a pen poised to write down required information about Leo: his parents' names, his mother's maiden name, where he was born, his birthday, and his Social Security number, and he asks you how many copies of the death certificate you will want. "Twelve is what most people get."

You go with twelve, too, although you wonder why you'd want twelve copies of a death certificate when you get only one copy of your birth certificate, and one birth certificate lasts a lifetime.

The expenses are itemized: the body retrieval, cremation, urn, death certificate (x 12), and tax.

Retrieving the body. Not yet dead, but already your husband is a body. *Lewy body.* Not yet dead, but long gone. And tax? Really?

You sign your name, here, here, and here, and initial there and there and there, and then the funeral salesman says, "We take Visa, Mastercard, American Express, and Diners Club."

Diners Club?

A Blast from the Past

Leo is not sleeping, but he's not what you'd call awake, either. You sit on the edge of the hospital bed and rest your hands on his shoulders and your head on his chest, not to listen to his lungs but to come as near as you can to giving him a hug without disturbing him, an approximation of a hug. Your eyes close, and that's how it is until Leo's hands are stroking your back, and then he's stroking your hair, and it's exactly the way he stroked your back and your hair whenever you were unhappy or upset over some foolishness or other; this was how Leo comforted you, consoled you.

Not now. Please, Leo. Don't be good to me now.

You ease out from under his caress, and with that, Leo puckers his lips to kiss you. Not the way you kiss him on the cheek or the forehead. Leo wants to kiss you on your mouth, your lips, which frightens you, but how could you not? So you do. Once, and then again, and after, you say to Larissa, "He knows who I am."

"Yes," Larissa says. "This can happen. I've seen it before. It's beautiful."

If this were a scene in a movie, the final scene, a sentimental tearjerker, or the last chapter of a treacly novel wrapped up in a feel-good bow, it would be an easy, cheap, sentimental, forgettable ending. But this is not a sappy movie or a cheap novel. This is your life, and it won't end until you are dead, too.

A Matter of Hours

Another day goes by. Larissa tells the hospice nurse what she told you, that last night Leo woke up around ten, and Larissa warmed up the chicken broth. "He ate some, not much, and then he fell back to sleep."

The hospice nurse says, "Soon. Later tonight, or possibly tomorrow."

The hospice nurse says that this is how it will go, how he will go: the way you breathe after running, short of breath, rapid breathing, followed by breathing so shallow as to seem as if he is not breathing, but then he will exhale. It will go like that, round and round until the last breath. The last breath will be deep. One long, deep breath. One last-ditch effort to take air into his lungs. In, but not out.

Together, you and Larissa sit vigil. You are holding his hand, and you kiss him like a bird pecking seeds from the ground, again and again on the forehead.

His forehead is hot.

The rattling in his chest is audible.

Larissa's weeping is audible.

He stops breathing. You hold your breath, too, but when he exhales, your shoulders sag, as if he has failed you, as if you were a personal trainer and that final breath is like that last push-up, come on, one more, one deep breath, and then you can stop.

It goes on this way for hours. "He was always stubborn." You try to smile, as if it were years from now, a time when it might be possible to look back.

"He's not ready to go," Larissa says. "He's not ready to leave you."

You wish she had not said that, because you are ready. For so long, you have been ready.

You don't know if he is suffering or not, but you ask Larissa to give him a morphine tablet. You want to ask her for a morphine tablet for yourself because what you do know for sure is that you are suffering.

How It Goes

For hours and interminable hours, you've been sitting vigil, and as if all these years have been amassed in this moment, you're tired. Tired, so very tired.

"Take a break," Larissa says. "Go home. Feed the cats. I'm here. I'll call you if something changes."

"I won't be long," you say. "No more than an hour."

You check to be sure you've got your keys, but before you leave, you go back to the bed to kiss your husband on his forehead, his cheek, and yes, his mouth, too, and you go home.

While you sort through the week's junk mail, you smell something rancid. The cat food? The smell of death? Or maybe it's you who stinks. You haven't showered in a week, if not more. You should take a shower, a quick shower.

Your clothes are in a pile on the floor. You're waiting for the water to get warm. The phone rings. It's Larissa. She says, "He passed."

In a frenzy to get dressed, you trip getting into your jeans, you put your shirt on inside out. It's faster not to hurry, and, really, there is no reason to hurry. Not now.

Take a deep breath.

One deep breath.

But you do hurry because Larissa is there alone, alone with Leo's corpse, still watching over him.

You look at your husband, dead, and quickly turn away.

Two men from the funeral home lift Leo onto a gurney. The

black plastic body bag looks like a garment bag, the kind of garment bag that you get when you buy a new coat. Before the two men zip up the bag, they ask if you want to say a final goodbye.

You shake your head. You've already said goodbye.

Day One

You detest Starbucks, but Larissa had asked you to pick up a frappuccino. You got an Americano for yourself, two grilled cheese sandwiches, and two brownies.

Neither you nor Larissa has an appetite for food, and you've yet to drink your coffees. You just sit there until Larissa says, "It's so empty here without him."

"I know. I wish you'd met him before, when he was himself. He would've been crazy about you. Of course, he was crazy about you from day one, but it would've been different. He would've really *known* you."

But he did really know her. *I'm with her now.* It was you he did not know.

You remind Larissa that she can stay in this apartment for as long as she'd like or needs to stay.

"Yes," she says. "I'll stay for another week or so."

"You got another job already?"

"No," she scoffs. "I'll need the time to pack and make my arrangements. I'm moving back home. Remember? To Jamaica."

You did not remember. You forgot. All these years, she delayed going home, to her home, all these years she sacrificed, for Leo, for you, and you forgot. "I'm so sorry," you say. "I wasn't thinking." You weren't thinking of her. You thought only of yourself, and you ask if she will forgive you.

"Forgive you? There's nothing to forgive you for. I loved Leo, and you were the best boss I've ever had."

"I wasn't your boss," you tell her, but you don't say, "You're my friend," because what if she doesn't say the same in return?

She asks if it would be okay with you if she were to take a few mementos, whatever you don't want.

Mementos you don't want? You want nothing from here; there's nothing you want to keep from these years, and you tell her to take whatever she would like to have. "I have so much at home."

"Thank you." She takes a few sips of coffee. "What about the furniture?"

"No. I guess I'll donate it somewhere."

"Would you mind if my aunt Jasmine took it? Her things are old, and she always tells me how she loves how I decorated here."

"Mind? Why would I mind? No, I wouldn't mind at all."

You drink your coffee, and you think about Leo, how despite not having been Leo for so long, his face remained unchanged, his hair was always white and thick, and his smile was his smile, and although he didn't have a clue as to what he was laughing at, his laugh was his laugh, and you ask Larissa, "Would you like to go out to dinner tonight? Someplace a little fancy?"

At home, after you make a reservation, you text Larissa: *I'll pick you up at 6:30.* You try to nap, but after a while, you know it's futile. Instead, you open your jewelry box, make a choice, and then you get your checkbook and find a pen.

At 6:35, you ring the doorbell.

You've never seen this Larissa before, all dolled up in a bright pink silk dress. Her lipstick and shoes are the same shade of pink. "Wow," you say. "You look gorgeous."

She does a slow turn to show you the back of her dress, which has a bustle and a bow.

"Absolutely gorgeous. We still have a few minutes. I have something I want to give you before we go."

Larissa opens the small velvet pouch where you put the necklace you selected for her. A diamond set in a gold nine-point star, an enneagram, which aside from being a geometric plane, not something you would have known but for Leo, represents perfection and unity. "It was a gift from Leo. Years ago. Before."

Larissa studies the star and says, "I can't take something that Leo gave you."

"He bought me enough jewelry to last me six lifetimes. It would've made him very happy for you to have it. In fact, he would've insisted that I give it to you."

"He was a good man," she says. "A very good man."

In the envelope is a note card. *Dear Larissa,* you wrote, *Our infinite gratitude and deep abiding love for you is beyond measure. Addie & Leo.* Along with the card are twenty-four checks, each made out for one month of her salary.

Larissa goes through each of the checks as if they were a packet of index cards, and then she says, "No. This is too much. Much too much."

"It's definitely not too much. Leo would've been furious with me if I'd given you even a penny less." Then you tease her, "Let's just hope none of them bounce." But they won't. No more checks to write for rent, no utilities, no cable, no more bills coming in from the credit card she used, and now, you have money in the bank and the promise of more to come. "I'm joking," you say. "I'm good for it."

"You can't imagine. You know, I save and save. I was going to buy a house." She's wiping her eyes. "With this, in Jamaica I can buy a palace. Live like a queen."

"You *are* a queen but go fix your makeup. Your eyeliner is smudged."

Larissa goes to the bathroom. You stare at your feet because you don't want to look around, you don't want to see this apartment, not now, not ever again, and when Larissa comes out of the bathroom, she says, "Okay. Let's go."

You walk out first, and behind you Larissa locks the door.

PART SEVEN

1

After the Facts

L eo's ashes are in the urn on the top bookshelf flanked by old medical texts along with the cuckoo items from his drawer of treasures, and the two Mass cards from Denise. The Cerulean blue bag with the unopened box inside is up there, too, as is the purse that preceded it.

To look at the shrine you put together for Leo requires that you crane your neck and tilt your head back, the same as to see the fireworks from the window on the Fourth of July. A conscious, deliberate effort, one you don't often make, but when you do look, you turn away before memory takes hold.

It's curious that throughout this long ordeal, you did not rid your apartment of any of Leo's possessions, as if not ridding yourself of his things compensated for ridding yourself of him. Even after he died, not to keep it all felt as if it would be an act of betrayal. Eventually, although it was the proverbial drop in the bucket, you did fill a suitcase with books, and as if the books were salmon returning to their place of birth to die, you sold them back to the Strand. His two suits, ties, white shirts, and dress shoes you carried all the way over to First Avenue to donate them to the thrift store where the proceeds go to animal shelters.

Then you disposed of more books, his six university ID cards, his Waterpik, and an old pair of sunglasses.

You set aside his passport and his driver's license, the legal proof of his identity. And then you stopped.

Today, it's time.

You start with his filing cabinet, those seven drawers stuffed well past capacity, the tops of papers jutting out like buckteeth. In the extra-large black trash bags purchased expressly for this purpose, you stuff the reams of papers written by other scientists and the six hundred zillion articles he never got around to reading. You'll never read the papers that Leo authored or co-authored, but those you return to the file cabinet. The second drawer's folders are filled with cards, every birthday card, anniversary card, and Valentine's Day card you made for him, including the ones you signed *Roberta*, and the earlier ones from Elaine, your cat who died before you adopted Roberta. You can't throw those away, either. Not now. Not yet. Should you, or should you not, keep the greeting cards from Denise? Store-bought cards for every conceivable occasion. You and Leo would practically die laughing over the insanity of their precision: *Happy Halloween to My Brother Who Ate All My Candy* and *Merry Christmas to My Older Brother Who Told Me There Was No Santa Claus* and *Happy Anniversary to My Sister-In-Law Who Puts Up with My Brother.* "Where does she find these?" Leo would ask.

After some deliberation, you put most of them, most but not all, in the garbage bag. Next, you throw away magazines, newspaper clippings, more papers written by people you've never heard of and some by people whose names are familiar, some with whom you'd had dinner. Garbage.

The last file folder, the one in the back of the fourth drawer, seems to be empty, but when you open it, three pieces of paper stapled together flutter to the floor.

The Seven Stages of Lewy Body Dementia

√ *Vivid Hallucinations*
√ *Aphasia*
√ *Trouble Keeping Track of Dates*
√ *Brief Losses of Lucidity*
√ *Intermittent Difficulty with Simple Tasks*

The check marks are small and written in pencil, pencil that can be erased, pencil marks that will fade over time.

He knew.

He knew and he didn't tell you.

Or did he tell you? Twice, three times, he said, "I'm not ready." Not ready for what? You never asked. Was he not ready to leave, to leave you, his life? Did he want more time, more days, just a few days, a few weeks, a few months more, like you had before? Before he had to go.

Was he playing the odds?

Did Leo miscalculate the timing of the inevitable?

He was not ready, but he knew that he'd be leaving.

Oh, Leo. You knew.

Leo, my love, why didn't you kill yourself?

You should have killed yourself.

No One Was Saved

I t's an unmistakable sound, the sound of glass as it shatters
on the floor, that wakes you from your sleep. You sit up and
listen, and again, you hear glass, more glass, crash and shat-
ter. Unless you are having an audial hallucination, someone has
broken into your apartment. To interrupt a robbery in progress
is like asking to get killed, yet wearing only a T-shirt, you get
out of bed to look, which is the most stupid thing to do, even
more stupid than having left the windows open, including the
one that leads to the fire escape, which is a stupendously stupid
thing to do. Not all the way open, just two inches, enough to
let in some fresh air without any possibility of the cats getting
out, but to leave your windows open, particularly the window
that leads to the fire escape, even as little as two inches, is to put
out a welcome mat: *Come in, come in, mi casa es tu casa.* You don't
even ask that they wipe their feet.

The not-stupid thing to do would be to grab your phone,
get back into bed, burrow under the covers to muffle the sound
of your voice, call 911, and whisper, "Someone is in my apartment." But you don't do the not-stupid thing. As if it will make
a difference, as if you won't get killed if you are stealthy in your
approach, you tippy-toe into the living room, where you come
face-to-face with a squirrel.

It's possible that you would prefer to be face-to-face with a
rapist.

Defender of wildlife, of all living creatures, you have, many
times, sat in the park, watching the squirrels go about their

business, scampering up tree trunks, digging holes in the ground to bury food for when winter comes, but that is a whole other order of business than finding one perched on your bookshelf, staring you down as if you were the intruder. On the floor are the shards of what had been an antique crystal inkwell, along with a shattered Pyrex beaker that, until now, had been shaped like a bong, and a glass globe, a paperweight of the world. Leo's things.

What if this squirrel has rabies? Rabid squirrels bite, and the cats, where are the cats, and how would you break up a fight between a cat and a squirrel? You don't see your cats, but you're not about to go looking for them now. Although clearly two inches was all it took for the squirrel to get in, you throw open the windows, all the way open, and, as if the squirrel understands what you're saying, you're yelling, "Get out! Get out," but that squirrel isn't going anywhere. You try pleading. "Please. Please, please, just go away."

Maybe if you offer him a bribe, if you put haute-cuisine squirrel food on the fire escape, he will take the bait, but you don't have peanuts or almonds or sunflower seeds. You do, however, have peanut butter, chunky-style, but just as you turn to make a mad dash for the kitchen, the squirrel jumps from the bookshelf onto the coffee table, which is no closer to the windows, but near to the floor, which is when your panic goes into overdrive. Roberta is here, and she's puffed up to three times her normal size. A cat puffed up like that is a cat ready for a brawl. She doesn't jump on the coffee table, but she's squinting at the squirrel as if staring him down, daring him to a fight. The squirrel is either very brave, very fierce, or maybe he's just a moron because, all puffed up like that, Roberta looks like she could kick that squirrel's butt, like it wouldn't even be a fair fight. Except for the fact that squirrels can crack walnuts with their teeth.

You nudge your cat with your foot. "Go away. Go, go," but Roberta pays no more heed to you than the squirrel did. She skulks around the coffee table, taking a few slow steps forward, a quick step back, then forward, and then as if she's no longer a small cat, albeit a small cat all puffed up, but rather a well-trained border collie, she herds the squirrel to the window, and it scampers off into the night.

Although your heart has yet to quit beating like a drum solo, and your hands are trembling no less, you're somewhat rational, rational enough to shut the windows and lock them. Then you get on your knees to heap praise upon Roberta, who has de-puffed; smaller in size but Herculean in your esteem. You're cooing at her. She raises her head for you to scratch her under her chin, which you do until it hits you: Howie. Where is Howie?

He's not in the bedroom, and he's not in your studio or in the bathroom, and although there's no way he could've crawled inside the cabinet under the kitchen sink, you look there anyway. "Howie," you call out repeatedly. "Wee-Wee." You double back to the bedroom and again look under the bed. "Wee-Wee?" Could it be that he followed Roberta into the living room? But he's not under any of the chairs nor under the couch, where Roberta is now lounging on the cushion, looking as blasé as Renoir's *Reclining Nude*. She yawns.

Where could he be? Where could he possibly be? *No, no, he didn't, he wouldn't, but he might have.* Howie *is* on the dim side of bright, but could he be *that* dim? You unlock one window and climb out onto the fire escape, scouting left and right and up and down. If he's reached street level, he'll never find his way home. *Please don't be lost, Howie. Please, please don't be lost.*

Skip the underwear, socks, and shoes. Zip up your jeans. To know that you'll need a flashlight indicates a presence of mind, but the absence of a sound mind sends you racing to the bathroom, because, sure, doesn't everyone keep a flashlight in the medicine cabinet? The flashlight is not in the medicine cabinet, but as if it were here, somewhere in the bathroom, your eyes dart in every direction until they land on Howie. As if he and Roberta both had been to Wonderland, where Roberta ate the EAT ME cake and grew big, and Howie downed the DRINK ME Kool-Aid, your huge cat is compressed to the size of a newborn kitten, so small as to have inconceivably wedged himself between the back of the toilet and the wall.

You get down on your knees and try to coax him out to no avail. Then you take hold of his paws and pull, but he refuses to budge, and you conclude that it's best to let him be, let him stay where he feels safe. You can only hope that he emerges before he grows big again and gets stuck back there.

With a glass of wine in hand, you join Roberta on the couch. It's been quite the night. A horror story turned adventure story turned slapstick, a story that begs to be told, from start to finish, to be shared with friends and with loved ones, from beginning to end. You stroke your cat's back. "Roberta," you say, "You would not believe what happened tonight. I woke up to the sound of glass shattering. I was sure that someone had broken into the apartment, but did I do the smart thing? No, of course not. I got out of bed to see who was there. The stupidest thing you could do. But it wasn't a burglar or a rapist. It was a squirrel. A *squirrel*. Sitting there on the bookshelf, resting on his hind legs, like he was expecting me to offer him refreshments. Leo's crystal inkwell, his glass globe, and the Pyrex beaker in shards on the floor."

You ask Roberta if she remembers Leo, and you remind yourself to sweep up the glass before one of you gets cut, and then you go back to your story.

"I don't know if it's true, but I've heard that squirrels are often rabid. Even if this one didn't have rabies, he had squirrel teeth. Cats have sharp teeth, but I don't know that sharp teeth are any match for teeth that can crack walnuts. I was frozen with fear, but then it occurred to me to put food on the fire escape, that food would entice him to leave. Squirrels love nuts, except I didn't have any almonds, but there is peanut butter in the refrigerator. I was just about to go get it, but—and this you really won't believe—in comes Roberta, all puffed up to three or four times her normal size."

Roberta, in third person. Roberta, as if she were not the heroine, as if she'd played no part whatsoever in this drama. Roberta in the third person, because isn't that how stories are told?

"Then, as if she were a border collie instead of a cat, she herded that squirrel to the window, and out he went. And where was Howie throughout this ordeal? Wee-Wee was hiding behind the toilet. Roberta saved us."

No one was saved.

The whole story, start to finish, because who else is there? Who else could you tell? Who else is there to listen? There is no one else, beginning to end.

Acknowledgments

Infinite thanks to my stupendous, true-blue agent Joy Harris; Mark Doten, editor extraordinaire and saintly; Bronwen Hruska, Rachel Kowal, Lily DeTaeye, and everyone at Soho Press for their support, faith, and patience; my adored friends (in no particular order) for keeping me going throughout it all: Carlie, Claire, Mike, Johanna, Richard, Kristina, Timothy, Deborah, Wally, Barbara, Nalini, Lauren, Tree, Liza, and Lynn; my students who do me proud; Barry and Brenda for forever reminding me why I opted to be a child-free cat lady; and lastly, but firstly, with abiding love and gratitude always, William Wadsworth.